ALL
ENEMIES

ALLAN
LEVERONE

All Enemies is dedicated to the people who believe in a country worth fighting for and who do so, often at great personal cost, sometimes resulting in the ultimate sacrifice.

Special thanks to:

Scott Carpenter for the outstanding cover art, to editor Jessica Swift of Swift Ink Editorial Services, who worked her purple pen to the bone to make a good book great, and to Robert Shane Wilson, for the formatting and design of the ALL ENEMIES print edition.

I

Sunday, September 6, 1987
2:00 p.m.
Baghdad, Iraq

The leader sat at the head of a long table. Smoked-black sunglasses covered his eyes although the conference room was dimly lit. The level of lighting was irrelevant to the leader; the glasses were a necessary part of his carefully crafted image. He sat ramrod-still as the room began to fill with his top advisers and military men.

Saddam Hussein stifled a grin as he watched the familiar dynamic play out. It was always the same. The early arrivals hurried to take the seats farthest away from him—Iraq's president and revolutionary command council chairman. As places at the table became scarce, the latest-arriving council members were forced to occupy the seats closest to their leader.

The men always pretended not to mind, always did their best to act casual and relaxed, but Saddam never failed to note their underlying uneasiness at being so close to him. He never failed to enjoy their discomfort.

When the last man had seated himself and opened his briefcase, Saddam wasted no time bringing the meeting to order. The tension was palpable, as most inside this room were already aware of the grand plan being considered by their country's bold and aggressive—and some would say unstable, although they would *never* say it aloud—leader.

"It is time," Saddam intoned gravely. "I have been informed

1

that our operatives are in place and awaiting the 'go' order."

He eased his sunglasses down his nose and gazed over the top of the frames at one of his most senior military men, Revolutionary Guard General Kareef Fakhouri. "Are we prepared to strike when the time is right?"

The general did his best to hold Saddam's stare. A career officer and high-ranking member of the Revolutionary Guard, Fakhouri was typically strong and confident, but dealing with Iraq's unpredictable leader had a way of making him feel uncertain and even a little afraid. After a moment he was forced to drop his eyes. "Yes, Your Excellency. We have massed our available troops as close to the attack area as we dare without arousing the suspicions of the West. We will be ready."

Saddam nodded and replaced the glasses on the bridge of his nose. "Good."

The man cleared his throat unhappily. It was clear he wanted to say more but did not know how to begin.

Saddam glared. Unanticipated questions were always unwelcome, especially in front of his innermost circle. "What is it?" he grunted, his voice a short staccato bark.

"Your Excellency, our conflict with the government of Iran has been militarily and financially draining. The fighting has dragged on for years, and while there have been dozens of treaties and cease-fires proposed, they rarely materialize, and the ones that do never seem to last. Mr. President, while we fight an active war on one front, I am concerned that engaging another foe on a separate front might spread our resources too thin."

Tentative nods and murmurs of muted assent followed the statement, and Saddam concentrated on controlling a flash of anger. He slid his sunglasses down his nose again. It never failed to be an effective gesture of intimidation. "You are concerned," he repeated.

Fakhoury cleared his throat and nodded uncertainly. "Yes, Your Excellency."

"Your 'concern' is irrelevant. You are here for one reason, and one reason only: to execute the tactical decisions made by others. Is that clear?"

"Of course, sir. I merely thought that our use of finite troop resources should be a factor in our calculations before beginning—"

Saddam held up a hand and General Fakhoury stopped speaking instantly.

The Iraqi leader turned to a man sitting across the table. The man was wrinkled and stooped, elderly, with thinning white hair combed messily across his forehead. Ghalib Bishara had been a mentor and advisor to Saddam since his early days in the Baath Party. He had accompanied Saddam to Syria and Egypt after Hussein's unsuccessful assassination attempt on Iraq's then-president in 1959, and was one of only a handful of people—perhaps the *only* one—to hold the Iraqi president's complete trust. "Please," Saddam said to the old man, "for the benefit of those who do not seem to have faith in their president, would you repeat what you told me a few weeks ago?"

The old man looked up. His eyes were rheumy and tired, but when he spoke, his voice was strong and his words clear. "The end is nearing in the long conflict with the Iranians. A negotiated settlement is nigh, and when it is finalized, the full force of our military—one of the finest in the world, as all at this table know—will be available to us. Moving forward with our annexation plan at this time, as President Hussein suggests, will not be a problem. Quite the opposite, in fact. There will never be a better time to proceed."

Bishara lowered his eyes to the table once more, dropping his head and remaining still. The room was hushed. No one coughed. No papers were shuffled. Saddam let the portentous silence stretch out, feeling the tension rise inside the room, playing the moment like a musical instrument.

Finally he drilled a gaze into General Fakhoury's eyes. "Does that address your 'concerns,' General? Or should I find someone with a little more faith in his superiors to fill your position?"

Fakhoury swallowed hard. "I-I was not aware of—"

"Thank you for making my point. You were not aware." Saddam stared down the flustered general a moment longer and then swept the room with his icy gaze, making eye contact one by one with every man at the table. "Are there any other questions?" he said coldly.

No one spoke. No one moved.

"Good." He turned to a man sitting at the far end of the table. The man was dressed all in black and had not spoken since his arrival. "Tell our people to begin the operation immediately."

The man nodded once. Then he rose and exited the room.

2

Monday, September 7, 1987
7:20 a.m.
Leningrad, Russia

Tracie Tanner lowered her head and concentrated on sweeping the crumbling sidewalk south of Leninskiy Prospekt. Her nerves were humming. She knew her quarry—a Soviet diplomat named Boris Rogaev—would soon leave his apartment on Leninskiy Prospekt and walk to a cabstand a hundred feet south of her position. From there he would ride the short distance to Pulkovo Airport to catch his 8:00 a.m. flight to Moscow and his job at the Kremlin as Undersecretary for Military Acquisitions.

It was Rogaev's Monday routine. He had made the trip hundreds of times before.

Today he would not reach the airport.

Tracie had chosen to conduct her surveillance from the sidewalk in front of an abandoned ice cream shop. The small wood-frame building was run-down, like much of Soviet Russia, but it featured a plate glass window that, miraculously, had not yet been smashed out or boarded up. Her goal was to blend in with the early-morning activity, to look like a typical Russian shopkeeper preparing for another business day.

Residents who had been paying attention would know the shop had been closed down, but Tracie's experience operating in the Soviet Union had taught her one thing without question: Russian peasants tended to mind their own business. They had long since learned that interfering in the affairs of those outside their own, carefully controlled circle of family and friends was never a good thing. Few, if any, would question her sudden appearance. Besides, if her timing was right, she should only have to maintain the ruse for a few minutes.

Tracie surreptitiously checked her watch. Rogaev should be along soon.

Dressed in a shapeless plaid shift reaching well below her knees, she knew the drab rust-and-tan colored wool dress would make her as good as invisible. She completed her harried shopkeeper illusion by stuffing her long, lustrous mane of flame-red hair into a fur Cossack hat pulled low on her forehead. The overall effect—she hoped—was that of a young Russian woman struggling to survive in the faltering Soviet economy. Tracie's goal was to look like any of ten thousand similar women in Leningrad.

She kept a sharp eye to the north as she swept, peering out from under her hat for any sign of Rogaev as she tirelessly swept the same section of cracked concrete over and over. After being turned by the CIA with offers of cash, Boris Rogaev had been a valuable source of information regarding Soviet military hardware and specifications for the past five years. But, recently, the KGB had become suspicious of him. The Soviets had been amassing proof of Rogaev's disloyalty for months.

Last Friday, an intercepted communiqué had convinced those at the highest levels of the CIA that it was time to extract their asset. It had become apparent that the KGB intended to arrest Rogaev Monday morning—today—upon his arrival at the Kremlin.

There had been no consideration given within the agency to abandoning Rogaev. Rescuing him would serve two purposes: it would permit the CIA to continue mining intelligence from the informant, and would clearly demonstrate to other undercover assets of the United States that they would not be abandoned if and when their covers were blown.

The operation had been hastily planned, with Tracie flying in just yesterday. This was her first op since being medically cleared to return to work after she suffered injuries thwarting an assassination attempt on President Reagan last June, so she felt more butterflies than she had in years.

Now that she was actually on the ground and working, she

felt more of the old confidence returning with each passing minute. She was in her element. Her mind briefly flitted to Shane Rowley, as it still did dozens of times a day, and her heart ached for a moment, again as it did dozens of times a day. Then she pushed away all emotion and refocused on the job before her.

Tracie glanced in the direction of Lenisnkiy Prospekt again. Still no sign of Rogaev. He would have to appear soon or he would miss his flight to Moscow, and the first vague thread of worry began to worm through her. What if the intel they had received was inaccurate and the KGB had already taken Rogaev, removing him from his apartment over the weekend?

She continued to sweep, glancing casually to the south, and froze at the sight of a handsome young Red Army soldier striding purposefully along the sidewalk, heading straight for her. He locked eyes with her, no trace of a smile on his chiseled face.

Tracie looked away, continuing her work, developing a plan to deal with the worst-case scenario: that Rogaev had been interrogated by the KGB already and had somehow set her up. It didn't seem likely, the bureaucrat shouldn't have known Tracie was even *in* Leningrad, but after the bizarre events of last May and June, events that revealed numerous leaks and betrayals inside the CIA, she wasn't prepared to take anything on faith.

She quickly considered her options. She was unarmed, which could pose a problem if the soldier was smart enough to stay out of reach.

Loosening her grip on the broomstick, Tracie prepared to strike at the soldier's throat. She would crush his Adam's apple and take his gun, then spin and prepare to defend herself against the second soldier who she knew would already be approaching from the other direction if she had, in fact, been set up.

Seconds passed. The soldier was nearly upon her. She forced herself not to look, waiting instead for a gruff voice to challenge her in Russian.

Nothing.

Finally she glanced up. The soldier was almost next to her, but he didn't seem intent on capturing her. He was still watching her, but now the trace of a smile played on the corners of his mouth. Just as he was passing, he veered directly into her, knocking her to the sidewalk.

She felt a flare of pain in her elbow as it took the brunt of the fall on the concrete. She glared up at the Russian soldier, who grinned coldly and said, "Idiot bitch, look what you've done to my boot. It's scuffed now. Why don't you watch where you're going?"

It wasn't a setup after all. He was just an arrogant bully used to throwing his weight around against intimidated Russian peasants. Tracie fought the urge to kick out with her heel and shatter his kneecap, or to clench her fists into a hammer and crush his balls. As satisfactory as either option would be, acting on either one would draw unnecessary attention and probably force the mission to be scrubbed.

Already she was conscious of passersby staring in sympathy, although she was not surprised that no one stepped up to help her. She swallowed her pride and shot the soldier a shame-faced look. "I am so sorry," she said, aware of the rustiness of her Russian and hoping it would go unnoticed. "Please excuse my clumsiness."

She reached into the pocket of her shift and pulled out a small handkerchief, then licked the fingers of her right hand, wetting a nearly indistinct smudge on the soldier's boot and buffing it out.

The gesture seemed to satisfy him, and when she finished, he said imperiously, "Yes, well, you must learn to be more careful." Then he strutted away, leaving a frustrated Tracie Tanner on her knees in his wake.

She cursed to herself and climbed to her feet.

Dusted off her dress.

And spotted Rogaev.

She shook her head, angry with herself. She had become distracted by the Red Army officer and had damned near missed seeing her target. He wore an ill-fitting suit, the material worn at the elbows and seat of the pants. It had to be at least fifteen years old. He had placed a faded maroon tie loosely around his neck, to be tightened when he arrived in Moscow, but not, apparently, a moment before.

He was moving fast in her direction, passing the Russian soldier who had assaulted Tracie. She bent to pick up her broom but then thought better of it. She straightened quickly, leaving it on the sidewalk where it had fallen. She paid no attention to the target until he swept by, eyes focused straight ahead, utterly unaware of her presence. Then she waited two seconds and fell in behind him, scanning the crowd to ensure she wasn't being observed.

After a moment she picked up her pace and soon had taken up a position slightly to the side and just behind Rogaev's right elbow. She leaned forward and said quietly, in Russian, "Comrade, it is a shame that the price of vodka has risen so sharply." It was the phrase Rogaev had been taught to expect any CIA contact to use.

The bureaucrat stiffened and slowed, and for a moment Tracie thought he would stop walking entirely. Then he regained some of his composure and continued on. He gave the proper response: "*Da*, I may have to switch to coffee."

They shared an awkward laugh and then the man said under his breath, "This is highly improper. Are you trying to get us killed?" His anger was plain.

Still smarting after the incident with the arrogant Russian officer, Tracie was in no mood to coddle the man. She replied coldly, "I'm trying to *save* you from being killed."

Now the man did stop walking. He turned to face her on the busy sidewalk. "What are you talking about?"

She smiled and took his arm, instantly playing the role of the adoring girlfriend. She coaxed him forward. To continue loitering would be to encourage the wrong kind of attention. A public sidewalk in Leningrad was the worst place to be having this conversation, but it was clear Rogaev had no intention of following her without at least some idea what was happening. She supposed she didn't blame him.

Glancing around furtively, Tracie kept the smile on her face. When she spoke, her voice was barely above a whisper. "The KGB is waiting for you in Moscow, where they will arrest you the moment you step off your plane. You're to be charged with treason. We both know what that means: a show trial followed by your immediate public execution."

Rogaev went ghost-white as the blood drained from his face. Tracie felt a stab of sympathy for him. More gently she added, "Don't worry, you're not getting on that airplane. You're not going anywhere near Moscow. Your plans have changed."

"Wh—Where am I going?"

"You're leaving this country forever. You will be transported to the West, where you'll start a new life." It was a lot to put on the unsuspecting bureaucrat's shoulders, but there was no way to avoid it. Time was at a premium.

To his credit, and to Tracie's surprise, Rogaev didn't fall apart. His panic was clear, though. "I'll never get out of Russia alive," he whispered bitterly. "The minute I don't show up at the Kremlin, the authorities will put out an alert. They'll blanket every airport. Search every plane. I don't stand a chance."

Tracie smiled tightly, eyes on the alert, her scan constant. She gripped his arm tightly and turned away from the busy main avenue and onto a much quieter side street. "That's why you're not leaving by plane," she said.

"What do you mean?"

"You're going to be out of the country and gone *before* you're supposed to arrive in Moscow."

"I do not understand."

"You don't have to. Just follow me." They walked as fast as Tracie dared without drawing attention to themselves. She hoped they looked like a typical Russian couple enjoying some time together.

They crossed busy streets, moving steadily northwest through neighborhoods filled with drab Soviet apartment buildings as far as the eye could see, basic square cement block construction with all the charm and appeal of prison cellblocks.

After twenty minutes spent traversing these steadily deteriorating neighborhoods, they arrived at a busy commercial shipping terminal on the easternmost shores of the Baltic Sea. The terminal was shabby and faded, many of the buildings temporary Quonset hut construction that over time had become permanent. Strips of peeling paint hung off rust-covered walls, the entire complex ringed by an equally rusted chain-link fence.

"Over we go," Tracie said, waving at the fence like a game show model.

"Climb over?" Rogaev asked incredulously. "That is your big plan? We will be seen by security. They will call authorities and we will be arrested!"

"Come on, Boris," Tracie answered. "You've lived in the glorious Soviet state your whole life, you know how things work. Grease the right palms and almost anyone can be persuaded to look the other way. We have," she glanced at her watch, "another six security-free minutes. I suggest we make the most of them."

Rogaev shook his head in obvious disbelief but turned immediately to the fence. He tried to force the toe of one of his dress shoes into one of the small chain link gaps, but his foot was too big to fit.

Tracie sighed and intertwined her fingers, forming a cradle, then braced herself against a fence support and held her hands at knee level. The Russian bureaucrat unsmilingly stepped onto the makeshift stepstool, reached up and clung to the top of the fence. He then grunted and swung awkwardly over, dropping heavily to the ground on the other side.

Tracie was up and over the fence before Rogaev had even regained his footing. "We're almost there," she said. "But we have to hurry."

They moved fast, abandoning all attempt at stealth, and trotted across the shipyard. Cranes roared, unloading huge wooden crates from mammoth ships, all of which seemed to be rusting as badly as the shipyard itself. Engines whined and voices bellowed. Men swore lustily almost nonstop.

Tracie knew she was being watched by at least half the men in the yard, shapeless dress or no shapeless dress. Not many females came around here. They would remember her, but it couldn't be helped. By the time it occurred to the authorities to question the shipyard workers, she and Rogaev would be safe and sound across the Gulf of Finland.

She hoped.

They crossed the yard, Tracie finally spotting the vessel she was looking for. She made a beeline for a small fishing boat bobbing at the end of a long, rotting wooden pier, Rogaev right on her heels. The boat's dual outboard engines were already running, burbling quietly as the two-man crew watched them approach, their faces giving away nothing.

One crewman, an ancient-looking Russian with shaggy hair and a long salt-and-pepper beard covering most of a weather-chapped face, helped them into the boat. The moment their feet touched the deck, Tracie said, "Go!" tersely, in Russian.

The crewman stepped onto the dock and unhitched a single rope from a cleat, tossing it onto the boat. Then he climbed back aboard and nodded to his counterpart at the helm. Instantly, the engines increased in pitch to a throaty roar and the boat leapt away from the dock, moving toward open water at a much livelier pace than seemed possible for such a beat-up old tub.

"Stealth wasn't an option?" the Soviet bureaucrat muttered to Tracie.

She grinned. "Speed seemed like the better option."

Worry lines etched Rogaev's face. "This crew will eventually be questioned by the authorities. What happens then?"

"To you personally? Nothing. You'll have long-since disappeared. And you needn't worry about these men. They've worked with the agency many times. Once we're safely ashore in Finland, they'll relocate to a very private port where their boat will be repainted and renamed. In less than twenty-four hours, there will be no evidence this craft ever existed."

"And me? What happens after I arrive in Finland?"

"There is a car waiting to drive us to Vantaa Airport in Helsinki, where we'll be flown by private jet to Ramstein Air Base in West Germany. You'll be debriefed there for several days and then flown to the United States, where you will be given a new identity and where you will start a new life."

Bewilderment gradually changed to gratitude in the Russian's eyes. "I...I don't know how to thank you for risking your life for me."

Tracie smiled. "No thanks necessary. I'm just doing my job."

She gazed at the rapidly receding Leningrad shoreline. She had been uncertain whether she ever wanted to return to CIA clandestine operations after the disaster in Washington that had taken Shane Rowley's life and forever changed hers; the tragedy that had left a permanent hole in her heart. But she realized now that she had missed the excitement of her old life.

Things would never be the same as they had been before. She accepted that.

Still, she was glad to be back at work.

3

The old man meandered slowly along the sidewalk. He took small, careful steps in an effort to avoid stumbling, although in this area, roads, sidewalks and city light fixtures were scrupulously maintained. Residents demanded it. The old man had a better chance of tripping over his own feet than over a crack or depression in the cement.

It was warm and muggy in the mid-Atlantic region of the United States, and yet the old man wore a light jacket over his standard attire of white dress shirt and grey polyester slacks. Both items had been ironed with military precision and featured razor-sharp creases. His body listed slightly to the right as he walked, and he leaned heavily on a cane, planting it with care prior to every second step. The man moved laboriously, painfully.

In his left hand he held a Styrofoam cup of coffee. Its plastic lid was tightly sealed, but a trace of steam found its way out through a small vent-hole and trailed the slow-moving man like steam from an old-time locomotive before dissipating in the heavy night air.

Most of the homes in this section of Georgetown were dark and still at this time of night, their owners fast asleep, but in one townhouse a light still burned in a single downstairs window, though it was nearly invisible behind a thick screen of lilac bushes.

13

After a glance in the direction of the lighted townhouse, the old man adjusted course, angling across the sidewalk toward a nondescript white sedan. The car was parked directly in front of the townhouse he had just passed. The interior of the vehicle was dark, but the old man knew it was occupied.

Whenever U.S. Secretary of State J. Robert Humphries overnighted at his Washington residence—the one where the light still burned—this car or one exactly like it was posted on the street. Inside it would be a Bureau of Diplomatic Security Special Agent tasked with providing security for the secretary of state.

The old man had been bringing a late-night coffee to the agent for the better part of six months now. The first couple of months had been an exercise in frustration, as he had spent night after night trudging along the sidewalk, offering coffee and a smile only to be rebuffed.

Finally, on an unseasonably cold late-April night, the agent had accepted the coffee, rolling down his window just enough to allow the old man to pass the cup through. Then he had asked the old man what he was doing out on such a blustery evening.

The old man was ready for the question; he had expected it. What else would the agent ask? That one question had been the opening he was waiting and working for.

He had responded that as a former civil servant himself he felt a certain kinship with the agent, stuck all alone outside the secretary of state's house, earning his living with the thankless protection detail. "The least I can do," he had said with a smile, "is bring you a coffee while getting my exercise."

The agent had never come right out and admitted he was serving as Humphries's protection detail, but he hadn't denied it, either. An admission hadn't been necessary. The old man was well aware of the agent's duties. He may have been more aware of them than the agent himself.

Every night since, on the occasions Humphries occupied the townhouse, the old man had struggled along the sidewalk, coffee in one hand, cane in the other, timing his appearance to ensure that the agent would be inside his vehicle upon the old man's arrival rather than patrolling the grounds.

And every night since, that agent had accepted his gift of coffee with a smile. On the nights that agent was off-duty, his replacement—an unsmiling hulk of a man—not only refused the coffee but also brusquely advised the old man to take a different route on his nightly constitutionals.

The old man didn't care. Eventually he stopped going out on the nights he knew the unsmiling hulk of an agent was working.

He didn't need that agent. He had the other.

Tonight he knew the *friendly* agent was working. Sure enough, the minute he reached the side of the vehicle—a Chrysler K-Car with U.S. government plates, kept so sparkling clean the old man thought the agent must run it through a car wash every day on his way to work—the passenger window rolled smoothly down.

"Evening, Mr. Jefferson," the agent said from the driver's side, his voice warm with recognition.

"Good evening, my friend," said the old man, whose name was not Jefferson, in what had become an established routine. "I happened to be out for some exercise and thought you might appreciate a little pick-me-up, from one working man to another."

The agent said, "Very kind of you, sir, and thank you." The old man knew the agent was smiling, despite his face being obscured by the darkness of the car's interior. He could hear it in his voice.

The agent slid across the front seat and reached up with two hands to accept his coffee. When he did, the old man simultaneously dropped the cane out of his right hand and the coffee cup out of his left. The cane clattered to the sidewalk and the coffee cup dropped to the road where it burst open, spraying hot coffee on the old man's feet.

He paid it no attention.

The agent said, "Mr. Jefferson, are you all right?" concern evident in his voice.

The old man didn't answer. He was too busy for conversation and there was nothing to say, anyway. He reached under his jacket and withdrew a Russian-made Makarov 9mm semi-automatic pistol with a long black sound suppressor screwed to its barrel. He pulled the gun clear of a custom-made Czechoslovakian leather shoulder holster and brought it to bear on the agent's face.

Before the agent had a chance to reach for his own weapon,

before he could even register surprise, the old man squeezed the trigger twice, firing point-blank into the agent's upturned face. Two muffled *pops* sounded at the same time the agent's head was exploding, splattering the inside of the vehicle with blood, bone and human tissue. The car's interior looked as though a water balloon filled with fruit punch had exploded.

The assailant wasted no time by admiring his handiwork. He dropped the arthritic old man act and moved like an elite athlete, opening the door and rolling the agent into the passenger side foot well. He picked the agent's windbreaker up off the front seat—it was covered with blood but still better than nothing—and used it to cover the still-bleeding, nearly headless corpse as best he could.

He examined the mess inside the car with a critical eye and wrinkled his nose in distaste, recognizing immediately that he could not afford the time it would take to clean all the gore off the windows. He was going to have to trust that the lack of activity on the quiet street at this time of night, combined with the car's location—positioned almost precisely between two street lights and covered in shadows—would prevent all but the nosiest of passersby from seeing the devastation and alerting police.

Eventually the body would be discovered, but the assailant wasn't concerned. He only needed a few minutes to complete his chore.

The no-longer-old man holstered his weapon. Then he bent and picked up his cane and the now-empty coffee cup off the sidewalk. Both would contain fingerprints but he didn't care. He tossed them into the back seat of the K-Car, then locked the vehicle.

The man then closed the window and gently shut the door. He looked up and down the street and was rewarded with exactly what he was hoping for: absolutely no activity. A quick scan of the townhouses lining the street showed darkened windows in all but the secretary of state's home.

The assassin turned away from the car and strolled casually along the sidewalk until passing a stately elm tree that he guessed had been planted around the time of the Gettysburg Address. Still seeing no suspicious neighbors, he eased left and melted into a small opening between two shrubs in a row of immaculately trimmed hedges.

A moment later he emerged in J. Robert Humphries's front yard. He crossed the yard in a matter of seconds and moved noiselessly along the side of the house. He bypassed the window with the light burning on the other side, careful not to make a sound as the window had been propped open several inches to allow fresh air inside.

At the rear of the house a sliding glass door overlooked a red brick patio. The assassin stepped to the door and looked down through the glass, unsurprised to see an adjustable metal bar placed along the base. The bar was a common tool used to prevent an intruder from opening the slider and gaining access to the home.

The assassin smiled. The bar would be utterly ineffective.

A thin gauze curtain had been pulled across the inside of the door, but the assassin could see through it to the vague outline of a man writing at a desk. The man's back was to the door, and he was bent over his work in concentration.

The assassin reached into his pants pocket and removed a small diamond-tipped glasscutter attached to a suction cup by a sturdy metal chain. He licked a finger and moistened the edges of the suction cup before placing it against the glass door at roughly chest height.

He pushed the cup carefully against the glass until it was it was firmly attached to it. Then he very slowly scribed a circle on the glass with the stylus, maintaining a steady pressure. A slight rasping noise accompanied the act, but the assassin was unconcerned. He assumed the man at the desk would be so engrossed in his work he would not even notice the barest hint of sound.

Even if Humphries did detect it, there was virtually no chance he would be able to identify the source of the noise before it was too late.

When he had scribed a full circle, the killer removed the stylus from the glass and eased the diamond tip under the rubber suction cup, breaking the seal. He capped the glasscutter and replaced the tool in his pocket. Then he stepped back and breathed deeply, allowing himself a moment of satisfaction for a job well done.

So far.

After the ten-second break, the assassin refocused and got back to work. He again removed his Makarov from its holster. He placed the butt of the gun's grip against the glass and tapped firmly, still unconcerned that the noise would attract any unwanted attention. A four-inch circle of glass fell away from the door, dropping to the interior floor of the townhouse where it spun like a coin before settling to a stop.

This time, the noise did get Humphries's attention, which was exactly what the assassin wanted. The secretary of state rose from his chair, turned, and scanned the empty room behind him. The killer could see only the vague suggestion of a body through the gauze curtain, but what the man was doing—and thinking— was as clear as day.

The killer crouched, still as a statue, and waited while the townhouse's occupant tried to locate the source of the noise. Finally Humphries spotted the small circle of glass on the floor. He crossed the room, his form clarifying through the sheer material of the curtain as he approached.

The secretary of state knelt and picked up the glass. He examined it for a moment and then made the decision that sealed his fate. He reached up and slid the curtain open, exposing himself to the assassin waiting as patiently as death on the other side of the door.

The assassin took a half-second to appreciate the look of stunned disbelief etched on J. Robert Humphries's face as he gaped into the barrel of the Makarov, which must have seemed as big and threatening as a cannon from his position just inches away. The killer said, quietly, "You're going to reach down and remove that steel bar, and then you're going to open this door. You're going to do it in the next two seconds or you will die."

The look of surprise on Humphries's face was replaced almost immediately with one of indignation followed by steely-eyed determination. "I can't," he said simply. "If I slide the door open my security alarm will activate, and I assume you wouldn't want that."

The killer was thrown off his game for a moment. He had expected his victim to panic, perhaps try to run, perhaps beg for his life. What he *hadn't* expected was this kind of calm, quick-witted response, but he adjusted quickly. "Not true, Mr. Secretary. I am well familiar with your alarm system. It is rudimentary, and cannot be activated until all of the doors and windows on this floor are closed. I passed an open window on my way here, therefore the alarm is off. Now, do as I say. You will not receive another warning."

For a long moment the standoff continued as the two men regarded each other. The assassin could see the secretary of state considering the odds of survival should he make a play for the Makarov's barrel and try to divert it long enough for him to duck away.

The assassin let him go through the mental exercise. He had left no more than an inch of sound-suppressed barrel poking through the hole in the glass, not nearly enough for Humphries to grab hold of without losing most of a hand—or more—to a 9 mm slug.

Humphries finally realized what the assassin had known all along—he had no reasonable options. He glared at the assassin in an attempt at defiance and then reached down and lifted the steel bar out of the door's track.

"Good. Now take two steps back and then stand perfectly still," the assassin instructed in his heavily accented English.

Humphries did as he was told.

The assassin slid the door open, keeping his weapon trained on his prey as he did so. When the door had opened far enough to provide access, the assassin moved with a practiced fluidity, pulling his Makarov back through the hole and then stepping to the left and into the townhouse.

The moment the assassin started moving, Humphries took one quick step backward. His next move would be to turn and run through the house in an attempt to reach the front door, but there was no time. The assassin entered so quickly that he was inside before Humphries could even turn. The secretary of state froze without being told. "Now what?" he said with just the slightest quaver in his voice.

"Now we take a little trip," the assassin answered. Humphries hadn't changed for bed yet and was still wearing a fitted off-white dress shirt and charcoal-grey slacks. His coat and tie were nowhere to be seen, but the assassin appreciated the fact that he wouldn't have to waste time waiting for his prey to get dressed. The dead protective agent out at the street would be expected to check in with his office soon, if he hadn't been already. When his superiors were unable to contact him via radio, they would send more agents out, and the assassin knew he had to be long gone before that happened. Time was running short.

"There's no way you'll get away with kidnapping me," Humphries said flatly. "There are agents watching this place even as we speak."

The assassin smiled icily and shook his head. "Not anymore, there aren't. There was only one man, and he will not be watching anything ever again."

Humphries's face, already pale, turned stark white. "You didn't—"

"Shut up," the assassin said, and gestured with his gun. "Put your shoes on." While the United States secretary of state did as he was told, the assassin used his shirt to wipe the Makarov clean, then he tossed it onto the floor behind the desk chair. He immediately drew a second weapon from an ankle holster. This gun was identical to the first but without the sound suppressor.

By now Humphries was ready, and the two men strolled through the townhouse and out the front door. In the unlikely event anyone looked out a window at the wrong moment, the killer knew the pair would look no more sinister than a couple of old friends reconnecting.

When they had walked halfway to the street, a dark blue sedan rolled to the curb. It stopped directly behind the K-Car holding the dead agent. The assassin opened the rear door and with a gesture that was almost formal in its stiffness, waved Humphries into the car.

He hesitated and the killer whispered. "Open your mouth to scream and you will die right on this curb. Then I will get in this car and disappear. Your death will never be anything more than an unexplained mystery."

Humphries glared at the killer, but seemed to recognize the futility of his situation. A moment later he lowered his head and slid into the back seat, his lips set in a grim line.

The assassin followed him inside and the vehicle accelerated smoothly away.

4

The mood inside the Oval Office was grim.

President Ronald Reagan half sat on the edge of his desk, tie loosened, looking every bit like a man in his seventies. Sitting somberly in a ragged circle around a highly polished walnut table was a small group of the president's most trusted advisers.

Minus one.

The meeting started with bluntness from the president. "Let's get right to the heart of the matter. What the hell happened to our secretary of state?"

There was a moment of utter silence during which no one seemed to want to be the first to speak. CIA Director Aaron Stallings decided to get the ball rolling. "Well, Mr. President, as far as we can tell, he was working alone in his townhouse last night when an intruder or intruders accessed his home and removed him."

"Who took him? There must be ransom demands; what are they?"

Stallings shrugged and shook his head, his massive jowls wobbling as he did. "The answer to both questions, sir, is nobody knows. There has thus far been no contact from the kidnappers."

Reagan glared at the floor as he digested this information. Then he lifted his head wearily. "Who knows the secretary of state is missing?"

"Only Humphries's family," Stallings said after a short pause. "No one else. The media's been told the secretary is slightly under the weather and is recovering at his home in North Dakota. Even the D.C. police are unaware. As far as they know, it was nothing more than a break-in at Secretary Humphries's local residence. The police are, of course, investigating the murder of the diplomatic security agent."

"Does the agent have a name?" Reagan asked.

"Of course, sir."

"Good. Find it and use it. That's a real human being who gave his life protecting J.R. Humphries."

"Yes, sir. It's, uh…" Stallings paused as he shuffled through a sheaf of papers stacked on the table. He felt his face flush bright red from the dressing-down. He prided himself on being unflappable and coolly analytical, and forced himself to regain his composure. "Ah, here we are. Special Agent Philip Hughes."

The president said, "Don't the police want to know what a Bureau of Diplomatic Security agent was doing outside an empty house?"

"Of course, sir, but we told them the agent was there as part of a routine drill. They don't believe us, but they're accepting it. For now. This isn't the first time we've stonewalled them. They're used to it."

FBI Director Matt Steinman cleared his throat, and Stallings felt a stab of relief when Reagan turned his gaze away from him to look at the other man. "Yes, Matt?"

Steinman was rail-thin, relatively young but severe-looking, like a banker with indigestion. He pushed his glasses up onto the bridge of his nose and said, "Sir, the Bureau is in the process of taking over the investigation. Once we've secured the scene and taken possession of all the evidence, we'll freeze the D.C. cops out. We'll cite national security concerns, which certainly won't be an exaggeration. That should buy us a little more time before word of the kidnapping is inevitably leaked."

"Unless the kidnappers choose to alert the media themselves."

Another uncomfortable silence.

Reagan's Chief of Staff Fulton Moore said, "There is that possibility, Mr. President. Obviously, it's entirely out of our control. We should consider whether to alert the press to the kidnapping ourselves, if only to control the flow of information and get ahead of the issue politically."

Reagan shook his head. "Get ahead of the issue politically? What are you talking about?"

"Well, sir, if the kidnappers spring it on the world in some dramatic way, say with a newspaper photo of the murdered U.S. secretary of state, and the world learns we knew Humphries was missing beforehand but said and did nothing, it makes you look weak and indecisive. If you release the information yourself, in the time and manner of your choosing, you can spin it, make yourself look better."

Reagan stared at his chief of staff, the intensity of his gaze unnerving even to Aaron Stallings, seated all the way across the Oval Office. "Spin it. Make myself look better."

"Yes, sir."

Aaron knew what was coming, and while he appreciated the fact that his own gaffe would now be forgotten, he still felt some sympathy for Moore. The president said, "Let's get something straight. I don't give a *damn* about how this makes me look politically. I don't care if I look weak or strong or anything in-between. What I care about is finding out what happened to the United States secretary of state and getting him back. I've known John Robert Humphries for thirty years. I consider him a close friend. I do not want to have to explain to his widow—another close friend, by the way—how he was taken right from under our noses and murdered. *That's* what I care about. That is *all* I care about. Am I making myself clear?"

Fulton Moore had gone chalk-white. "Yes, Mr. President. Of course. I didn't mean to infer..." His voice faded away.

Reagan stood up and began pacing in front of his desk, deep in thought. "Okay," he said, ignoring Moore. "I want all your best guesses. Who took J. Robert Humphries and for what purpose?"

FBI Director Steinman spoke up again. "A weapon was recovered from the scene, sir."

"And?"

"And while it had been wiped clean of fingerprints, we're certain it didn't belong to Secretary of State Humphries. It was a Russian-made Makarov 9mm semi-automatic pistol, Mr. President. That model is popular with both the KGB and Russian

Special Forces."

"Are you telling me the *Soviets* kidnapped my secretary of state? To what end?"

"It would appear so, Mr. President," Assistant Secretary of State Joseph Malone said. "We don't know why yet, and the Soviets have yet to respond to our official inquiries regarding the matter."

Reagan stopped pacing and glared at the men. "They have yet to respond? I'll call Gorbachev myself. I'll have a response within the hour. It may not be one we want, but they'll damned well talk to us."

The president leaned against his desk, concentrating hard. Aaron Stallings thought he looked considerably older than he had at the start of the meeting. "All right," Reagan said. "Everybody get back to work. I want hourly updates from everyone, whether you have anything to report or not. And I don't mean from your flunkies, I want to hear from each of you personally. Understood?"

Everyone murmured their assent as they rose en masse and began filing out of the Oval Office. "Aaron," the president said.

He turned. "Yes?"

"I'd like to talk to you alone if you can spare a moment."

"Of course, Mr. President," he said, utterly unsurprised.

* * *

"Bureaucracies," Ronald Reagan said, "operate slowly. They're ponderous and unwieldy, and while I have no doubt the mechanism of the federal government, in the form of all our various departments and agencies, will ultimately get to the bottom of who kidnapped J.R. Humphries and why, I'm afraid it will take much too long. I fear we'll be too late. Aaron, I do not want to bring my friend back to Washington in a body bag."

The CIA director waited for the president to finish. He was clearly leading up to something, and while Aaron Stallings had a pretty good idea what that something might be, he didn't think that talking over his boss would be a smart move, career-wise.

Reagan shut his mouth and stared expectantly and he knew it was now his turn. "Mr. President," he said, "I'm sure you realize Secretary of State Humphries may already be dead. The fact that we haven't heard a word from the kidnappers since the secretary disappeared, a span of..." he glanced at his watch, "...more than eight hours, means that, in fact, is the most likely possibility."

"I do understand that," Reagan answered. "But if the goal was to kill Humphries in order to advance some political cause or to publicize some fanatic's agenda, why not just shoot him in his home? Why go to all the trouble of removing him? Why take that added risk? And where could they have removed him *to*?"

Stallings started to answer, but the president raised a hand to cut him off.

"In any event," Reagan continued, "all of that is beside the point. Yes, I recognize the *possibility* that J.R. may be dead. But I refuse to accept that he's been murdered until I see clear, incontrovertible proof. In the meantime, I intend to operate as though he is alive. And I expect everyone else to do the same. Which brings me to why I asked you to meet with me alone."

Stallings waited, saying nothing.

"I want you to choose one of your agents to conduct a parallel investigation. Alone. Undercover. A lone operative working outside the constraints of the bureaucracy stands the best chance of success. It may be our only chance of success, given the time pressure we're operating under. Obviously, this would have to be someone who has demonstrated the ability to work solo, under intense pressure, with little or no organizational backup."

"An off-books op."

"If that's what you choose to call it."

Stallings cleared his throat. "Mr. President, what you're asking me to do is—"

"Yes, I know what it is. It's illegal."

"I don't understand," he said. "Why aren't you having this conversation with Steinman? Surely the FBI has agents who could handle the job, and they're tasked with operating within the boundaries of the United States, which the CIA is not."

"It's very simple," Reagan said, holding Aaron Stallings's eyes with his steady, intense gaze. "The FBI is intrinsically embedded in the unwieldy bureaucracy I just referenced. I don't trust that any Bureau special agent would be given the freedom operationally to do what will likely have to be done."

"Sir, the CIA is just as much a part of the bureaucracy."

"Granted. But here's the difference: I'm asking this of you as a personal favor. No official request. No paper trail. Just you and me alone in this room. I'm asking you to assign one agent, someone you feel is up to the task of tracking down whoever kidnapped the United States secretary of state, and bringing him back alive. That's the favor. What do you say, Aaron?"

Stallings paused for effect. He had suspected from the moment Reagan asked him to stay in the Oval Office what was going to be asked of him. Of the CIA. While he had no particular affection for the president, Aaron Stallings was well aware of the close personal relationship between the old man and J. Robert Humphries. After a second or two, he said, "Of course, sir. How could I refuse?"

Having gotten the answer he wanted, the president smiled. Even in his seventies, after nearly two full terms holding down the most pressure-filled job in the world, he still possessed those matinee-idol good looks and the commanding Hollywood leading-man presence that he used to such political advantage. "Good man," he said, clapping Stallings on the back. "Do you have a man in mind for the job?"

Now it was Aaron Stallings's turn to smile. "Oh, yes sir, I do. Except . . ."

"Except what?"

"She's not a man."

5

Tracie Tanner rapped her knuckles once against the frosted pebbled glass of CIA Director Aaron Stallings's office door. She waited a half-second and then entered without invitation. After cooling her heels for nearly an hour in an anteroom waiting for the Great Man to see her, she had lost all patience by the time Stallings's personal secretary—a blocky woman somewhere between the ages of fifty and eighty-five, with the bluest hair and most severe face Tracie had ever seen—glanced up from a mountain of paperwork and smiled acidly, telling her, "Director Stallings will see you now."

The door was already half open before Stallings looked up from his paperwork. He stared unblinking, not bothering to hide his expression of extreme distaste, as she crossed the room and sat in a chair permanently positioned in front of his desk.

It was almost unheard-of for a lowly field agent to be invited inside the plush confines of Aaron Stallings's office, and this was the second time in a matter of months Tracie had been. She knew she was supposed to feel honored, or special, or something, but couldn't manage to summon up the requisite emotion.

The last time she had been inside this office had been an unmitigated disaster. Stallings admitted straight-out that if he had his way, she would be brought up on charges of treason for opening a Top Secret document entrusted to her for delivery only. President Reagan had personally interceded on her behalf—justifiably so, Tracie thought, given the fact she had saved him from assassination—but Stallings had made a not-so-veiled threat about what would happen to her career once her protector was out of office.

It had not been pretty.

This time, an urgent call had come in while she was accompanying the reluctant Soviet defector Boris Rogaev to West Germany aboard the Gulfstream G-4. She had been instructed to release Rogaev into the custody of another agent when the plane touched down at Ramstein and was then to immediately continue on to Washington where she would meet with Stallings.

No details were given as to *why* Tracie was being summoned to D.C., but a one-on-one meeting with the agency's head man was such a rarity that her interest had been piqued from the start. She doubted the meeting would consist of good news, though. Based on personal experience, she knew she should be ready for anything.

She sat quietly in Stallings's office, hands folded in her lap, waiting for him to talk. As was typical for the man legendary in Washington political circles for his bluntness, he didn't bother wasting time on greetings or congratulations on her successful return to the company. He simply glared at her for a moment like he suspected her of committing some heinous but unspecified crime, and then began his pitch.

"We've got a situation," he said.

"I assumed as much," she answered coolly.

"Secretary of State Humphries has been kidnapped."

"What?" Tracie exclaimed, momentarily dropping her veneer of guarded calm. "Who's claimed responsibility? Do we know where he was taken? What are the ransom demands?"

Stallings raised his hands to stop her flood of questions, the flabby skin under his arms flapping like a turkey's wattle. "We don't know who's taken him or where he is. There have been no demands made as yet. No one has claimed responsibility."

"But you assume he was taken out of the country?"

"No, we do not assume that. Just the opposite, in fact. We believe he is still inside the borders of the United States, likely within a few hours of D.C."

Tracie shook her head, confused. "Then what am I doing here?"

"We want you to find J. Robert Humphries and return him safely to D.C."

"Sir, that's not a mission for the CIA unless and until it can be shown Humphries has been taken abroad."

Stallings glared down his nose at Tracie. She didn't care. She had seen his tough-guy act before and it didn't intimidate her any more now than it had back in June. He said, "I don't need a lecture on the mission of the CIA, and I don't need your suggestions about how to run the agency."

"Then what *do* you need?" she shot back.

"I already told you. Locate our missing secretary of state and bring him home safely."

"Director Stallings, not three months ago, I sat in this very office while you threatened me with arrest and prosecution for treason, *after saving the president of the United States from assassination*, specifically because I opened a classified document from the Soviets and ran an op here in the U.S. Now you're telling me you want me to run another clandestine Central Intelligence operation inside the borders of this country? Are you out of your mind? Why on earth would I even consider doing that?"

"Because," Stallings said smugly. "Your protector, President Ronald Reagan, the man whose life you saved back in June, wants it done. He doesn't believe the FBI can move fast enough to save Humphries, if in fact the secretary is even still alive, and he is willing to, shall we say, push the boundaries of the law a bit."

"Push the boundaries—"

"Yes. He and Humphries are very close friends; they've known each other for decades. Nancy is very close to Humphries's wife, Sara. The president wants this done and he asked me to pick the right agent to complete the mission. My choice was you."

"And if I'm caught, or if something happens to me?"

"You'll receive the full support of the president and everyone here at the agency."

He was lying.

Tracie knew it.

And Stallings knew that she knew. He smiled thinly. "It goes without saying that time is of the essence. I'll need your answer now, so I have time to find a suitable replacement if you opt out of the mission."

"And if I say no?"

"Then you can tender your resignation with Mary on your way out."

The CIA director's threat was irrelevant. Tracie had already made up her mind. Ronald Reagan had stood up for her and was the only reason she wasn't at this very moment rotting away inside an eight by twelve cell in Fort Leavenworth, Kansas. Her sense of personal loyalty was strong. She could no more abandon the president after he had asked for help than she could cut off her own arm.

"I'll do it," she said impassively.

"Good," Stallings replied with a cold shark smile, as if he hadn't known all along what her answer would be. "I've had Mary prepare a packet for you of the evidence recovered thus far in the case, as well as the contact information of all the principal investigators. Pick up the packet on your way out and get started immediately."

"Yes sir," she said, rising slowly. "Who will be my CIA contact?" Her handler for the first seven years of her career, Winston Andrews, was dead. He had committed suicide just a few months ago after having been unmasked as a Soviet collaborator.

"Me," Stallings said. "My private number is listed in your packet of information. Memorize it and then destroy it. The line is secure and you can get ahold of me any time, night or day."

Tracie groaned inwardly. She would truly be operating alone. Stallings despised her. But more to the point, he was a political animal, a decades-long Washington insider. His guiding principle, like that of most Washington insiders, was self-interest above all else. Any illusion that the CIA or any other government entity would come to her rescue should she falter, vanished.

She turned and walked to the office door, determined not to show any concern. She refused to give Stallings the satisfaction. She placed her hand on the knob and then turned to look back at her now-direct superior. The CIA director was gazing at her shrewdly. "Why me?" she asked.

"What do you mean?"

"There are plenty of operatives who've been working longer than me, who would probably be better-suited to save the life of the man fifth in the line of succession for the presidency. What made you choose me?"

Stallings stared at her a moment, his eyes cold and calculating. She was certain he would give a bullshit answer, but he surprised her. "You managed to elude a team of trained Soviet assassins and take out an experienced sniper on top of the Minuteman Insurance building ..." She thought of Shane and her heart ached. "But, more than anything else, I picked you because you're expendable. You're a throwaway. We can lose you and not miss a beat."

She regarded him from the doorway. His arrogant smile remained pasted in place. "I appreciate your honesty," she said evenly, then opened the door and walked out.

6

J. Robert Humphries had been left mostly alone by his kidnappers for what felt like a very long time after being deposited inside a partially remodeled corner of a big empty building. Their only interaction with him had been to escort him to the bathroom a few times and to bring him some food and water.

Conversation was kept to a minimum during these visits, but he had been surprised—and disheartened—to discover that the kidnappers consistently allowed him to see their faces while providing his food and bathroom breaks. The hood that had remained in place over his head was pulled off for the duration of these too-short breaks. While he was thankful to be able to see and to breathe normally for a few minutes, that small pleasure was overshadowed by the knowledge that felons allowing the victim of their crimes to see them, and thus identify them, could mean only one thing: they didn't expect him ever to get that opportunity.

After being escorted out of his home by the man with the handgun, J.R. had been shoved unceremoniously into the back seat of the automobile that had pulled up behind his murdered protective agent's car. A sack had been pulled over his head and when he complained, the response had been, "Shut up, or you will end up like the dead agent."

Although his permanent home was in Fargo, North Dakota, J. Robert Humphries had spent most of the last three decades in the Washington, D.C., area. He had been determined to follow the turns of the kidnap vehicle, to map their route in his head. Sooner or later he would have an opportunity to contact rescuers—he hoped—and he wanted to give the authorities the best possible chance of locating him.

Despite a nearly encyclopedic knowledge of the layout of Washington D.C., with the bag pulled tightly over his head he became lost and confused almost immediately. The driver made several left and right turns in rapid succession and that was the end of Humphries's plan.

Then they had driven for what seemed like hours.

The car stopped once to refuel. When Humphries heard the distinctive *clunk* of the nozzle sliding into the gas tank, he thought for one brief second about screaming for help and trusting fate or luck that someone would be within hearing distance. But then a gun barrel had been placed against his temple, the pressure hard and unyielding and terrifying, and a soft voice had whispered through the cloth on his head, "Not one word or you die."

And J. Robert Humphries had closed his mouth. By the time they arrived at their destination, he knew the sun was rising because he could sense the brightness through the sackcloth. But whether they had driven hundreds of miles away from D.C. or taken a circuitous route just to confuse him and ended up near where they had started, he could not guess.

He was being held in an abandoned schoolhouse, made obvious to him through his supervised trips to use a bathroom that would be recognizable to anyone who had grown up in the United States in the last hundred years and attended a public school. The building was old and musty and had clearly been empty for years. Maybe decades.

But this was more than just an abandoned school building. Construction work had been done in the area he was being held. It had been built to look like any bedroom in any anonymous American home. The work was shoddy and the materials cheap, but the illusion was fairly persuasive if you ignored the fact that only three-quarters of a room had been built. The effect was jarring.

The "room" was sparsely furnished, with an iron-framed bed which he assumed he would be handcuffed to when he slept, if he lived that long. There was also the chair to which he was currently manacled and a small bedside table with nothing on it. The white sheetrock walls of his "bedroom" held a couple of unremarkable paintings, reproductions of artwork undoubtedly mass-produced, that likely decorated the interiors of cheap motels all over the country.

When allowed to use the bathroom, he had been escorted a short distance along a typically wide school hallway, dark and barren, and then been locked inside a metal-walled stall to do his business. When he finished, he knocked on the door and waited for it to be unlocked and opened by one of his captors while the man leveled a handgun in his face. Then he was escorted back to his bedroom, where he was once again manacled, wrists and ankles, to the heavy wooden chair with the sackcloth secured over his head.

The same routine had taken place twice thus far. It hadn't varied. After the first occasion he had asked why the sack was necessary—the bedroom windows had been boarded over and the door to his makeshift cell was locked from the outside. Additionally, he had to assume an armed guard had been posted outside the door.

The answer had been a terse, "Shut up!"

After the second trip to the bathroom he hadn't bothered to ask again. He assumed at that point that the sack was meant to increase his sense of isolation and thus his fear. Humphries further assumed that if his first request to have it removed had gone unheeded, it was pointless to try again, and he refused to allow them the satisfaction of telling him once more to shut up.

It was a small victory. Likely a meaningless one as well.

The rest of his time had been spent alone and undisturbed, giving Humphries plenty of time to think. Fear was a constant, although after the initial spike of terror he had suffered last night in his townhouse upon seeing the business end of a pistol shoved in his face, it had receded to a more or less manageable level.

For the time being.

He wondered what time it was, and knew that by now the president would have been informed that he was missing. The forces of the United States government would even now be mobilizing to find and save him.

Humphries found the prospect less than inspiring. As a longtime Washington political insider, he was intimately familiar with the capabilities and limitations of Uncle Sam's massive bureaucracy, and while government force could be a fearsome and awe-inspiring thing, he knew all too well that it could be cumbersome and slow to respond to individual crises.

He was considering the fate of the Bureau of Diplomatic Security agent, ashamed to admit to himself he wasn't even sure which agent had been assigned to guard his residence, when the sound of the heavy lock turning in the door refocused his terror immediately.

The door opened and he heard heavy footfalls crossing the room. It was the sound of a man moving with a purpose. A second later the cloth sack was ripped off his head.

It took a moment for his eyes to adjust. He blinked rapidly despite the relative darkness of the room, lit only by a single low-wattage bulb screwed into a floor lamp against the far wall. The building's power had been disconnected years ago, Humphries assumed. His captors must have set up a generator somewhere, although he could hear nothing that sounded even remotely like the running of a small engine.

When he was able to focus, Humphries saw a man standing before him holding a newspaper and a camera. It was the same man who had accompanied him on both bathroom trips, and who brought him food and water. "I hope you are not camera-shy," he grunted.

Humphries took a deep breath, hoping his heart wouldn't explode inside his chest and send him to the grave before his kidnappers could. He glanced at the paper and then up at the kidnapper. "Proof of life, I assume?" he said, willing his voice not to shake. He would be damned if he was going to give these lawbreakers the satisfaction of knowing how frightened he was.

The man smiled at the question. "Something like that," he said. He inserted a key into the cuff securing Humphries's left hand to the chair and unlocked it. Then he held out the newspaper for Humphries to take.

Humphries looked at the front page and blinked in stunned surprise. It wasn't the *New York Times* or the *Washington Post* or the *Los Angeles Times*. In fact, the newspaper wasn't even written in English. Covering the entire page was the distinctive Cyrillic script used in Russian dialects.

Humphries was floored. The idea that foreign nationals might have kidnapped him for political purposes didn't come as any surprise; it was the first thing he had considered. It would explain the choice of victim—the U.S. secretary of state—perfectly.

But the possibility that the kidnappers might be agents of a Soviet-bloc country hadn't even occurred to him. The three men he had seen since his kidnapping were all physically very similar: olive-skinned and swarthy, with curly dark-brown, almost black hair. Complexion-wise, they were the exact opposite of what he would have expected of Russians or Czechs or East Germans. And their accents sounded not even remotely Russian.

The kidnapper's eyes narrowed in annoyance. "What do you think you are looking at?" he said.

Humphries shook his head silently. He was mystified, more so than he had been two minutes ago.

The kidnapper eyed him a moment longer and then demanded, "Hold the paper up, just under your chin, front page out."

J.R. did as he was told and the kidnapper stepped back to snap a photo. J.R. stared directly into the camera with what he hoped was a defiant look, knowing the picture would likely be on the front page of every newspaper as well as being the lead story on every television newscast within a matter of hours.

The shutter clicked and the flash popped, and then the kidnapper stepped forward again and ripped the newspaper out of Humphries's hand without another word. He yanked the hood back down over Humphries's head and stalked out of the room.

The door closed and the lock clicked into place.

And J. Robert Humphries sat in solitary terror, wondering what the hell was happening.

7

Tracie accepted the packet of evidence offered by Stallings's secretary and hurried to an empty conference room. She had two hours to absorb as much information as she could before a scheduled noon briefing with FBI and D.C. police officials on the search for Secretary of State J. Robert Humphries.

It was not nearly enough time. Everyone else involved had more than a twelve-hour head start, and Stallings had made it clear he expected immediate results from her, regardless of anyone else's progress.

And she had precious little experience in locating missing persons.

She had no law enforcement experience at all, really. When she thought about it, she realized most of what she had done in service to her country over her seven-year career would be considered by most objective observers to be on the *wrong* side of the law, at least technically speaking.

That was not to say she felt any guilt. The process of defending the world's preeminent democracy when many governments would stop at nothing to undermine it, even topple it, was inevitably a messy one. It came as no surprise, at least to Tracie, that it often involved actions some would find distasteful. Morally objectionable. Even repugnant.

But that didn't mean they weren't necessary.

However, her operational CIA experience rarely involved *finding* persons of interest. More often her work involved taking some specified action *against* persons of interest: Intimidating them. Bribing them. Occasionally saving them, as she had done with Boris Rogaev back in Leningrad. Almost always, though, she knew exactly *where* to find them.

She sipped a coffee purchased from a break room vending machine—it had the sludgy consistency of well-worn motor oil and was hot enough to melt steel—and spread the materials across the conference table in front of her.

There was a copy of the responding D.C. police officer's report, as well as of the FBI lead investigator's report.

There were crime scene photos of the murdered Bureau of Diplomatic Security agent and the interior of his car.

There were contact names and telephone numbers.

There were dozens of photos of the secretary of state's townhouse, both interior and exterior shots, from all angles. Most of the photos focused on the downstairs study, where Humphries was believed to have been working when he was taken.

Tracie scanned the mass of evidence and pictures of Humphries's house, and one thing caught her attention immediately. Featured prominently in several of the crime scene photos was a handgun that had apparently been dropped on the carpet behind Humphries's desk.

And it wasn't just any handgun. It was a weapon very familiar to Tracie, she had seen dozens of them up close over the years and had been shot twice with an identical weapon just three months ago, not far from where she sat drinking scalding hot coffee.

It was a Russian-made Makarov 9mm semiautomatic pistol.

* * *

Tuesday, September 8, 1987
12:00 p.m.
FBI Headquarters, Washington, D.C.

Precisely at noon Tracie walked into a plushly appointed conference room located on the third floor of the J. Edgar Hoover FBI Headquarters Building. Milling around the table were roughly a dozen bureaucratic types, all dressed in nearly identical

Brooks Brothers—or maybe knockoff—suits. Tracie had the absurd thought that all of the men must shop at the same clothing store.

Every other occupant of the conference room was male, and all of their heads turned as if on swivels to check out the new arrival. Tracie was used to being ogled. Unless she intentionally dressed for anonymity, as she had done in Leningrad while waiting to ambush Boris Rogaev, she was fully aware of her stunning good looks and their effect on men. She had taken advantage of those good looks many times in the field.

Now, however, she would face the opposite problem. A woman's ability to be taken seriously by men seemed inversely proportional to her beauty. She knew instinctively, based on long experience, that at some point she would have to demonstrate that she was more than just a pretty face—she was someone to be taken seriously.

A man with unevenly dyed black hair and an officious bureaucratic bearing stood at the head of the table. Tracie recognized him as FBI Director Matt Steinman. Upon Tracie's arrival, Steinman cleared his throat and said loudly, "All right, everyone is *finally* here, so please take a seat and let's get started."

Tracie knew every eye was on her. She made a show of checking her watch and then said, just as loudly but with a chill to her voice, "Unless my watch is off, I'm right on time. Keep your editorial comments to yourself." She stared down Steinman, pulled out a chair, and sat at the table.

The FBI director's face reddened and Tracie wondered whether he'd blow up or get himself under control. It didn't matter to her. Either way, she'd just established control. Steinman couldn't come close to intimidating her after some of the things she'd seen—and done—in the field. Plus, she'd stood up to CIA Director Aaron Stallings, a man renowned in political circles for his explosive temper, more than once.

"Excuse me, miss?" Steinman finally ventured.

"You heard me. I'm precisely on time, so I'll thank you to keep your unnecessary and unproductive comments to yourself. Or am I wrong in assuming we have more important things to do than measure each other's dicks?"

Nervous laughter came from around the table. From everyone except Matt Steinman, who fixed her with a glare she steadfastly returned. Apparently stumped for a response to her challenge, he dropped his gaze and continued on as if nothing had happened. "All right everyone," he said. "Quick introductions and then we'll begin."

The men went around the table introducing themselves and their government agency or law enforcement connection. When it was Tracie's turn, she said simply, "Candice Clayburgh, special liaison."

"Liaison to who?" Steinman demanded.

Jesus, Tracie thought. *Wasn't he advised of the confidential nature of my mission?* "I'm not at liberty to say," she answered coolly after a short pause. "Weren't you informed I would be attending this meeting?"

"Of course."

"And I assume you're aware of who informed you?" Tracie hoped even an entrenched, decades-long bureaucrat like Matt Steinman would have enough sense and operational awareness to recognize and understand the concept of plausible deniability. It was critical her White House/CIA connection remain private.

The room became so quiet Tracie was sure she could have heard a pin drop, even on the carpet.

Comprehension dawned on Steinman's face. He glared at her but said, "Welcome aboard, Candice," making it perfectly clear he meant no such thing. Then, "We have a lot to do. Let's get started."

Every official sitting at this table knew, or at least could reasonably guess, that she was there clandestinely. The sharper ones would likely even be able to deduce for whom she was working. But their deductions were irrelevant. Nothing could be proven, and thus everyone above her in the food chain was protected.

It was comforting for everyone but her.

* * *

The meeting droned on. Evidence analysis was followed by a discussion of various theories regarding the secretary of state's abduction. Tracie fully understood why the president had asked Aaron Stallings to take action outside normal bureaucratic and law enforcement channels: utilizing those channels would be slow and cumbersome.

But the meeting did prove helpful in some ways. She learned that President Reagan had personally contacted Soviet General Secretary Mikhael Gorbachev to protest in the strongest possible manner Humphries's kidnapping. The Soviet leader had responded unequivocally that the U.S.S.R. was not in any way involved in the secretary's disappearance, and that furthermore they resented the implication of impropriety. Tensions were skyrocketing, with rumors of war preparations already flying.

She also learned that in a matter of hours State Department representatives would accompany FBI investigators to the Russian embassy to discuss the kidnapping with Soviet representatives in an attempt to gauge the truthfulness of their denials. No one doubted they would deny involvement, echoing the statement of their leader, despite the Russian-made weapon that had been found at the scene.

"The fact of the matter is," intoned FBI Director Steinman, "that the Makarov recovered at Humphries's residence demonstrates virtually without question that if a Russian wasn't involved, another Soviet bloc state almost certainly was. None of those Soviet satellites operate independent of Moscow, and Gorbachev is full of crap if he expects us to buy the whole ignorance schtick he's trying to sell."

Tracie listened, as she had for most of the afternoon, without speaking. Her reason for attending was to gather information, not to speculate wildly, though wild speculation seemed to be the order of the day. Having spent much of her career operating in and around Soviet bloc states, it was obvious to her that Steinman was speaking as a bureaucrat rather than an investigator.

But finally she couldn't take it anymore. She said, "Explain to me again why we're so certain Humphries was kidnapped by the Soviets?"

At the head of the table, Steinman rolled his eyes. Tracie sensed annoyance from the men around the table, even from those who had been solidly in her corner after she smacked down the FBI director.

She didn't care.

Steinman sighed theatrically and then said, "Have you even been paying attention Miss…"

"Clayburgh," she reminded him helpfully.

"Yes, Miss Clayburgh. Have you been listening? A Makarov semiautomatic handgun was found on the floor of the room from which we believe the secretary of state was taken. You're obviously unaware of the significance of that fact, so I'll spell it out for you, and I'll speak slowly so you might be able to keep up. A Makarov is a *Russian gun*. Its presence in the home, when we know with certainty that J. Robert Humphries owns *no* guns, indicates almost beyond all doubt that a Russian, or at the very least, a Soviet-bloc representative, was responsible for Humphries's disappearance." He shook his head in exasperation when he had finished speaking.

"Why?" Tracie said.

"Excuse me?"

"I said, why does the fact that a Russian gun was found at the scene demonstrate that Humphries was taken by a Russian?"

"*It's a Russian gun!* How many Americans do you think own Makarov pistols?"

"I don't know, probably not many. But you're missing the point."

"Jesus, lady, I understand we're not supposed to know why you're here, but I feel confident in saying whoever you're working for wouldn't want you impeding the investigation and slowing things down. And that's exactly what you're doing. So why don't you just sit back and keep your mouth shut and let the professionals handle this?"

Tracie nodded thoughtfully. "Okay," she said. "I'll be sure to let my superiors know you weren't interested in hearing what I had to say. I'll make my point to *them* and they can determine its value for themselves."

Steinman exhaled explosively, his face reddening just as it had at the beginning of the meeting. "Fine. What's your goddamn point?"

"Good decision," she said sweetly, "and I'll be as quick and concise as I can, so you professionals can get back to work. Has anyone determined exactly *how* that Makarov ended up on the floor behind the secretary of state's chair?"

"The kidnapper obviously dropped it in his haste to escort Secretary of State Humphries out of the home."

"Shouldn't we assume that the Soviets would send their best

men on such an audacious mission, to kidnap the United States secretary of state out of his own home, right under the noses of the Bureau of Diplomatic Security, *in Washington, D.C.*, of all places?"

"I think that would be a fair assumption," Steinman conceded reluctantly. "So what?"

"Well, doesn't it strike any of you professionals as a little . . . I don't know . . . *unlikely* that one of the Soviets' finest covert ops teams would execute such a bold and complicated plan nearly to perfection, only to accidentally forget one of their weapons as they're exiting the house? Does anyone at this table really believe they'd be that sloppy, particularly when the most difficult part of the mission has been accomplished?"

Tracie saw thoughtful expressions on the faces of the men ringing the table. But Steinman simply shook his head in disgust. When he replied, his voice was scornful. "It's not your fault that you don't understand how these things work," he said. "But agents with operational experience know that things go wrong on every mission. Events happen that just can't be planned for. That's obviously the circumstance here. One of the Soviet agents got a little too overconfident and screwed up. It's a lucky break for us, and one we will most certainly take advantage of. If you had any real-world experience," he added bitingly, "you would have realized that."

"I see," Tracie said. "Thank you for helping me understand how things work in the real world." She struggled to keep the sarcasm out of her voice. She had probably seen more fieldwork in her seven-year career than all these men put together, and she figured Steinman's real-world experience had likely been limited to a year or two as an FBI special agent before beginning his climb up the bureaucratic ladder.

"But," she continued before anyone could cut her off, "has anyone given any consideration to the possibility that we were *supposed* to find that weapon, that the kidnappers used Makarovs specifically so that they could throw one down at the crime scene and implicate the Soviets?"

"*What?*" Steinman's already red face was turning purple now. "Are you trying to tell me this kidnapping is a setup?"

"I'm not trying to tell you anything. I'm just asking a question."

"What purpose would anyone have in setting up the Soviets in this manner? And furthermore, *who* would do such a thing?"

"All good questions," Tracie answered with a shrug.

"That theory is preposterous," Steinman said. "We have to conduct this investigation on the basis of the evidence uncovered, not on some wild flight of fancy concocted out of thin air."

"So your answer is no, then. No one has given my scenario any consideration."

"My answer," Steinman said, his voice rising, "is that there's no reason to assume this kidnapping is anything but a Soviet operation, their official denials be damned. Now, if no one has any other unsupported theories to toss out, I suggest we wrap this up and go find one missing secretary of state."

No one spoke and Steinman nodded, lowering himself into his chair at the same time everyone else at the conference table began to stand. Tracie was relieved to note that his complexion seemed to be returning to normal. She had needed to put him in his place, but sending him to the hospital wasn't part of the plan.

Papers were being shuffled into briefcases and the buzz of a half-dozen individual conversations filled the room when there was an impatient knock at the closed door.

Steinman looked up, puzzled, and said, "Yes, come in," just as the door burst open and a harried young man in a suit similar to those worn by nearly everyone else in the conference room hurried in. In his hand he held a manila envelope. He ignored the agents and law enforcement representatives milling about and walked briskly to Steinman, handing over the envelope without a word.

Tracie—along with everyone else in the room—watched with interest as the FBI director unsealed the envelope and withdrew a single sheet of paper. He stared at it for a moment before lifting his head to gaze directly into Tracie's eyes. He held the sheet of paper up and turned it outward so those gathered in the room could see it.

"Still think the Soviets are being set up?" he asked acidly.

On the paper was a reproduction of a photograph of United States Secretary of State J. Robert Humphries. His right wrist was manacled to a chair. His left hand was free, and in it he clutched a newspaper, holding the front page just under his chin. The newspaper was printed in Cyrillic.

Russian.

8

Before leaving FBI headquarters, Tracie received a mimeographed copy of the Humphries photo, which she tucked into her briefcase along with copies of all the other related evidence. There was no question the dramatic picture had once again convinced most, if not all, of the investigators that the Soviets were behind the kidnapping.

Tracie, however, remained skeptical. Something about the Russian newspaper in the photo bothered her, although she couldn't quite put her finger on what it was. But more to the point, why would the KGB be so up-front about advertising their involvement in a kidnapping plot just hours after denying it at the highest levels?

And why send the chilling photograph along to the Department of State—which had forwarded a copy immediately to the FBI—without any written communication attached?

Why would the Soviet Union risk such a dangerous undertaking without a clear objective in mind, and if they *had* such an objective, why not state it?

The last question bothered Tracie the most, and she chewed on it as she exited the building. The more she considered the issue, the more she came to the conclusion that there *was* a clear objective. And it was exactly what she had voiced at the meeting: to throw the weight of suspicion onto the Soviets and away from whatever country had actually kidnapped the secretary of state.

It was the only option that made sense, at least to Tracie. But before she was willing to place all her eggs in that particular basket, she would have to convince herself beyond all doubt of the truthfulness of the Soviets' assertion that neither they, nor any of their allies, had kidnapped Humphries.

She knew tense discussions had been taking place all day at the Soviet embassy between State Department officials and Russian diplomats regarding the Humphries situation. She knew also that those discussions would yield nothing of value. Experience had taught her that there was no way on God's green earth the Russian ambassador was going to counter Gorbachev's personal denial to President Reagan about the kidnapping.

Not unless that diplomat had a desire to be recalled to Moscow and hanged.

But Tracie had an advantage. She was no State Department official. No bureaucrat. The diplomatic niceties and official protocols the diplomats were expected to adhere to meant nothing to her. She wasn't bound to any code of conduct when it came to extracting the truth.

And she knew just where to find the man she needed now.

* * *

The Heart of Moscow Café was located less than a block south of the massive, heavily secured Soviet Embassy complex on Wisconsin Avenue in northwest D.C. Tracie drove past the restaurant and then pulled her CIA car to the curb roughly halfway between the Heart of Moscow and the embassy grounds.

She locked the vehicle—a plain, beautifully anonymous white Chrysler K-Car—then began walking briskly south along Wisconsin. She was thankful for the sharp-looking business suit she had worn to the briefing at the Hoover Building. With a little imagination, she could easily transform her professional attire into something more appropriate for what she had in mind.

Although the Heart of Moscow billed itself as a "café," in reality it was an upscale Washington dining establishment catering to the area's Soviet diplomatic presence. Its interior featured rich walnut wood tones, plush carpeting, and gleaming brass accents that offset the dark wood. Tracie had eaten at the

Heart of Moscow once or twice while in D.C. for mission debriefs, and it reminded her of nothing more than an old-fashioned men's club. The only thing missing were buffalo heads hanging on the walls.

All of Tracie's CIA fieldwork, prior to June's run-in with the Soviet sniper attempting to assassinate President Reagan, had taken place off U.S. soil. Nevertheless, she was well aware of Soviet Ambassador to the United States Anatoly Grinkov's love for the Heart of Moscow. Part of her responsibility as a field agent specializing in Eastern European affairs was to familiarize herself with all of the Soviet Union's major players in the world of politics as well as espionage, as the two were inextricably linked.

Thus, she knew a number of key facts about Grinkov: he was inaccessible behind the high walls and iron gates of the Soviet Embassy, and he preferred to eat most of his evening meals at the Russian-themed restaurant. Although security was heavy while he dined, Grinkov was known to enjoy the authentic Russian vodka served at the Heart of Moscow—often too much of it—and U.S. intelligence officials had verified numerous incidents of Grinkov sneaking away from the restaurant in the company of top-tier prostitutes.

With no form of security.

American intelligence officials had long been aware of this security weakness and had been waiting for the right time to exploit it. Tracie thought the current situation fit the bill perfectly. She wasn't sure Aaron Stallings would agree—was virtually certain the CIA director would *disagree*, in fact—so she hadn't yet bothered checking in with her contact. Failing to receive permission was a whole different ballgame than asking for it and being denied.

The last Tracie knew, Soviet Ambassador Grinkov had not missed a weeknight meal at the Heart of Moscow in months. She had remained as current as possible with intelligence reports while completing rehab for the wounds she suffered in her life-and-death struggle on the roof of the Minuteman Mutual building in June, and while she had no way of knowing for certain that Grinkov would be here tonight, it was well worth spending a couple of hours to find out.

After leaving the Hoover Building and before getting into

her car, Tracie had walked straight to a phone booth on the corner of Ninth and D Streets and called in a dinner reservation for one at the Heart of Moscow. It would have been quicker and easier to do it from one of the many phones at FBI Headquarters, but there was no way in the world she was going to leave a record of *that* particular call.

Now, as she navigated the crowded sidewalk, Tracie reached up and removed the barrette that had been holding her hair in a bun. The conservative style she had sported for the FBI briefing was the exact opposite of what she wanted to achieve now. Her thick mane of lustrous red hair tumbled over her shoulders and she shook it out, then pulled it all to one side where it caressed her neck and nestled softly against her right breast.

The temperature was still warm as the late-summer sun began to fall below the horizon. Tracie opened her blazer and unfastened the top two buttons of her sharply creased white blouse. She glanced down and muttered, "Ah, what the hell," and unbuttoned a third. The blouse was not exactly sheer, but with a hint of a lacy bra that would show every time she leaned forward, Tracie felt she stood a good chance of getting Grinkov's attention. She wished her skirt were a little shorter, but there was nothing she could do about that. When the time came, she would make sure to flash plenty of leg.

Her heels clicked on the pavement and she picked up her pace. She wanted to be in place at the Heart of Moscow prior to the arrival of Grinkov's dinner party, should he show up. At the café's entrance, she adopted a sultry expression and, affecting a thick Russian accent, said to the hostess, "You have reservation for me, yes? The name, Ekatarina Zharykhin?"

The hostess, a young raven-haired woman Tracie took for a Washington-area college student earning extra spending money, eyed her coolly. It was the look women reserve for other women they believe are dressed inappropriately. Tracie resisted the urge to smile. *Perfect*, she thought. *The hooker persona is working.*

The hostess took her time answering, leaving no doubt her message of disapproval was received loud and clear. Finally she said, "Will anyone be joining you for dinner, Miss Zharykhin?"

Tracie smiled wickedly. "The reservation is for one, but who knows how night will progress, eh?"

"Right this way, please." The overmatched hostess took one

final glance at Tracie's low-cut blouse, met her eyes and then looked away, before leading her to a tiny table near the back of the restaurant. It was exactly where Tracie had known she would be seated, as it was the only place in the dining room with tables small enough to seat a single diner.

It was also the perfect location from which to intercept Ambassador Grinkov. He would have to walk directly past her table to reach the men's room, and once he started drinking vodka, it would only be a matter of time before he made that journey.

Tracie eased into her seat and ordered a drink. All she had to do now was wait.

9

Tracie was lingering over dessert when she got her chance. The restaurant had filled up shortly after her arrival and had remained busy ever since, and she was beginning to fear the staff would ask her to leave before Grinkov made his first trip to the men's room.

And then, there he was.

Anatoly Grinkov was a bear of a man, with thick black hair and a scruffy salt-and-pepper beard he wore in a perpetual two-day growth, à la Don Johnson in *Miami Vice*. He appeared from around a corner, walking in a direct line toward the men's room like a man on a mission. He didn't stumble, didn't zig-zag or look in any way impaired, but a trace of an alcohol flush colored his face and, to Tracie, his eyes looked a touch glassy.

She waited until he was almost past her table before hiking her skirt halfway up her thighs and sliding out of her seat. She thrust her left leg out so that her bare knee just grazed the passing ambassador's shin, rubbing his leg through his dress pants. "Oh," she said, feigning surprise, still employing her thick Russian accent. "Excuse me, Comrade Grinkov, I did not see you coming!"

Grinkov glanced down at her and did a comical double take. Tracie watched as his eyes traveled up her legs. They lingered at the hem of her skirt, which had ridden even higher as she slid out of her seat, before examining her cleavage and finally reaching her eyes.

He stopped, seeming to forget his intention to use the men's room, and said, "How do you know who I am?" His tone indicated that of course she would know who he was, but that these little games must be played out.

Tracie didn't mind. "Everyone knows Anatoly Grinkov," she said, her voice a seductive purr. She ran a fingertip over the rim of her vodka glass and then lifted it to her lips, where she sucked off the moisture. Grinkov's eyes tracked her finger's journey. "The name 'Grinkov' means 'power' to me," she whispered, "and power is so . . . seductive. . ."

She lifted her eyes to Grinkov's face, parted her lips and ran her tongue over them slowly. The Soviet ambassador smiled widely and said, "Come with me." Then he turned his back and strode down the hallway toward the rest rooms, apparently never considering the possibility she might not follow.

Tracie glanced around the restaurant. One of the reasons the Soviet embassy personnel favored the Heart of Moscow, in addition to its fine food and authentic Russian vodka, was the layout of the dining area. Every table, even singles like the one where Tracie had been seated, was surrounded by heavily polished walnut barriers rising virtually to the ceiling. Thus, the dining room could be filled and still the diners at each table were afforded the utmost privacy.

She smiled and hurried after the Soviet ambassador, catching up to him just as he reached the restroom doors. The ladies room was on the left side of the hallway, the men's on the right. Grinkov leaned right and pushed the door open, took a quick glance inside the lavatory, then turned back to Tracie with a grin that she assumed was supposed to be seductive but looked downright creepy. "Time to enjoy some of that 'power,' eh?" he said before he disappeared into the lavatory.

Tracie glanced one more time down the hallway—still empty—and then followed the horny politician into the bathroom. It was scrupulously clean, with gleaming pale blue ceramic tiles on the walls and a floor that looked as though you could eat off it. Four urinals lined one wall, and beyond those fixtures were four toilets enclosed inside stalls separated by the typical institutional portable metal dividers running nearly floor to ceiling.

Grinkov stood in front of the farthest stall, creepy grin still plastered across his slightly drunk face. Tracie could see his suit trousers slightly tented and knew he was anxious to get started.

She pretended to be hesitant. "Comrade Grinkov," she said. "Right here? What if someone comes in?"

He laughed like a man who had had this conversation many times. Probably he had. "No one will care, darling, and if they do, I will pay for their entire meal. They will leave here happier than when they came in, trust me. The Americans call it 'profit motive,' da?"

Tracie forced a giggle and ran her eyes up and down Grinkov's body before following him into the stall. She turned and engaged the lock, while behind her, she heard Soviet Amabassador Anatoly Grinkov's fly unzip. She turned back to the Russian and sank to her knees while he very helpfully removed himself from his trousers.

This was the critical part of the operation. On her knees in front of him, Tracie was as close to defenseless as she was comfortable allowing herself to get. She had to ensure he remained preoccupied for just a couple more seconds.

She smiled hungrily and held his gaze, locking eyes with the bureaucrat while her right hand snaked around her back and under her linen jacket. She slipped her fingers under the waistband of her skirt, wrapping them around her tactical combat knife that was held securely in its leather scabbard sewn into a belt that wound around her waist. It made for a slightly uncomfortable fit, but Tracie didn't care. When needed, it was the perfect fashion accessory.

"What are you waiting for?" Grinkov growled. "My time is precious."

Tracie pretended to admire him. "You are very well endowed," she said, still in the thick Russian accent she had been affecting since entering the Heart of Moscow, but now she dropped the pretense and finished in her normal American dialect. "What are you going to do when it's gone?"

In an instant, she brought the combat knife out from behind her back and held it against Anatoly Grinkov's member, which immediately lost some of its luster. Not to mention size. "What do you think you are doing?" he said slowly, his voice low and menacing.

"Mr. Ambassador, we need to talk," Tracie said calmly. She rose to her feet, maintaining the knife's hair's breadth distance from the man's organ. Despite his intimidating tone, Grinkov had yet to move a muscle.

"Who are you?" he demanded, and then, without waiting for a reply, added, "I have nothing to say to you, whoever you are."

"We'll see about that," she said, her voice quiet but determined. "Now, very carefully, zip yourself up." She removed the knife from his crotch and before he could react, slid the razor-sharp blade under the back of his suit jacket, pressing it lightly against his spine. "Keep in mind that if you make one move I interpret as threatening, I'll gut you like a trout before you even know what hit you. Do you understand, Mr. Amabassador?"

Grinkov glared at her, hesitating only a moment before saying, "I understand."

"Good. We're going to leave the restroom and turn right. Then we'll walk down the hallway, through the bar and out the back entrance. Attempt to signal anyone and you die. Scream or yell or even breathe heavy and you die. Move in any way I don't like, and what do you think happens?"

"I understand," Grinkov spat, refusing to say the words.

"Let's go, then." Tracie knew time was precious. Grinkov had obviously pulled his Lothario routine many times before, so his security would not begin to get suspicious about his absence for a few more minutes, but the Russian's idea of romance wasn't exactly a drawn-out affair. Before too much more time passed, his security team would send someone to find him. When he wasn't located, the Heart of Moscow Café would be locked down like Folsom Prison within seconds.

The odd-looking pair shuffled to the men's room door and exited. To anyone who didn't look too closely, they would resemble a romantic couple walking through the bar, the young woman with her arm around her lover's back.

She hoped.

Ambassador Anatoly Grinkov was a regular here, so many people would recognize him if they were paying attention. There was definitely some risk involved. But the walk through the darkened lounge to the seldom-used rear entrance was a short one, and Tracie felt reasonably confident her bold play would work.

It did. Within seconds, they had pushed through the Heart of Moscow's back door and into the still-cooling night. The sun had long since set and lighting was minimal. Tracie felt the most dangerous part of the operation was now behind her.

And Anatoly Grinkov stopped walking.

"I am not going one step farther," he said, seeming to realize the farther away from his security detail he got, the worse his situation became.

In an instant, Tracie had pulled the knife out from behind the big Russian and grabbed his left wrist with her left hand. She stepped nimbly behind him and twisted his arm back and to the right, pulling it taut, his hand now immobilized painfully up near his shoulder blades.

With her right hand, she reached around and placed the tip of the combat knife against the ambassador's ample belly. The entire maneuver was completed in a single eye blink. "Walk or die," she said through gritted teeth. "It's your choice."

The Russian held his ground for a moment and Tracie increased the knife's pressure. She felt it slice through his dress shirt and t-shirt. He gasped as it drew blood, and then he began moving again, trudging forward like a condemned man on his way to the gallows.

Good. That was what she wanted him to think. She knew he would never talk otherwise.

IO

I nside the Oval Office, the mood had not improved over the course of the day.

The same participants as this morning—with one notable exception—had gathered for another situation briefing, and there was no good news to report to a president who was becoming increasingly frustrated.

Briefing packages were passed around. Included in each were copies of another photograph of Secretary of State J. Robert Humphries as well as the recently received list of the kidnappers' demands.

The list was handwritten.

In Russian.

Each briefing package included a typed translation placed directly below the photocopy of the list of demands.

As tense as the morning's presidential briefing had been, this one was much more so. CIA Director Aaron Stallings almost felt sorry for his FBI counterpart, Matt Steinman, because before Steinman could even begin, President Reagan said, "I want at least one bit of good news I can bring to Sara Humphries when I leave here. Someone had better tell me we've made progress locating J.R. Can anyone tell me that?"

The image of the kind grandfatherly figure Americans had twice voted for, the man quick with a smile and a quip, was absent tonight. Instead, the president appeared angry and worried as he sat behind his desk, his face set and determined even as his age lines seemed a little deeper than they had just a few hours ago.

"Well, Mr. President, there is cause for optimism," Steinman said. "This latest communication from the kidnappers confirms our earlier conclusion that the Soviets are indeed holding the secretary of state."

"Cause for optimism," Reagan repeated. "How so? Do we know *where* J.R. is being held? Do we know *how* we're going to get him back?"

"Well, no, sir," Steinman said, unconsciously reaching under his collar and pulling it away from his perspiring neck.

"Then, would you please explain why in the *hell* I should feel optimistic about anything?"

"Well, sir, now that we have direct confirmation that the Soviets are involved, we can begin putting pressure on them to release the secretary of state. They have to know that doing anything other than turning him over to us alive and well will be cause for war. I think everyone in this room would agree that's an outcome nobody wants, especially not the Soviets, and especially not at this point in time."

Reagan's eyes had been narrowing steadily as Steinman talked, and now he glared at the FBI director. Watching the exchange from the far end of the Oval Office, Aaron Stallings was intrigued. He didn't particularly like either man, but as someone who had been on the receiving end of Ronald Reagan's wrath, he could sympathize with Matt Steinman's position: forced to give bad news to a president who didn't want to hear it.

"*That's* your good news?" Reagan thundered. "We know the Soviets have kidnapped our secretary of state, but we don't have any idea where he's being held? Hell, they won't even officially admit to having him! How is *any* of that cause for optimism?"

"Sir," Steinman said. "I think it's fair to say the list of demands we received a few minutes ago eliminates any possibility we should take Gorbachev's denials seriously."

"About this list," a perplexed Ronald Reagan said after quickly reviewing the briefing package. He flicked his gaze from the package to Steinman's face and back again. "This is something else that makes no sense to me. The Soviet Union wants us to begin immediately disassembling our European strategic nuclear weapons arsenal? That's ludicrous!"

"That was our reaction as well, Mr. President."

"That subject's been under negotiation for years," Reagan continued, as if the FBI director had not even spoken. "The Soviets know it's not in our interest to remove even *some* of those weapons, never mind all of them. Has Gorbachev lost his mind? And why would he officially deny involvement in the kidnapping if he planned to hit us with these demands just a few hours later?"

Stallings cleared his throat before he spoke. "Mr. President, perhaps General Secretary Gorbachev is unaware of the Soviet involvement. The Communists' grip on power is slipping. The world is changing rapidly. It's not outside the realm of possibility that another faction inside Russia has taken Secretary Humphries."

"But to what end? It's beyond belief that *any* faction would think we would accede to demands as sweeping as these. Even as close as I am with J.R., I could never put our friendship ahead of the safety and security of our European allies."

"Apparently someone has decided to test your resolve on that issue, sir."

The president glared at Matt Steinman as if perhaps the FBI director himself had written the ransom demands. Despite the gravity of the situation, Aaron Stallings had to stifle a smile as the outmatched Steinman tried to meet Reagan's stare, only to drop his eyes after a second or two.

The briefing continued for another thirty minutes, despite the fact not one participant had anything of import to add. Stallings half paid attention while thinking about Tracie Tanner and whether she had made any progress in tracking J.R. Humphries.

He hoped so. He knew President Reagan would be expecting a personal briefing on Tanner's unofficial, unsanctioned op later, and he had no desire to have to face the withering gaze of the leader of the free world.

II

Battery Kemble Park was deserted this time of night, just as Tracie had known it would be. As the daughter of a high-ranking U.S. Army general and a career Washington diplomat, Tracie had spent her formative years in the D.C. area and knew that during daylight hours many locals considered the national park and former Union Army Civil War garrison a prime dog-walking location.

After sunset, though, the rolling hills and winding pathways of Battery Kemble Park emptied and the park became isolated and lonely, making it the perfect spot for what she had in mind.

After boldly snatching would-be ladies man Anatoly Grinkov out from under his security detail at the Heart of Moscow Café, Tracie had walked the reckless politician through an alley behind the restaurant to her waiting car.

She shoved him through the front passenger side door and then reached under the seat and removed a pair of handcuffs she had stored there. She forced him to lean forward and brought the tip of her combat knife to Grinkov's throat. "Put your hands behind your back," she whispered. "Do it now."

He hesitated and then complied. When he did, she cuffed his wrists together behind his back. Then she tore a six-inch slice of duct tape off a roll and slapped it over the Soviet ambassador's mouth.

She did all of this parked on the side of a relatively busy Washington, D.C., street while managing to look like just another young wife or girlfriend taking care of her man, who had had a little too much to drink and would face her wrath in the morning. Years of clandestine ops on foreign soil had taught Tracie that ninety-five percent of people saw exactly what they expected to see. It was the other five percent who were dangerous.

After securing Grinkov and hoping the dim nighttime light and movement of the vehicle would prevent anyone from noticing that her passenger's mouth had been sealed shut, Tracie walked around the front of the K-Car and slid into the driver's seat. Then she drove at a deliberate pace—no one is a better driver than a cautious lawbreaker—through northwest D.C. to Chain Bridge Road. There, she passed a series of stately homes on the right, set well back from the leafy road. Roughly fifty feet from the park's entrance Tracie cut her headlights and then turned left onto a narrow park access road.

Half a mile later she pulled to the side and killed the engine. Chain Bridge Road had long since disappeared in the rear view mirror and the only danger now would be if a patrolling park policeman were to see the Chrysler. The park police were notoriously understaffed, though, and from her youth Tracie knew nighttime patrols through Battery Kemble were sporadic at best.

Besides, she thought, *we won't be here long.*

The hum of the Chrysler's engine died away and they sat in silence, Tracie letting the Soviet ambassador stew in the juices of his imagination.

She waited one minute.

Two.

Then she turned to face Anatoly Grinkov. "It's time to 'fess up," she said coldly. "You understand what will happen if I remove the tape and you scream, correct?"

Grinkov nodded.

Tracie wasn't sure she believed the man, but she wouldn't be able to get the information she needed through osmosis, so she reluctantly reached over and ripped the tape off her captive's face. He gasped at the sudden pain and said, "You are crazy woman. You will pay for this."

She ignored the threat. "We know your people kidnapped Secretary of State Humphries, and you're going to tell me where he is. "If you don't, the next time anyone sees you, your bloated, lifeless corpse will be floating face down in the Potomac River."

It was obvious Grinkov was afraid but was trying hard to maintain a brave front. He shook his head, his movements jerky. He was blinking rapidly, breathing erratically, on the verge of a panic attack.

He swallowed heavily and said, "I have no idea what you are even talking about. We have kidnapped no one. But I tell you this: if you kill me, such an act of unprovoked aggression will result in all-out war."

Tracie snorted. "Unprovoked aggression? Did you really think you could kidnap J. Robert Humphries and not face consequences from the United States?" She examined the Russian's face closely as she talked and was unsurprised at what she saw.

He truly *didn't* know what she was talking about.

As a CIA clandestine ops veteran who had served in countries around the globe, Tracie's survival frequently depended upon her ability to read people, to gauge the truthfulness of their statements and to determine whether a perfect stranger represented a threat, often on little more than their facial expressions and body language.

And everything in Anatoly Grinkov's expression screamed *confusion.*

The notion that the Soviets had kidnapped the sitting U.S. secretary of state without their own ambassador to the United States being aware of the plan was ludicrous. If they had done it, he would know.

And he didn't know.

His eyes narrowed and then he confirmed Tracie's suspicions by saying, slowly, in his heavily Russian-accented English, "Secretary of State Humphries is missing? How long has he been gone?"

Tracie was nearly convinced that Grinkov knew nothing about Humphries's disappearance. But she had to be sure. She reached behind her back and retrieved her combat knife. Lifted it nearly to eye height, her movements slow and deliberate. Then she held it before his eyes and rotated her wrist. The lethal silver glittered and winked in the light of the moon streaming through the windshield.

With its black matte handle, curved tip, and partially serrated blade, it was an impressive weapon even to someone familiar with impressive weapons. Anatoly Grinkov was not such a man. His eyes widened. "Wh- What are you going to do with that?" he asked.

"Come on, Mr. Ambassador, get real. The kidnappers sent a proof of life photo of Humphries to the White House. In the picture, he's holding a newspaper. Today's date. Care to hazard a guess as to what language the newspaper is printed in?"

Grinkov's eyes flashed angrily. "I am telling you, I do not know what you are talking about."

"I don't believe you," Tracie lied. "And you're going to tell me where to find J.R. Humphries. You're going to tell me *right now*, or you're going to lose your most valuable possession. And when it's gone, there's no telling how long you'll live. I'm no first-aid expert, so I don't know how badly a severed penis will bleed. Then there's the issue of what people will say when they find your body in the morning, a semi-respected Russian diplomat bleeding to death in the middle of the night with his willy cut off."

She grinned at him as if sharing a private joke. "Wow," she said. "*Those* will be some interesting newspaper articles to read. Too bad you won't be alive to see them."

Then she gripped the knife in her teeth and slowly unzipped the ambassador's fly, removing his member from his trousers and holding it in her two hands. She glanced up into his panicked eyes and smiled sadly. "A little less enthusiastic than the last time I saw it, huh?"

Grinkov began sputtering denials, the skyrocketing stress level causing him to babble half in English, half in Russian. He leaned forward as if to head-butt her but Tracie was ready for it. She shoved him hard, forcing him against the seatback. Then she grabbed the knife out of her mouth with her right hand while maintaining a grip on his member with her left. In an instant, she had the razor-sharp blade pressed against the base of his penis. "Don't move a muscle," she hissed, "or you'll be singing soprano before you can blink."

By now Grinkov was crying, tears of rage and frustration and fear sliding down his face as he swore on his mother's grave he had no knowledge of J.R. Humphries's kidnapping saying that the Soviet government would never stoop to such a heinous crime.

Tracie hated to continue, but she had to play it to the end. "Liar!" she said, increasing her pressure on the combat knife just enough to pierce skin. Blood leaked out of the small cut and the ammonia smell of urine filled her nostrils as Grinkov's bladder voided, soaking Tracie's hand as well as his trousers and the K-Car's seat.

He screamed out one last desperate denial.

Tracie was convinced.

The Soviets were not involved.

12

Tracie was late checking in with CIA Director Aaron Stallings.

By the time she had driven the disheveled Anatoly Grinkov out of Battery Kemble Park, stopped the vehicle a half-block north of the Soviet Embassy, removed the Soviet ambassador's handcuffs and duct-tape gag, and pushed him out onto the sidewalk, it was more than thirty minutes past their agreed-upon check-in time.

Had she still been working with her previous handler, CIA veteran Winston Andrews, being thirty minutes late for a routine check-in would not have been an issue. Andrews had understood that almost nothing ever went as planned with fieldwork. Events were fluid, circumstances changed, and the operative adapted. Sticking to a hard timetable was all but impossible.

But Aaron Stallings was not just another handler. In the strictest sense he wasn't a handler at all—at least not of individual assets. He was the director of the Central Intelligence Agency, a man wielding tremendous power, who was subject to little or no direct oversight.

And who was not accustomed to being kept waiting.

By anyone. Ever.

Stallings was far sharper than FBI Director Matt Steinman, and had remained involved in the day-to-day operations of his agency, at least to the extent possible for someone in his position. Tracie had no doubt Stallings understood the elastic nature of clandestine fieldwork. Still, she knew he would not appreciate her being late barely twelve hours into her mission.

So she drove directly to Langley after dropping off Anatoly Grinkov. She was tired but anxious to report to the old CIA man what she had learned. He was expecting results and although she was no closer to determining where Humphries was being held, or even exactly who had taken him, eliminating official Soviet involvement in the kidnapping represented real progress.

She wheeled onto CIA property, knowing without a doubt that Stallings would still be holed up in his office, working. The director was legendary not just for his quick temper and abrasive personality, but for his workaholic nature as well. He had been married for over thirty years, but to Tracie's knowledge no one had ever met his wife. The joke around Langley for decades had been that the longtime CIA director's spouse was a fiction, created out of whole cloth to convince subordinates that their boss actually did have a life outside work, when the opposite was clearly the case.

In any event, even if Stallings had been a typical nine-to-five bureaucrat, there would be no question he'd still be manning his desk at this hour. With Secretary of State Humphries missing, it was all hands on deck. Nobody in a position of authority in the Reagan Administration was getting much sleep tonight. And that undoubtedly included the president himself.

Tracie returned the K-Car to a lot where it immediately slipped into anonymity, surrounded by dozens of other similar vehicles. The license plate would be removed and destroyed by an agency staffer within minutes. She retrieved all of her possessions, dumped everything into her own car, and then hurried into the massive agency headquarters building.

Accessing Stallings's office required being cleared through a second security checkpoint in addition to the one at the building's main entrance. The process had been slow and cumbersome each of the previous two times she had been summoned, but tonight one glance at her ID was enough for the security officer. He waved her through the checkpoint with an abrupt, "Director Stallings is expecting you."

Not an encouraging sign.

The hallways were mostly empty at this time of night, especially in the administrative wing. Lights had been dimmed to less than half their daytime wattage and the labyrinthine corridors of the big CIA Headquarters building felt strange and almost alien.

Tracie entered Stallings's office suite. The door directly into his office was closed. Stallings's personal secretary had long-since departed for the day, probably heading home about the time Tracie was unbuttoning the top three buttons on her blouse in preparation for her faux-seduction of Anatoly Grinkov.

She didn't hesitate. Didn't even slow down. The CIA director was a master of manipulation and intimidation and Tracie Tanner was determined not to give him the satisfaction of seeing the slightest weakness. She marched up to his closed door and rapped twice, loudly. Then she turned the knob and entered the office just as Stallings was barking, "Come in!"

The director's voice was gruff, angry, and unnecessarily loud. Tracie immediately recognized the implications: she had failed in her goal of reaching Stallings's office ahead of the official Soviet protest over the treatment of their ambassador to the United States.

In addition to being a horny old bastard, Grinkov was an efficient one as well; she had to give him that.

She had taken three steps across Aaron Stallings's carpeted office when he raised his head from a document he had been studying and said, "Just what the hell do you think you're doing, Agent Tanner?"

She met his gaze and said, "What you asked me to do."

Stallings slammed his fast down on his desk. It was one of his favorite tactics.

She saw it coming and didn't react.

He scowled. "You want to explain to me how threatening the life of the Soviet ambassador to the United States accomplishes *any part* of your mission? Christ, I send you out on an unsanctioned, unofficial operation and the first thing you do is attack the highest-profile Soviet bureaucrat you can find. What the hell is wrong with you?"

Tracie sat without being invited and said quietly, "Am I going to get the opportunity to respond, or would you prefer just to rant and rave at me?"

"You'll not only get the opportunity to respond, I *demand* a response. And it had better be good."

"Sir, you've been involved in the world of clandestine intelligence gathering since before I was born. In light of that experience, what does it tell you when a Russian-made Makarov semiautomatic pistol is found at the kidnapping scene of one of the highest-profile men in the world? And it wasn't just *there*, it was practically anchoring the crime scene. It couldn't have been more obvious if it had a flashing neon sign pointing at it."

Stallings said nothing. He continued to stare at Tracie unblinkingly. She considered his silence a marginal improvement over the yelling.

She continued. "Do you really think a team as professional and experienced as was necessary to pull off such a brazen kidnapping would have made that kind of basic error? They do everything perfectly, including getting the drop on an experienced Bureau of Diplomatic Security agent, managing to get close enough to him to blow his brains all over the inside of his vehicle without him even drawing his weapon, and then they *accidentally leave such a damning piece of evidence at the scene?* Do you really buy that? Because I sure don't."

"Mistakes happen, Agent Tanner," Stallings said evenly but without much conviction.

"That's exactly what FBI Director Steinman said," Tracie answered, intentionally tweaking her boss. The CIA director's views on his FBI counterpart were well known within the agency. Stallings scowled and she continued. "And I'll tell you what I told him. Of course mistakes happen. But the notion that elite Soviet field operatives would make that kind of egregious error with the success of the operation—not to mention their lives—on the line, I find simply impossible to believe."

"You do."

"Yes, sir, I do. And I've dealt with these people for a long time."

"Noted. But what does any of this have to do with you threatening the life of Anatoly Grinkov?"

"Come on, sir, with all due respect—"

"Just answer the question, Tanner!"

"I needed to confirm my suspicions, sir. I had to interview someone I could be certain would have knowledge *if* the Soviets were involved in Humphries's kidnapping. The obvious choice was Ambassador Grinkov. Nothing the Soviets do here in the states happens without his knowledge and approval."

"Forgetting for a moment how rash and reckless your little stunt was, do you really believe Grinkov would have admitted Soviet involvement in the face of Gorbachev's official denial, just because you asked him? That would be tantamount to committing suicide!"

"Agreed, and of course he wouldn't have admitted it. But one thing I've learned in seven years is how to read people. I know when someone is lying to me. I have to, because it's often the only thing that keeps me alive. And even when faced with the ultimate humiliation and the imminent loss of…body parts, and probably his life, I saw absolutely no indication from Anatoly Grinkov that he was lying when he continued to deny that the Soviets had kidnapped Secretary of State Humphries. None. Zero. I don't know yet who took Humphries, but one thing I *do* know is it wasn't the Soviets."

"You're one hundred percent certain, just based on reading the face of the man whose life you were threatening?"

"There's a lot more to it than just reading his face, and there's no such thing as being one hundred percent certain. But, having said that, yes, I'm as confident as I can be in my analysis."

"What about the photo of Humphries holding the Russian newspaper?"

"Come on, sir, you know that could easily be faked."

Stallings sighed. For the first time, Tracie felt as though she might be getting through to him. He said, "Yes, it could be faked, and my thoughts were exactly the same as yours when I saw the crime scene photo of that Makarov lying invitingly on the floor of Humphries's townhouse. But while you've been running around Washington threatening diplomats, there have been further developments."

Tracie's heart sank. "What developments?"

Stallings picked up the document he had been studying when she entered and tossed it across the desk at her. He remained silent until she had finished reading. It didn't take long. Thanks to Tracie's familiarity with the Russian language, she was able to read the original ransom note, rather than the English translation provided below it.

As had been the case when examining the photograph of Humphries holding the Russian newspaper hours earlier, something bothered Tracie about the letter—something she couldn't quite put her finger on. She pushed the unformed concern to the back of her mind for the moment, though, as the impact of the words hit her. She shook her head. "Am I reading this right? They want us to dismantle Western Europe's nuclear defense systems? Are they crazy? Reagan would never go for that, and if he did, our allies would scream bloody murder!"

Stallings shrugged. "I agree," he said simply. "But that's not relevant to the situation. The relevant point is that this seals the deal. This proves it. The Soviets are holding the secretary of state prisoner."

Tracie scanned the document, looking for a signature. There was none. She turned it over. Nothing. She spread her hands in confusion. "Who, specifically, is it from? It's unsigned."

Stallings said, "The official signature has been redacted in the copies provided to law enforcement and diplomatic agencies, but I had a brief opportunity to examine the original. The signature belonged to Soviet Foreign Minister Sergei Tamarkin. Assistant Secretary of State Joe Malone has dealt extensively with Tamarkin, and he says the signature appears legitimate. I requested to take possession of the original in order to have our cryptographers authenticate it, but was denied in favor of the FBI's experts. Let's hope they know what they're doing, but until we hear otherwise, we have to operate on the assumption that the signature is real."

"Presumably we've confronted the Soviets with all of this?"

"Of course. They're denying everything, which means nothing. We've demanded to speak directly to Tamarkin and, of course, they've refused. It all adds up to verification."

"Unless they're telling the truth."

Stallings's jaw dropped open and he leveled a look of incredulity at Tracie. "What? You're not still supporting this ridiculous notion that the Soviets are being set up, are you? Not in the face of all of this evidence, which includes what amounts to a signed confession."

Tracie shook her head. "None of this proves—"

Stallings exploded. "Now you listen to me, Agent Tanner. Enough with the hunches and wild goose chases. You've already wasted the better part of a day, and as far as I can see are no closer to finding J.R. Humphries than you were when I recruited you for this assignment. The Soviet Union has kidnapped our secretary of state. That much is obvious. Go get him back or pack your things and start looking for a new line of work, is that understood?"

"Yes, sir," Tracie said. "Understood."

"Good. Now take this copy of the ransom letter and get the hell out of my office. The next time we chat you'd better have made real progress, not stirred up a diplomatic hornet's nest."

Aaron Stallings glared at her before turning his attention to the mass of paperwork littering his desk. Tracie stood and exited without a word.

13

Back in her car, Tracie sat under the light of a sodium arc street lamp and studied the ransom note again. It was short, straightforward, and to the point. "Immediately begin disassembling all strategic nuclear weapons in Europe."

There was no, "Or else" attached to the ultimatum. But then again, there was no need for one. The Soviets knew that U.S. officials would recognize the threat implicit in their instructions. The "or else" was assumed. Begin removing the missiles or bad things would happen to Secretary of State J. Robert Humphries.

Chances were those bad things didn't include death, at least not immediately. Chances were he would lose a finger, or three, at various intervals designed to transmit a sense of urgency to the United States. Competent removal of Humphries's digits would not threaten his life but would make perfectly clear the Soviets' seriousness.

As plans went, Tracie mused, it wasn't bad, if undertaken in a vacuum. The problem, of course, was that it was not undertaken in a vacuum, but in the real world. Ronald Reagan had been president for better than six and a half years, more than enough time for the rest of the world—the Soviet Union in particular—to understand the man's approach to foreign relations.

Reagan would never allow himself to be bullied in such an

79

obvious and brutal fashion, not even with the life of his close friend on the line. The Soviets *had* to know that. They had seen Iraq release U.S. hostages they had held for nearly four hundred fifty days just after Reagan's 1981 inauguration, in part to demonstrate their contempt for President Jimmy Carter, but also out of concern over what the much more hawkish Reagan might do in retaliation if they *weren't* released.

Most recently, they had seen the president take advantage of a failed KGB assassination plot directed at him. President Reagan had gone on the offensive and called for the destruction of the Berlin Wall. The Soviets would be forced to comply with the demand or would risk the Americans revealing to the rest of the world how the KGB had utterly lost control of a number of their operatives.

To Tracie, whose career had dovetailed neatly with the Reagan presidency and who had spent most of her time as a covert ops specialist working in and around Soviet Russia and East Germany, this sudden, brutal change in tactics by the Soviet Union didn't add up.

Not that she didn't think they were capable of it. Of course they were. She simply knew that *they* would know it wouldn't work, that they would be risking war for nothing. And the Soviets were not stupid.

Tracie blew out a breath in frustration and read the ransom note again.

She reviewed the photograph of Secretary of State Humphries holding the Russian newspaper. Looked more closely at the headline. It was something about an eight-car pileup on a freeway near Moscow, an event that could be easily verified. The newsprint under the headline was too small and too fuzzy for Tracie to read the accompanying article with any real comprehension.

Something about the newspaper photo and the ransom note was not quite right. She still couldn't figure out what it was.

She rolled her shoulders and yawned. Ever since she'd been shot, her still-healing shoulders would stiffen and ache relentlessly when she began to get tired. She wished she could grab a quick nap. Not only would she feel better physically, but perhaps whatever was bothering her about the supposed Russian correspondence would come out of hiding and resolve itself.

She recalled what CIA Director Aaron Stallings had said about trying to authenticate the signature on the ransom note: *I requested to take possession of the original in order to have our cryptographers authenticate it...*

Authenticate it.

She tapped her fingers on the steering wheel and thought hard. Stallings had directed her in no uncertain terms to follow up on the Soviet connection to the case. There could be no mistaking his orders. He was quite clear.

Authenticate it.

For the second time in just a few months, she would be risking her career if she followed her instincts.

Authenticate it.

She had been given this assignment because the director of the CIA knew that following standard channels and standard protocols would likely result in one dead United States cabinet official, with the likelihood of war to follow.

Authenticate it.

Still deep in thought, Tracie returned the documents to her briefcase. She snapped it shut and started her car, motoring toward Alexandria, Virginia.

It was now nearly midnight and she had been going practically nonstop since smuggling Boris Rogaev out of Leningrad. She needed sleep.

Craved it.

She wasn't going to get it.

She needed to pay someone a visit.

81

14

The tiny ranch-style home was crammed onto a piece of property roughly the size and dimensions of a high school softball diamond. Overgrown ornamental shrubs were working diligently to take over a weed-strewn yard weeks overdue for a mowing, and pale yellow light flickered hesitantly from a rusting electric lantern set back from the road.

Tracie had to smile as she stood outside of her vehicle taking it all in. She hadn't visited this house in more than six years, but every detail of the exterior—at least what she could make out through the uneven light—looked exactly the same as it had the last time she had been here.

She navigated a rickety staircase, stepping up to a small front landing. Then she set her briefcase down and pressed the doorbell. A loud buzzing noise filled the house and then died away.

Silence.

She pressed the bell again.

Buzzing noise and then silence.

The resident was home; she knew it. He never went anywhere besides work if he could help it, and he certainly didn't do that after midnight.

She tried again, this time holding the button down while counting to ten in her head.

At last, through the door's decorative frosted glass window, Tracie saw a scarecrow-thin man stumble around a corner, moving more or less in her direction. The man, who had clearly been sleeping, ran a hand through his unruly mop of mud-brown hair before flipping a light switch. A floodlight mounted over the door blazed on and the man peered out the window. A confused look crossed his face before he blinked in surprise and smiled broadly. Then he threw the door open.

"Well, Lord Almighty, if it isn't my favorite student ever! Welcome, Tracie, come on in. I haven't seen you in...let's see...must be almost seven years. What in the heck brings you out here at this time of night? And by the way, would it kill you to call ahead first?"

Tracie grinned at the barrage of questions. Peter Brickley had been her favorite instructor when she was going through training at The Farm. "I'm sorry I couldn't give you any advance notice that I was coming to see you," she said as he led her down a short hallway and into a living room cluttered with books, newspapers and scholarly journals. "But I'm caught up in something classified and didn't even want to use an unsecured telephone line."

"Have a seat," Brickley invited, tossing assorted paperwork onto the floor and making just enough room on his couch for her. "Can I get you a drink or a bite to eat?"

Tracie smiled. "Thank you, Dr. Brickley, but I really have to get right down to business. My assignment is extremely time-critical and I desperately need your help."

"Okay." He nodded gravely and eased into an overstuffed chair placed directly across a small coffee table from her. "How can I help you?"

One of the reasons Tracie Tanner had been recruited by the CIA immediately following her graduation from Brown University in Providence, Rhode Island, had been her degree in linguistics. The outstanding grades she had earned in that field of study, combined with her athleticism, beauty, and family pedigree of service to country, had made her an attractive target for the agency specializing in foreign clandestine operations. The fact she was a quick learner and so talented at the job had been a pleasant surprise both to her handler, Winston Andrews, and to herself.

But even with her honors degree in linguistics and her

considerable field experience, Tracie knew she could not begin to compete with the knowledge of the man seated across the messy table from her. Dr. Peter Brickley was one of the most accomplished figures in the field of linguistics, a world-renowned lecturer and the author of dozens of groundbreaking treatises in his field.

And, unbeknownst to almost anyone in the world outside the company, he was a CIA contractor.

Tracie lifted her battered briefcase and set it atop the mess. She unsnapped the clasps and withdrew the top two documents, turning them around and placing them on the table. "I was hoping you might look at these two items and give me your impressions."

She waited in silence as Dr. Brickley leaned over the table. His eyes widened as he took in the photograph of Secretary of State Humphries. He looked up and stared at her for a moment, saying nothing, before beginning to study the sheets. Two minutes stretched into four, and then six. The linguist squinted hard and eventually searched around until locating a large magnifying glass. He lifted it to his face and returned his attention to the papers. At last, Dr. Brickley sat back in his chair and gazed at Tracie. "What would you like to know?" he asked quietly.

"Are these documents written by a Russian?"

A trace of a smile flitted across the professor's cadaverous face. "This is why I always felt you should have gone on and achieved a postgraduate degree in the field of linguistics," he said. "I would have loved to work with you. You have marvelous natural ability."

"So your answer is..."

"Let me ask you a question," Brickley said. "Why would you suspect these documents were *not* Russian in origin? All of the grammar, even what I could read of the newspaper article itself, is technically correct." He shrugged. "Why do you have a problem with it?"

Tracie thought for a moment. "I...I don't know. I can't really put my finger on it. I've spent a lot of time inside Soviet Russia and many of their satellite states since the last time I saw you, and I'm fairly comfortable with many Russian dialects, which can differ somewhat from region to region—"

"—Just as English dialects can differ from region to region

inside this country."

"Exactly. But after being exposed to as much Cyrillic as probably any outsider has been over the past half-decade, I can't say what it is that bothers me. Something just doesn't seem right about it. It seems somehow...contrived."

This time Brickley's smile wasn't just a trace flitting across his face, it was broad and proud, like a father watching his daughter excel in the school spelling bee. "Again, it's a shame you chose to move right into CIA fieldwork. You would eventually have made an outstanding linguistic analyst."

Tracie laughed. "And people shooting at me would have been a rare occurrence."

"Longer average career span, too," Brickley said seriously. "Anyway," he continued, "I can see from the photograph that the secretary of state's recent disappearance from the world stage isn't due to illness, as has been reported. You meant it when you said your assignment was time-critical if this evidence is indication, so I won't waste any more of your time.

"Your suspicions about the origin of these documents are one hundred percent on-target. They were written in Cyrillic but were definitely *not* composed by someone of Russian origin, or even by someone with significant Russian connections. There are subtle errors in phrasing that, while not distinguishable to a layman, are quite noticeable to anyone with an extensive background in the study of linguistics.

"That's why I am so proud of you," he added. "Despite being so long removed from your studies, you picked up on the phrasing problems, even though you were not able to recognize exactly what it was you didn't like."

"Thank you for confirming my suspicions," Tracie said. "Director Stallings thinks I'm misguided at best and a lunatic at worst."

"You're working directly with Stallings? What in the world is going on?"

Tracie met his gaze and said nothing.

"Uh, right," he stammered. "You can't talk about it. Sorry about that. In any event, don't worry about Stallings; you can handle him."

"Thank you," Tracie said. "Now comes the hard part. It's nice to know my suspicions were correct, but my next question is really why I woke up one of the world's preeminent linguistics experts in the middle of the night."

"Any time, for you," Brickley said sincerely.

"What I really need to know is this: if the documents weren't written by a Russian, who *were* they written by?"

* * *

The professor spent a long time studying the two photocopies. He leaned back in his chair, reading glasses perched on his nose, holding the papers just inches from his face. Then he leaned forward, plopping them down on the table before bending over them as if waiting for them to perform a trick.

Then he repeated the process. Twice.

"The Russian language is ancient, as are many languages," he finally began. "Due to the vastness of Russia's land mass, the differences in dialect can be significant from one part of the country to another. Complicating matters is that their language has been influenced to varying degrees by the dialects of Europe to the west, and of Asia to the south and east.

"That said, there are patterns that remain consistent throughout all Cyrillic dialects that are missing here. Their absence is subtle but recognizable, if you know what to look for."

Tracie glanced at her watch. Her mission was time-critical, but she knew that any attempt to hurry Brickley along would be pointless. Like many true geniuses, the linguist operated on his own wavelength, which was often very different from everyone else's. She knew that once he started his explanation, he would eventually give her the information she needed. All she could do was let him get to the point in his own way.

"This is why," the professor continued, "you were able to discern that something was not quite right in the phrasing of the Cyrillic. Your linguistic studies, combined with your exposure to real-world Russian dialects, made this...forgery...ring false to you."

His next words surprised her. "Have your agency travels over the past seven years ever brought you to the Middle East?"

Tracie blinked in surprise. "Well, yes," she said slowly. "I've spent a small amount of time there. But nothing significant. My lack of familiarity with their languages and customs makes me a less-than-ideal choice when it comes to field work in that region."

Brickley nodded, then sat quietly.

"Are you saying you think these papers were written by someone from the Middle East?"

"Yes," he answered simply.

Tracie sat back, stunned. A Middle Eastern connection to the kidnapping of a sitting U.S. secretary of state? That possibility had never even crossed her mind. Certainly there was no shortage of countries in that troubled region that would like nothing better than to attack the United States, but who would have the capability? The technical expertise?

She pushed her surprise aside for the time being, and asked Brickley, "What leads you to the conclusion this was forged by a Middle Easterner?"

"Speech patterns," he said, as if no further explanation was necessary. When Tracie didn't respond, he attempted to explain. "I can't really be too specific without getting into an in-depth discussion of the history of each language and culture, a scenario that would require a considerable commitment of time to the subject, which you say is something you cannot spare. Judging by the photograph I see in front of me, I'm inclined to believe time is of the essence. To put it as succinctly as I can, there are patterns in the phrasing of speech that are unique to each language, something you should remember from your own linguistic studies."

Brickley looked at Tracie expectantly and she nodded. "Well then," he said. "Suffice it to say that although I would have preferred a larger sample to work with than just one newspaper headline, the few sentences of text below it that I was able to make out, and a short, handwritten letter, I am confident that the phrasing patterns in the samples you provided me are most closely aligned with the speech patterns that would belong to a person of Middle Eastern culture."

Tracie shook her head, thinking hard. "Could you hazard a guess as to which Middle Eastern country we're talking about? Which language?"

"Middle Eastern cultures are among the oldest in the world, which means of course that their languages are ancient as well. Aramaic, for example, dates back more than three thousand years and survives to this day in the form of Neo-Aramaic languages.

Now, over the centuries, these Neo-Aramaic languages have splintered into two distinct formats: Eastern Aramaic, which has long been dominant, and Western Aramaic, which has more or less died out, with one significant exception: the Ma'loula dialect. When you consider—"

Tracie had studied under Professor Brickley long enough to know that if she didn't refocus him on the topic at hand, she would be treated to a detailed treatise on the history of the Aramaic language. As a former linguistics major, she thought the subject might be interesting, perhaps even fascinating, but the CIA covert ops specialist in her knew it was a subject for another time.

She cleared her throat and said, "Uh, professor, the documents? You were going to give me your best guess as to which Middle Eastern dialect the speech patterns most resemble?"

"Oh, yes, of course," Brickley said, pushing his glasses up to the bridge of his nose and blinking owlishly behind the thick lenses. "As I was saying, the languages in that part of the world are among the oldest in recorded history. Of course they've all developed differently, and adjusted to changing times at different rates—"

"Professor?"

"Uh, yes. I was doing it again, wasn't I? I'm sorry, Tracie, it's just that I so rarely get the opportunity to discuss these types of things with people who are actually interested in them that sometimes I get carried away. I'll get right to the heart of the matter. In my opinion, the speech patterns in both of these documents most closely resemble Iraqi Arabic."

"Iraq?"

"Yes. Now bear in mind, I am not as confident in that assessment as I am in stating that these documents *were not* authored by a Russian. If you hadn't asked for my best guess, I would never even have mentioned it because I don't want to be responsible for pointing you in the wrong direction. But you asked my opinion, and that is it."

Tracie tried unsuccessfully to stifle a yawn as she began gathering up the papers and shoving them back into her briefcase. The ache in her still-healing shoulders was now a constant throbbing, the pain radiating into her neck and igniting a headache that threatened to spiral out of control. She needed sleep.

She rotated her shoulders in an effort to loosen them, and Professor Brickley, who had been watching her closely, said, "You look exhausted, Tracie."

She smiled wanly. "I'm okay. Give me a few hours of uninterrupted rack time and I'll be fine."

"I heard you were injured recently."

"Where did you hear that?"

He smiled. "Grapevine. You know how it is."

"I can't talk about it," she answered too quickly, thinking of Shane. At the thought of him tears began to fill her eyes and she wiped them away angrily with the back of her hand.

Brickley raised his hands in a placating gesture. "I understand," he said. "I wasn't trying to pry. I was just wondering if perhaps you should have taken a little more time off before returning to operational status."

"The doctors cleared me, so I came back" she said, keeping quiet about the real reason she had returned to work so quickly. *Hanging around doing nothing, thinking of Shane and how much I miss him, was killing me. This job is all I have.*

Brickley got up from his overstuffed chair and walked around the coffee table. He shoved some more magazines and newspapers from the couch onto the floor and sat next to Tracie. "If you ever need to talk," he said, "my door is always open."

She smiled gratefully and said, "Thank you, Professor."

"Peter," he said.

"Okay, Peter. I'll take you up on your offer, too; that's a promise. But it can't be tonight. I've got a lot of work to do. You've given me plenty to think about and I have to map out some kind of strategy for moving forward. Thanks for all your help."

She rose from the couch and began walking quickly down the hallway. Professor Brickley got up more slowly and followed, struggling to match her pace. He started to say something else and she turned and flashed him a bright smile.

Then she opened the front door and walked into the night.

15

Wednesday, September 9, 1987
Time unknown
Location unknown

J. Robert Humphries was having trouble concentrating. His vision was blurry and he was thirsty beyond all reason. He wondered if he had been drugged, and if so, with what. He tried to determine approximately how long he had been held captive in the room that had been constructed to resemble a spare bedroom, but could not.

He had not been mistreated, not exactly. Not unless you considered being dragged out of your own home in the middle of the night at gunpoint and held in some undisclosed location by unknown assailants for some unknown reason, being mistreated.

J.R. changed his mind.

He *had* been mistreated. Badly.

But he guessed he had been fortunate, all things considered. The men holding him here had knocked him around a little—he had the bumps and bruises to prove it—but for the most part they seemed to be handling him with kid gloves.

He supposed that made sense. It was patently obvious, even in his confused and frightened state, that he had been taken for political reasons, undoubtedly by representatives of a foreign government hostile to the United States, and any leverage his captors might expect to exert over the Reagan Administration was dependent upon his continued good health. Killing him would be counterproductive, and injuring him badly would be nearly as much so.

J.R. thought he should be thankful for that small bit of good fortune, as well as for the fact that the kidnappers had stopped covering his head with the cloth sack. After his last bathroom break they had left it off. Still, he couldn't work up much enthusiasm for the concept of gratitude. His joints ached from being held in the same position for hours on end, he was queasy, he was suffering from a headache that refused to back down, and he had managed to doze for only a few minutes at a time. He was exhausted.

He tried to recall his American history, and whether a sitting U.S. secretary of state had ever been kidnapped and held for ransom. He didn't think so. If it had ever happened, it certainly wasn't in the modern era.

His body hurt and his head throbbed. His mouth was scratchy and dry.

After a while he fell into an uneasy slumber.

* * *

The door opened with a loud crash and J.R. Humphries awoke with a start. One of the kidnappers had apparently kicked it open after unlocking it, and it slammed back against the wall. The doorknob blasted a small crater into the sheetrock, sending powdery white residue floating into the air. It looked like confectioner's sugar.

J.R. blinked rapidly, trying to regain his senses. He couldn't tell whether he had been dozing for ten minutes or three hours, and although it didn't make a damned bit of difference to his current situation, it bothered him that he didn't know.

But what happened next bothered him even more.

A new man was here, someone he had not yet seen. The new arrival glanced in J.R.'s direction for a moment as he strode into the room. His eyes were filled with both disdain and amusement. In one hand he carried a plastic bucket, like a housewife might use when mopping her kitchen floor. He moved to a point directly in front of J.R. and dropped the bucket. It landed with a thud, and spun on its edge and stopped. Then the man left the room without a word.

J.R.'s sense of disorientation began to turn to alarm when the same man returned a moment later carrying first-aid supplies. Gauze pads of varying sizes. Adhesive tape. Antibacterial cream.

These supplies he dropped on the floor next to the bucket. He stood and stared wordlessly at J.R. It occurred to J.R. that he should ask the kidnapper why he hadn't just carried the supplies inside the bucket and saved himself a trip. Then he began to suspect that the man hadn't *wanted* to save himself a trip. He had wanted to drag the moment out, to build a sense of tension.

And it was working. J.R. felt his pulse quicken. He tried to return the kidnapper's steady gaze, but after a moment he looked away. He hated himself for doing so but he couldn't help it.

The kidnapper left the room again. This time when he returned he was carrying just one item, but that single item was enough to turn J.R.'s alarm into full-fledged panic.

The man was carrying a hedge trimmer.

It was a heavy-duty professional model, big and sturdy, with thick wooden handles featuring rubber handgrips so the user could avoid slippage when sweating in the hot summer sun. Its cutting jaws had been sharpened to a razor's edge. J.R. could see them glittering in the dim light even as the kidnapper carried the tool across the room.

In almost any other setting the clippers would look utterly benign, but at this moment, to J.R. Humphries, they were dark, deadly, threatening.

Or maybe it was the look in the kidnapper's eyes. He sauntered across the room, hedge trimmer in one hand, held down at his side, swinging it casually as he walked. When he reached the spot where he had dropped the other supplies, he stopped and stood directly in front of J.R.

The man still had not said a word, and J.R. knew he had to quell his rising panic or risk a heart attack or stroke. John Robert Humphries was in decent shape for a man who had done no significant amount of manual labor in more than three decades, but nevertheless, given the current stress on his sixty-three-year-old heart, it wouldn't surprise him if the organ simply exploded inside his chest.

He swallowed heavily and forced himself to look into the kidnapper's eyes. They were dark. Hooded. Threatening, like the sky before a thunderstorm. J.R. tried his best to keep his voice steady as he said, "What's the meaning of this? What are your intentions?"

The words sounded silly as he said them. They sounded too formal, out of sync with the setting and the situation, but he said them without stuttering or shaking too badly and he was proud of himself for that.

For a moment he thought his questions would be ignored. But then the man smiled thinly, his face devoid of any warmth. "We have a job to do," the man said.

"We?"

"Yes. We. You and me. My contribution to this job consists of performing the manual labor, the 'heavy lifting,' as you Americans might say. And your contribution..."

J.R. knew the man was playing with him, drawing out the moment. He resolved not to fall for it. He would not give this clearly sadistic bastard the satisfaction he was seeking.

But he crumbled almost immediately. He couldn't help himself. He was a career politician, a diplomat, a man more comfortable in the world of high-stakes negotiation accompanied by fine brandy served in crystal decanters than in the world of guns and garden tools. "Yes?" He was unable to keep the tremor out of his voice and he hated himself for it.

"Your contribution to the job," the man continued, "is to endure the pain."

J.R.'s breath began coming in short gasps and he felt as if he were suffocating. He was hyperventilating, his panic and fear choking him as the man dropped to his knees in front of the chair. Dimly, he realized the man had not just been carrying the hedge trimmers on his third trip into the room. He had been holding a roll of duct tape in his other hand.

He watched in dread fascination, unable to take his eyes off the silvery roll as the man ripped off a long strip. The sound of the tape pulling off the roll was abrupt and grating, and J.R. jumped involuntarily, causing his steel handcuffs to clatter against the chair.

The man slapped the strip of duct tape over J.R.'s right wrist and then quickly wound it around the chair arm. Not only was J.R. bound, but the minimal amount of mobility he had previously enjoyed in his arm was gone.

The man ripped off another strip and placed it over the knuckles of J.R.'s right hand, slipping it in the gap between his thumb and pointer finger before once again securing it firmly to the wooden chair arm.

His right arm was essentially useless. The best J.R. could do was waggle his fingers. He began to get a sense of the inevitable, and he started talking, babbling really, gulping just enough air to make promises he knew he could not keep, if only the unknown men who had taken him would just release him.

"Put the bag over my head and drive me away, drop me anywhere. I don't know your names, so I can't hurt you. Furthermore, I *wouldn't* hurt you! All I want is to go back to my family. You needn't worry about me; I won't say a word to anyone. And I can get you money! All the money you could ever want. You'll have to release me, of course, in order for me to access it, but I have it, plenty of money, and—"

Somewhere inside J.R. knew he was nearly incoherent, but he couldn't help himself and didn't care. He had held it together for much longer than anyone should ever have to, but now, in the face of…whatever atrocity was about to be committed, he just could not keep himself under control.

"Enough!" the man said, stopping the flood of words. "I don't care about your money. There is nothing you can give me that I want, besides what you are providing right now."

The man shut his mouth and went back to work, once again as stoic as ever. He doubled up on the strips of tape he had already placed around J.R.'s forearm and hand, and then quickly secured the secretary of state's left arm to the other side of the chair. He didn't bother taping down that hand.

J.R. had stopped talking because he didn't want to anger this obviously dangerous man any further, and talk was clearly not going to accomplish anything anyway. But he couldn't stop himself from hyperventilating again. He was panting, gulping air. He felt a tightening in his bladder and wished he could be escorted to the bathroom, but knew that was not going to happen.

Prep work apparently done, the man rose to his feet. He towered over J.R., who felt even more helpless than he had before, as senseless as that seemed. The man slid the bucket with his foot across the dirty tile floor until it was positioned directly under J.R.'s right hand.

J.R. was crying freely now. The no-nonsense United States

secretary of state, a man who had stared down bloodthirsty dictators across negotiating tables around the world, who had drawn metaphorical lines in invisible sand on nearly every continent, wept like a child, ashamed of his weakness but helpless to stop his tears.

His captor didn't seem to notice. The man appeared to take no pleasure in his work, but it didn't seem to bother him much, either. He looked J.R. in the eye. "It is clear you know what is to come next. I would like to say I am sorry, but that would be a lie. You would not want me to lie to you, would you, Mr. Secretary?"

J.R. ignored the question. There was nothing to gain by answering.

The man shrugged.

He bent and picked the hedge trimmers up off the floor.

He placed the jaws around the little finger of J.R.'s right hand, snugging the razor-sharp cutting edges as close to the knuckle as possible. J.R. tried to resist, but his hand had been so completely immobilized the best he could do was waggle his fingers, accomplishing nothing but putting himself in danger of cutting off his own digit.

Without warning, the kidnapper violently snapped the hedge trimmer handles together. The high-torque, highly sharpened blades flashed, neatly snipping through J.R. Humphries's little finger with little more resistance than would have been offered by a decent-sized twig.

J.R. watched in shock and disbelief, his brain unable to process the images his eyes were sending it. His finger disappeared. A half-second later a light *thunk* signaled it had reached the bottom of the bucket.

Blood spurted but there was no pain. Not yet.

The man calmly placed the hedge trimmers on the floor and picked up the medical supplies. He began removing gauze pads from their packaging and unrolling an Ace bandage.

And J.R. screamed. First from the shock and then from a rolling wave of pain. It began in his now-nonexistent little finger and radiated toward his body, racing into his hand and up his arm.

The man ignored him, working diligently, preparing, presumably, to stanch the flow of blood from J.R. Humphries's suddenly misshapen hand.

J.R. felt a rush of bile rising into his gullet and knew he was going to be sick. He tried to tell the man, but before he could get the words out his brain decided it had seen enough. Everything went black and the world disappeared.

16

Tracie yawned and tried with little success to rub the sleep out of her eyes. There had been no real alternative to getting a few hours of sleep—the body can run only so long on coffee and adrenaline—but now she wondered whether sacking out for just a few hours had been a mistake. Sleep had not vanquished her headache and her shoulder throbbed just as badly now as it had last night.

She rolled her shoulders in a vain attempt to loosen them and showered quickly, then dried off and padded to her bedroom, towel wrapped around her. There would be no young urban professional woman business attire today. She picked out a comfortable pair of jeans and a loose-fitting grey top, then slipped into her clothes and was out the door less than fifteen minutes after waking. It was going to be a busy day.

* * *

Marshall Fulton was one of the CIA's top analysts on Middle Eastern affairs. Tracie had met him years ago at a company

Christmas party and the pair had hit it off immediately, spending most of the evening discussing their mutual interest in rock music and noir films. It had been one of the truly rare instances when she had been able to shed her natural reticence and fully enjoy a night out.

She had seen him occasionally over the intervening years, always at Langley during the few times she had been called back to Washington. Their relationship, Tracie knew, would barely even qualify as a casual friendship. They certainly weren't close enough to justify her requesting backdoor intelligence from him.

But that was exactly what she was going to do.

Whether he would agree to help her was anyone's guess. The CIA was the ultimate "need-to-know" entity—for an operative to access intel through unofficial channels was considered a major offense, punishable by immediate termination and potentially even criminal prosecution.

It was the sort of thing that could end not just Tracie's career, but Marshall's as well. He would have no reason to talk to her without a specific order or formal Information Request from a superior. CIA data analysts were always busy, swamped with the sheer volume of information being funneled through Langley from hot spots around the world, and the likelihood of Marshall Fulton agreeing to waste his valuable time on the hunch of a field operative—disregarding the possibly felonious aspect of the request—was slim.

Still, it was worth a try. The Middle Easter connection to Humphries's kidnapping was becoming increasingly clear to her if not to anyone else, and her expertise simply did not extend to that region. She knew she needed help.

Tracie parked at the CIA complex and entered the labyrinth of hallways and offices crisscrossing the massive headquarters building, saying a quick prayer that she would not bump into Director Stallings. The odds of that happening were infinitesimal—her boss's office was located in an entirely separate wing, and with something big going down he wouldn't have time to stroll through the operational areas of the complex—but being seen by someone she knew *was* a possibility. Which would be almost as bad.

If word got back to Stallings that Tracie was still investigating a theory she had been told specifically to abandon, the response from her boss would be thunderous and immediate. Even her presence in the building was risky. The CIA director had made it clear he expected results—the sooner the better. In his bureaucratic mind that meant pounding the pavement and rounding up the kidnappers, not drinking coffee and chatting with a young, handsome data analyst.

Stallings wouldn't consider the problem of how she was supposed to know what pavement to pound. It wasn't his concern. He had given her an assignment and she would carry it out. Period.

Tracie wound her way through the corridors until she reached a mammoth room located behind a set of reinforced glass double doors. The room was the size of a gymnasium, dissected by movable partitions erected to form dozens of workspaces.

Inside the resulting cubicles were men—and occasionally women—who looked no different than typical midlevel corporate office workers. Their workspaces included desks, telephones, printers, small televisions all tuned to CNN, most muted, and the occasion clunky computer monitor. Reams of paperwork cluttered the desks, and shelves and filing cabinets lining the walls testified to the sheer volume of intelligence being monitored and interpreted by the analysts.

But unlike the typical midlevel office worker, these harried men and women daily handled information of the most sensitive nature. Information considered top secret and which affected national security.

Tracie wound her way through the room. She knew who she was looking for but not where his workstation was located. Most of the analysts ignored her as she passed, occupied as they were writing reports, speaking with contacts on secure telephone lines, or studying data.

Finally Tracie spotted Marshall Fulton. A massive black man, Fulton looked far too big for his cramped workstation, like if he leaned back in his chair and stretched he would knock the flimsy partition right over. He was youngish, good-looking—she guessed he might be about thirty-two—dressed impeccably in a sharply tailored charcoal suit, cream-colored dress shirt and lavender tie. A thin sheen of perspiration covered the rich chocolate skin of his forehead. Tracie thought he looked more like a high-powered stockbroker than an overworked CIA intelligence specialist.

His was talking on the telephone, half-turned, leaning against his desk as she approached. He didn't see her coming. She stood for a moment, watching him work, until he seemed to sense her presence and looked over. His expression of puzzlement lasted approximately one second then transformed into a wide smile of recognition. "I'll have to call you back," he said into the phone. "Something critical just came up. Yep. Talk to ya later." And just like that he hung up.

"Something critical?" Tracie said, returning his smile.

"Everything's relative," Fulton said. He lifted his hands, palms up in imitation of a set of scales. "Do I hang up and engage in conversation with a beautiful woman—" he raised one hand and lowered the other "—or make small talk with an eighty-five-year-old Jewish bookie in Georgetown?" He waggled his eyebrows suggestively. "It's no contest, really."

Tracie laughed knowing there was absolutely no way in the world Marshall Fulton's telephone conversation had been with a gambler, unless that gambler was somehow involved in a Middle Eastern bookmaking ring with national security implications. She also knew she wouldn't have handled the situation any differently, had their positions been reversed.

"The lovely Miss Tracie Tanner," the analyst said amiably. "I bet I haven't spoken more than twenty words with you since...let's see . . . must have been Christmas Eve, 1983."

"Close," she said with a grin, secretly pleased he had remembered her name after nearly three years. "You have the right holiday, but the wrong year. It was 1984."

He snapped his fingers. "Dammit. Almost said '84. Winston Andrews's townhouse," he continued. "As I recall, we shared a couple of drinks and commiserated that our personal lives were so pathetic we had to spend the holiday in the company of a geezer old enough to be our grandfather." His smile faltered. "Sorry to hear about Winston. The way things ended for him was horrific."

Tracie nodded. "Thanks." She had gotten somewhat used to the awkwardness of dealing with CIA associates aware of her former mentor's suicide. They weren't privy to the exact circumstances of his death, of course—Tracie was the only person left alive who carried that awful memory—but agency people were among the few in the world who could comprehend the bond between a field agent and her handler, so they had an instinctive understanding of the pain she would feel at his loss.

Fulton sensed her discomfort and hurried to change the subject. "So," he said, crossing his arms and gazing shrewdly at her. "What brings a big shot field agent all the way down to the dungeon to commingle with us little people?"

Tracie laughed, taking in his muscular appearance. "Little? I don't think you qualify."

"Point taken. Still, I know you're not here just to pass the time, as pleasant as that thought is to me."

She lowered her voice and squeezed into the cramped space next to the analyst in an attempt to secure a little privacy. "I need some information."

Fulton wrinkled his forehead and spoke quietly. "I know you spend most of your time battling the bad guys, but I also know you're well aware of how intelligence gets processed. I don't see an Information Request Form in your hands, and I'm certain I'd remember if I had received one prior to your visit."

Tracie cleared her throat. This was where things would get a little dicey. She would either get what she needed or he would tell her to pound sand. Marshall Fulton had been a CIA analyst since before Tracie was hired, and he had a sterling reputation in the agency. The few times Tracie had interacted with him he had seemed like a true professional. So she had no real reason to believe he would be willing to put his career on the line for a casual acquaintance, and that was exactly what she was about to ask him to do.

"No," she admitted. "I didn't send you an InReq. The information I'm looking for would be of a more…unofficial nature."

Fulton stared at her openly, his handsome brown eyes questioning but not angry or suspicious. For a long moment he said nothing, and she was beginning to think she had made a mistake by coming to see him. Then he glanced at his watch and said, "You know, time sure flies when you're busy. I've been hard at work for hours on end. I'd say it's long past time I took a break. Care to join me in a cup of coffee?"

* * *

The cafeteria was big, crowded, chaotic, and noisy, filled with agency employees eating breakfast, drinking coffee, gossiping, and passing the time. Short of leaving the CIA complex entirely and driving to a local coffee shop, it was perfect.

They found a table in one corner of the massive dining hall and sipped coffee. Tracie grinned at her colleague. When she spoke, it was in a voice barely above a whisper. "Hard at work for hours on end? It's not even nine-thirty in the morning! What time did you get here, four?"

Marshall laughed. "Okay, you got me. I've only been here since eight. Still, I'm one hard-working dude. An hour of work for me is like three for anyone else." He lowered his voice. "Plus, as I'm sure you're well aware, you never know who might be listening. Depending on what you want to know, we may not even be safe having the conversation here."

She shrugged. "We'll be okay as long as we keep our voices down. There's a lot more ambient noise here than in your cubicle. And while I'm certain we're being watched, I doubt the company is going to waste the really good surveillance equipment on their own spooks eating in the agency cafeteria."

"Okay," he said reluctantly. "I'll yield to your experience. Now, I have to admit you've piqued my curiosity. What can I do for you? And be aware, I may get up and walk away at any moment."

"Fair enough," Tracie said. She took a deep breath and tried to decide how to approach the issue. "Your area of specialty is the Middle East."

"I remember," Fulton said, and they both laughed.

"Have you seen any…unusual activity…in the region over the last few weeks?"

Marshall Fulton raised one eyebrow. He took a big bite of a cinnamon roll and eyed Tracie curiously. "You're going to have to be more specific. The Middle East is a powder keg. People have been worried about the Soviet Union and the Cold War for decades—and rightfully so, I guess—but in my opinion, the region we really ought to be concerned about is North Africa and the strip of land between the Mediterranean and the Arabian Sea. Maybe it's because I've spent many years analyzing intelligence from there, but people in the Middle East have been butchering each other for thousands of years, and I believe it won't be much longer before things reach critical mass there."

"You make the situation sound hopeless."

"Maybe 'hopeless' would be overstating it a bit, but I'm very serious about my concern. I'm afraid the Iran hostage situation of a few years ago might be just the beginning. At least with the Soviets we can understand their motives, as much as we may disagree with them. In many cultures of the Middle East, people do not operate with thought processes or logic that we understand. If we don't begin to shift our perceptions in that part of the world, we are headed for big trouble."

Tracie was silent for a moment as she considered Marshall Fulton's statement. He was clearly passionate about the subject, and as a CIA intelligence analyst, he was closer to the situation in that region than almost anyone else in the world who was not experiencing it firsthand.

But did that give him more credibility, or less? Maybe he was *too* close to things happening there.

"Be more specific," she repeated to herself, speaking even more quietly. Then she looked up at him. "Okay, let me try this. Intelligence gathering over a long period of time in any region reveals traceable patterns of behavior by individuals, as well as by governments and military forces. Has any intel coming across your desk recently led you to raise your suspicions or to suggest that something out of the ordinary—even if 'ordinary' is typically strange or chaotic—might be happening?"

A trace of a smile crossed Marshall's face and then disappeared. "Now we're getting somewhere," he said. "Surely you are familiar with the Iran/Iraq war."

"Of course," she said. "As a specialist in Soviet-bloc affairs, undoubtedly I'm not as well-versed on the subject as you are, but it would be a poor covert-ops specialist, maybe a suicidal one, who wasn't aware of something as significant as that. That war's been ongoing for years."

"That's right," Marshall agreed. "Seven years, to be exact. It's the longest-running war of the twentieth century, and has been particularly brutal and bloody."

"Okay," Tracie said, wishing the analyst would get to his point but not wanting to push too hard and change his mind about sharing information that was likely classified.

"Well, your point about patterns emerging is particularly apt, given the way the war has dragged on." Marshall's voice was barely louder than a whisper now, and he glanced furtively around the cafeteria before continuing. "Over the last couple of weeks, I've noticed what I interpret as a significant migration of Saddam Hussein's troops."

"Migration?" Tracie asked, thinking it an odd choice of words.

"Yes. Men and equipment have been moving slowly but steadily south from the Iran/Iraq border, where the fighting has been raging, toward Iraq's border with Saudi Arabia."

"Why?"

Fulton shrugged. "That's the sixty-four thousand dollar question. I have no idea."

"But what about the front lines? Won't the Iraqi troops and equipment be missed when it comes to fighting the Iranians?"

"You would think so, but there have been continuing attempts at diplomatic solutions—cease-fires and peace talks and the like—in an effort to stop the fighting over the years. Ultimately they've all been unsuccessful. But maybe Hussein knows something we don't. Maybe he anticipates an upcoming diplomatic effort that will stop the fighting for good."

"Isn't that a dangerous gamble for him to take?"

"Absolutely."

"Why would he do it then?"

"Again, good question. I don't know."

"What have your superiors said? Surely you've passed this intelligence on to them."

"Of course," Fulton said. "But as far as I know they haven't even acknowledged that these troop movements are taking place."

"*What?* Why not?"

"You have to understand," Fulton said. "These movements are not major, dramatic personnel shifts. If I weren't monitoring the situation extremely closely I would never have even noticed anything at all. It's more like a very subtle change in their focus. No one seems to consider it significant except for me."

Tracie sipped her coffee and stared down at the table, thinking hard, trying to make connections between seemingly unconnected events.

The brazen kidnapping of a sitting United States secretary of state, seemingly by representatives of the United States' major geopolitical enemy, the Soviet Union.

The vehement denial of responsibility, offered up under duress, by a Soviet official who would be in a position to know the details of the kidnapping.

The assertion by the CIA's foremost linguistics expert that the author of the kidnappers' list of demands was likely someone with Middle Eastern roots—an Iraqi, to be specific.

And Iraq's apparently illogical positioning of military assets *away* from a war zone and toward one of the most strategically important countries in the world in terms of oil production, a critical component of the economic well-being of the United States and the rest of the industrialized world.

As she tried to puzzle it out, Marshall Fulton sat across the table, sipping his coffee and eating his cinnamon roll. The longer she considered everything, the more the connections seemed to become clear.

She knew what she had to do next. And she wasn't looking forward to it.

17

"Excuse me?" Aaron Stallings said. His eyes were dark and his voice strained with the effort as he attempted—without much success—to control his anger. "I thought I made myself clear last night when I told you to forget about this goddamned notion you've fallen in love with that someone other than the Soviets is responsible for the kidnapping of J. Robert Humphries."

"Sir, please," she said. "If you'll just give me a chance to explain."

"Explain? There is no explanation! I gave you *specific orders*: follow the evidence and recover Secretary of State Humphries. Instead of doing as you were told, you go off on some wasteful and unwarranted wild goose chase." He shook his head disgustedly. "Iraqi troop movements my ass. Every minute you spend on this fantasy is a minute colder the real trail gets. Before long Humphries will be dead, and you'll still be worrying about Saddam goddamn Hussein."

"Sir—" she repeated, but the CIA director cut her off, slamming his fist down on the surface of his desk. Pens jumped and papers shuffled, and a stapler that had been hanging half off the desk toppled to the floor, landing with a muffled thud on the thick carpet.

"Don't 'sir' me," he said, spitting the words out with an angry

109

snarl. "We've started to receive body parts now. Before long we'll have to piece J. Robert Humphries—a close personal friend of the president, in case you needed a reminder—back together like a goddamn jigsaw puzzle!"

Tracie shook her head. "What are you talking about?"

"Oh, you hadn't heard?" he said, relishing her confusion, his expression icy. "The Department of State received a package this morning. Inside the package was a human finger, a finger that had been recently removed from its owner."

"A finger? But there's no reason to believe it belonged to Humphries. It could have come from anyone, as gruesome as that sounds. A cadaver, even."

"No," Stallings said abruptly. "The finger was accompanied by a photograph of Secretary Humphries. In the photograph his hand is displayed. The hand is covered by a bloody bandage, but the little finger is clearly missing." He scowled at Tracie. "While you've been chasing fantasies, the Soviets have been dismembering our secretary of state."

'But...' Tracie said. "None of that makes sense from a tactical standpoint. If Humphries was taken by the Soviets, what do they have to gain by cutting off his finger, especially when they continue to deny their involvement in his disappearance? They have to know such an act of aggression would push us to the brink of war."

"Those kinds of philosophical questions don't concern you. Or at least they *didn't* concern you," Stallings corrected himself ominously. "Your job was not to analyze intelligence, or to look for logic where no logic was to be found. Your job was to locate and recover J. Robert Humphries. You know, to do what you were trained to do. I can see I grossly overrated your ability to carry out this mission, and now I'm left having to explain to the president of the United States why we're sitting idly by while Mikhail Gorbachev mails our secretary of state to us in pieces."

"Sir, I still believe—"

"Don't interrupt me! I should have known better than to trust the operative who smeared the memory of Winston Andrews with unfounded charges of treason—and eventually drove him to take his own life—with an assignment this critically important. It was my error in judgment, and one for which I'll surely pay dearly.

"But I'm nothing if not flexible," Stallings continued, almost as if speaking to himself. "I'll find another operative to do the job you were so unprepared to handle, and with any luck we can still get Humphries back before he's killed or we go to war with the Soviets or both.

"In the meantime," he said, glaring at Tracie, "you're finished here at CIA. I've had it with your insubordination. You'll never work in this agency again. Turn in your ID and weapon downstairs and then leave the property. Don't try to return until you're called back here for out-processing, because you'll be arrested if you do. Now get the hell out of my sight."

* * *

Tracie threaded her way around the partitions, moving quickly, knowing she had only a couple of minutes. Stallings would have notified the security agents of her termination the moment she stalked out of his office, and if too much time elapsed before she showed up to turn in her ID and weapon and be escorted out of the building, she knew they would come looking for her.

Once that happened, there would be no talking to Marshall Fulton.

She hoped to hell he had returned to his desk after their coffee break. When she had reached a point roughly halfway across the cavernous room, Tracie spotted the big man hunkered down at his desk, suit jacket off, writing diligently. She walked up behind Marshall and slid into the cubical.

He jumped in surprise and then smiled. "Well, isn't this my lucky day," he said. "I don't see you for years, and then I hit the lottery twice in an hour and a half. It's a lucky break, though, because there's something I need to tell you."

He glanced into her eyes and the smile froze on his face. "What's wrong?" he asked, lowering his voice instinctively.

"Listen," Tracie said urgently. She spoke quietly but quickly. "I don't have much time. Here's my home number." She jotted it down on a slip of paper. "I'd really appreciate it if you call me as soon as you get out of work. We need to talk."

"No problem," he said, folding the paper and sliding it into the breast pocket of his dress shirt. "Like I said, I have some information you need, anyway. But what do you mean you don't have much time? What's going on?"

"I just lost my job," she said.

18

"What in the world is going on?" Marshall asked. He had done as she had asked, calling the number she gave him at precisely five minutes after five. They had agreed to meet at a small diner-style restaurant off Macarthur Boulevard, not far from Battery Kemble Park, where Tracie had interrogated Anatoly Grinkov.

Thirty minutes later the CIA analyst slid into a booth across from Tracie, moving with the grace of an athlete. Concern was evident on his face as he eyed Tracie. "You said you lost your job? What is that supposed to mean?"

She shrugged. It didn't seem like the sort of statement that could be easily misinterpreted. "Like I told you this morning, I got fired. Stallings tore me a new one and then had me escorted out of the building like a criminal. He said if I came back, I'd be arrested on the spot."

"Wait a second, back up," Marshall said, going silent when a young, bored-looking waitress came over to fill their coffee mugs. He continued after the waitress had walked away without taking their order. "*Stallings* fired you?"

Tracie nodded.

"Aaron Stallings himself? The big cheese?"

"The one and only. And I don't think a very complimentary reference letter will be forthcoming should I need one."

Marshall laughed. It came from deep inside his barrel chest and sounded to Tracie like a volcano preparing to blow. "As if." The reality was that a reference letter for a former CIA covert field operative would *never* happen, no matter the circumstances of her dismissal. What could it say?

After taking a moment, letting their nervous laughter break the tension, Marshall said, "What have you gotten yourself into? It's not like Aaron Stallings typically hires and fires the help. I've never even spoken to the man, and I've been at the agency longer than you."

"Count yourself lucky," she said. "Contrary to his jolly appearance, the director is not exactly soft and cuddly."

"I'm serious, Tracie," he said. "What have you gotten mixed up in?"

"First things first," she answered. "Before I got booted out of Langley you said you needed to tell me something. Since you weren't comfortable blurting it out at your desk, I assume it's related to what we talked about at lunch."

"It is. But now that you're out of work, I suppose it's irrelevant."

"Not necessarily," Tracie said. "Why don't you tell me what it is and I'll make that determination?"

Marshall leaned on his elbows, staring across the table at her uncomfortably. "Uh, listen," he said. "If you don't work for the company anymore, I probably shouldn't say anything. I mean, I really shouldn't have been passing along classified information anyway—"

"You could lose your job."

"Exactly," he agreed miserably. "And I was willing to take that risk for you. But now, with you out of work and all…"

"I understand," she said gently, letting him off the hook. "And if I were in your position, I would feel exactly the same way."

She knew she was going to have to fill him in on the situation with J. Robert Humphries's kidnapping if she was going to have any chance of securing his cooperation. And at this point, she needed his cooperation. *If he thinks sharing intel on troop movements in the Middle East is taking a risk, he'll never go along with what I'm about to do.*

After the bored waitress had returned and taken their dinner order, wandering off toward the kitchen afterward like she was in some kind of permanent semi-haze, Tracie started talking. She didn't stop until their food was gone and the dishes taken away.

She left nothing out.

She hoped she hadn't made a grave mistake.

Marshall whistled softly when she finished her story. "This thing is a ticking time bomb," he said. "A CIA op inside the United States? To recover a kidnapped cabinet official? Why in God's name did you ever agree to do it?"

Tracie spread her hands. "I didn't have a choice if I wanted to keep my job."

Marshall snorted. "You see how well that worked out."

"You know what I mean. The director of the fucking CIA personally gives you an assignment, and threatens your job, you have two options: do as he asks or look for work. Since I'm not qualified to do anything else, I did as he asked."

"And now you're out of work," Marshall reminded her helpfully.

"Thanks. I haven't forgotten."

"So, what are you going to do?"

"What can I do? I'm going to get J. Robert Humphries back. Nobody at Langley wants to hear about a Middle Eastern connection to his kidnapping. They're going to ignore that possibility as long as they can. Eventually someone, either at the CIA or the FBI, will recognize what I already see clearly, but by then it will be too late. We'll have a dead secretary of state on our hands and we'll probably be at war with the Soviet Union."

"You're going to get Humphries back."

"That's right."

"All by yourself."

"You heard me."

"But what are the odds Humphries is even still in the country? It's been a couple of days now since he was taken. Don't you think it's much more likely he's been moved somewhere?"

Tracie shook her head. "No, I don't think that at all. In fact, my guess is he's still relatively close by."

"Why would you think that?"

"Put yourself in their shoes for a minute, Marshall. J. Robert Humphries is one of the most recognizable men in the world.

He's on the news regularly, he gives speeches on all continents, negotiates with America's friends and enemies. Even people who don't follow politics closely know his face."

"So?"

"So, the farther his kidnappers try to move him, the greater the likelihood their plan falls apart because somebody recognizes him. The risks of trying to smuggle J. Robert Humphries out of the country are just too great, and if they're not going to attempt that, why keep him out in the open any longer than they have to? My guess is that he's within a couple of hours of D.C. right now, and that wherever he is he was stashed there the night he was taken, with no plans to move him again until the heat dies down."

"I suppose," Marshall said. "But even if that's all true, how are you going to find him?"

"I'm not sure yet. But the first step is to hear what you were so anxious to tell me this afternoon, before I became persona non grata at the agency. You may be surprised to hear this, but I didn't unburden myself to you because you're such a great listener. I did it so you would know what I'm up against and so—hopefully—you would decide to pass along whatever intel you have.

"I don't like to beg, Marshall. I'm the same person I was ten hours ago, with the same goal I had ten hours ago. I took a huge risk telling you about Humphries. Doing so could get me a life sentence in Fort Leavenworth. I'm in a real bind here, and I wouldn't ask if I didn't need your help. Please, tell me what you know."

Marshall Fulton sighed heavily.

He ran a hand through his closely cropped hair.

Straightened his tie.

Started talking.

"Okay, here's the deal, and from what you've told me, it may be more important than even I realized. I'm sure you know that three years ago, the U.S. government officially reestablished diplomatic relations with Saddam Hussein and the Republic of Iraq, correct?"

"Of course."

"Well, during those three years the company has maintained a more or less continuous surveillance on the Iraqi embassy over on Massachusetts Avenue."

"More or less?"

Marshall shrugged. "You know how it goes. Resources are finite—budgets get cut and then restored and then cut again. Sometimes we have the manpower to do it, sometimes we don't."

Tracie nodded. "Been there. But weren't you the one who just a little while ago claimed to be so shocked about me running an agency op inside the boundaries of the United States? How is this any different?"

"Technically, the embassy of any nation is sovereign territory, so we're not *really* operating inside the U.S."

Despite the seriousness of the situation she found herself in, Tracie struggled to suppress a smile. "Kind of splitting hairs there, Sport, don't you think?"

"Sure," Marshall agreed readily. "But it's not my call. That decision was made by someone far above my pay grade. All I do is analyze the data that come across my desk."

"Understood," Tracie said. "So, I'm assuming, since you mentioned this 'technically legal' surveillance operation, that it's been active recently."

"Right you are."

"And that it turned up something that's raised your suspicions."

"You're one sharp cookie. No wonder you've survived so long working in hostile environments."

Tracie let the compliment go. Things were starting to get interesting. "And what did this on-again-off-again technically legal surveillance turn up?"

Marshall sighed again. "Remember, it might mean absolutely nothing."

"I get it," Tracie said, exasperated. "I'm willing to deal with a dead end, if that's what it turns out to be, but I've got to start somewhere."

"Okay," Marshall said, lowering his voice as he had done inside the employee cafeteria at Langley. "The last few weeks, there's been a significant uptick in embassy activity after hours."

"After hours? What does that mean?"

"You know, like in the middle of the night. People coming and going at two, three, four a.m."

"And where do these people come from and go to at that time of night?"

Marshall shrugged. "Who knows? The agents conducting the surveillance weren't instructed to follow them. They did, however, make note of this activity as being extremely unusual."

"Hmm."

"Exactly. And the activity has increased even more in the last three days."

"Three days? That would be the day before Humphries disappeared."

The data analyst nodded as Tracie digested the information. To his credit, Marshall remained quiet, not wanting to break her concentration. A minute stretched into two, and then five, and finally he said, "What do you think? Could the Iraqis possibly be holding J. Robert Humphries hostage inside their own embassy?"

Tracie shrugged and shook her head dubiously. "I don't know. Granted, an embassy is sovereign territory as you said, but it's hard to imagine anyone being that bold."

"We are talking about Saddam Hussein here. He's a loose cannon; there's no telling from one minute to the next what that man is going to do."

"Understood. But it still seems unlikely. Are the Iraqis really sophisticated enough to pull off something like the kidnapping of the U.S. secretary of state while at the same time framing the Soviets for the crime? And why would they go to such lengths? What's their ultimate goal?"

"That I can't tell you," Marshall said. "But don't sell them short. I've been working the Middle East for a long time, and although in some areas Iraq has barely risen out of the Stone Age, in others they are as cosmopolitan and sophisticated as any European nation."

"I guess," she said, still unconvinced.

"So what are you going to do?"

She thought for a moment. "I'm going to conduct a little surveillance of my own. When people start coming and going, I'm going to follow them. I want to know what the hell they're up to, and whether it has anything to do with J. Robert Humphries."

19

The Republic of Iraq's embassy complex was located along Massachusetts Avenue, not far from Norway's embassy and slightly north of the United States Naval Observatory. Immediately after her meeting with Marshall Fulton Tracie had driven to the neighborhood, which was largely residential once she exited busy Massachusetts Avenue. She wanted to get a feel for the area before night fell, specifically to nail down the number of potential embassy egress points besides the main entrance.

As far as she could tell there was only one. A small paved alleyway, barely wide enough to accommodate a vehicle, snaked out from behind the tree-lined fence surrounding the Iraqi mission. There was no way from Tracie's brief drive through the neighborhood for her to determine whether any other, more clandestine, entrances studded the property. It was hard to believe there weren't any, but if the CIA's occasional surveillance had captured an increase in nighttime embassy activity, Tracie felt it was fair to assume that activity had probably occurred through one of the two public entrances.

Following her quick tour, Tracie had gone home to nap. She tried without much success to avoid dwelling on the circumstances of her firing, or to consider just how far her CIA star had fallen in such a short time. Just a few months ago, Tracie

119

Tanner had been a busy covert ops specialist, highly regarded within the agency, mentored and handled by one of the longest-tenured and most accomplished CIA men in history, Winston Andrews. Then had come a seemingly simple mission: recover a top-secret document from an informant in East Germany and hand-deliver it to the White House.

Simple.

Tracie had pulled off far more difficult assignments, dozens of them over the years, without a hitch.

But this one had begun unraveling almost immediately, and before all was said and done, she had been attacked and nearly killed, forced to go on the run with no agency backup, fallen in love, seen her mentor kill himself before her eyes, gotten into a deadly gun battle atop a Washington insurance building during which she had taken two bullets, and watched as her newfound love sacrificed his own life to save hers.

In the end, she had delivered the document and stopped a shocking assassination attempt, but only President Reagan's intervention had saved her job, and she had fallen into a morass of self-pity and self-recrimination as she recovered from the surgery that repaired the bullet wounds in her shoulders.

The wounds inflicted on her heart were less easily repaired. She missed Shane Rowley more than she could ever have imagined missing anyone, and only the prospect of returning to the job she loved had given her any semblance of hope for the future.

And now, even that hope was gone. She was jobless, with no relevant work experience that would translate into other gainful employment. She supposed her desperate resolve to continue the search for the kidnappers of J. Robert Humphries was her way of avoiding the recognition of how screwed-up her life had become over the last three months. But even in her state of denial, she knew that one way or the other, this silly notion of saving the secretary of state all by herself would end soon enough, and she would be left with nothing.

And no one.

She fell into a fitful doze on her couch, tossing and turning and dreaming about Bangor, Maine, and a handsome air traffic controller who changed a young woman's life and then disappeared forever. She dreamed about loyalty and betrayal and sacrifices large and small, and when she awoke, night had fallen and her series of intense dreams had become nothing more than a hazy mishmash of heartache and tears.

She sat up and checked her watch.

Showered.

Ate.

And trudged to her car, where she would force herself to do the only thing she could think of.

Her job.

20

Tracie parked on a quiet side street that ran perpendicular to Massachusetts Avenue. She found a curbside spot covered in shadows that offered an unobstructed view of the paved alleyway running behind the Iraqi embassy. It would be impossible to watch both the main entrance and this one, and she reasoned that if the Iraqis were involved in the disappearance of Secretary of State Humphries, their operatives would want to come and go in a less obtrusive manner than via the main gate.

A light drizzle had fallen while she was sleeping, and the air was muggy, heavy with the threat of more showers. Tracie hoped they would hold off. She had parked a fair distance from the embassy and reduced visibility would severely hamper her ability to maintain effective surveillance.

She shut down the engine and settled back in her seat, trying to get comfortable while also exposing as little of her body as possible to anyone who might be paying attention. The neighborhood seemed utterly still, but there were no guarantees the Iraqis didn't have someone keeping watch.

Once situated, she used her time to review what she had learned about the kidnapping of J. Robert Humphries. Much of it seemed to make no sense. She could accept the theory that a Middle Eastern government had been behind the kidnapping, even in the absence of any logical explanation why they would

123

do so, because over the years she had seen plenty of ops that would have seemed nonsensical to any observer except the authority who thought them up. And that included plenty of American operations.

What she didn't understand was why the *Iraqis* would be involved. An Iranian plot against the United States at least made sense from a strategic point of view. Even after the Ayatollah Khomenei's 1981 release of the American hostages who had been taken toward the end of Jimmy Carter's presidency and held for a year and a half, relations with the Iranian government had been strained, to say the least.

That the Ayatollah and his followers would try to strike at the "Great Satan" again, given the opportunity, went without saying.

But Iraq? The U.S. had provided weapons and support to Saddam Hussein in his seven year (and counting) war against Iran. Tracie knew him to be unstable and thus untrustworthy. But the idea that he would mastermind a plot as complex as the Humphries kidnapping without having some strategic benefit in mind commensurate with the risk involved made no sense whatsoever.

Still, Marshall Fulton's intelligence report suggesting increased covert activity around the Iraqi embassy coincided precisely with the timing of Humphries's disappearance. And Professor Brickley's educated guess that the Russian ransom documents were most likely written by an Iraqi couldn't be coincidental.

A siren wailed from somewhere across the city, muffled by distance and the muggy night air. She had cracked the driver's side window in her little car after parking, both to allow some fresh air into the vehicle and to monitor the ambient nocturnal sounds of the slumbering neighborhood. A cat meowed plaintively. A television set blared out an open window, the volume cranked up much too loud. Tracie couldn't tell which house it was coming from.

The Iraqi embassy complex—or at least the portion Tracie could see—remained still and quiet. It had now been almost an hour since she had pulled to the curb and in that time not a single soul had come or gone via the narrow alleyway.

The time was nearly two a.m. Tracie knew she would have

to maintain the stakeout at least until sunrise, since Marshall's intel regarding the embassy indicated the potential for covert activity until at least four a.m.

She wished she could have reviewed the surveillance reports turned in by the agents covering the embassy, but hadn't even considered asking Marshall for them. Accessing them herself was now impossible, given her status as an ex-CIA employee, and Marshall had already risked far more on her behalf than she had any right to expect. Sharing classified documents with a civilian—Tracie thought about the term and was overcome by a wave of sadness—would be grounds not just for Fulton's termination but for criminal prosecution.

She could not ask that of someone who had treated her so well.

She began to wonder whether maybe she had shown up too late. Perhaps whatever was going to happen—if anything—had already gone down. Tracie had assumed any kidnapping-related activity would not occur until the quietest part of the overnight. It was the most likely possibility, according to Marshall's intel.

But who really knew? Tracie was grasping at the most unlikely of straws anyway; maybe she had misread the situation entirely and the Iraqis had already left for wherever they were holding J. Robert Humphries. Maybe they were even now cutting off another of the man's fingers.

Or maybe Humphries really was being held inside the embassy complex. Maybe no one would leave the grounds at all because the secretary of state was trussed up like a Thanksgiving turkey in a soundproof room inside a hidden underground bunker deep beneath the mission grounds.

Or maybe they weren't involved in Humphries's disappearance at all.

A sense of hopelessness crept into her thoughts. What the hell did she think she was doing? She had been fired from her job, kicked out of Langley like a common criminal, and yet here she sat, alone, maintaining surveillance on the sovereign territory of a foreign government in the vain hope of . . . What? Catching masked Iraqis as they prodded the terrified J. Robert Humphries out the back door of the embassy at gunpoint?

She yawned and shook her head at her own foolishness, and that was when she detected a furtive movement out of the corner of her eye. She came immediately alert. Focused her attention on the shrubs lining the fence along the alleyway.

For a moment nothing happened, but as she began to question what she had seen—*Maybe I'm batshit crazy in addition to being tired*—she saw it again.

There. A hint of motion behind the screen of bushes, sensed more than seen.

Then, to her astonishment, she caught sight of a car, moving slowly, headlights extinguished. It stopped at the chain-link fence and idled for a moment. Then the gate swung open, apparently operated remotely, and the vehicle nosed into the alley and crept slowly along the path lined by shrubs, almost-but-not-quite invisible.

The car—it was either black or dark blue or perhaps forest green—rolled the length of the alley and then stopped just short of the road, lights still off. Tracie resisted the urge to slide farther down in her seat. She knew there was no way she could be seen by the occupants of the mystery vehicle; the angle was wrong and her car was bathed in nighttime shadows.

But here was exactly the sort of suspicious activity Marshall's surveillance reports had been referring to. She squinted and tried to see inside the car, which was long and wide, a Lincoln Town Car or something similar. She didn't think she would be able to and she was right. No luck.

The car sat a heartbeat longer and then eased onto the deserted side street. The headlights blazed on. It rolled to the Massachusetts Avenue intersection and stopped again. Now directly under the glare of a streetlight, Tracie could see her speculation was correct—the vehicle was a Lincoln Town Car. It turned right, accelerated past the embassy complex and disappeared into the night.

Tracie started her engine and counted to ten. This section of Massachusetts Avenue was long, wide, and straight, meaning that at two a.m. the Town Car would be visible for a long distance unless it had turned immediately onto another side street.

Tracie rolled the dice and assumed the driver would remain on Mass. Ave., at least for a while. The lack of traffic that would make it easy to keep the car in sight would make it just as easy for the driver to spot a tail if she wasn't extremely careful.

Finally, she pulled out of her curbside spot, executing a

quick K-turn and rolling the short distance to the Massachusetts Avenue intersection. She peered along the mostly empty thoroughfare and saw the red taillights of the Lincoln a quarter-mile ahead, now traveling at full speed, moving north out of D.C.

Tracie flipped on her headlights and followed.

21

J. Robert Humphries awoke with a start. An ex-marine, he had served with distinction in World War II and the early days of the Korean conflict, and until a few days ago had always viewed himself as strong and tough. Steely eyed. Stoic. Able to take whatever life threw at him.

The qualities that had made him a good marine and had seen him through tours of duty in two wars, one declared and one undeclared, were the same qualities that had made him so valuable to Ronald Reagan when it had come time for the president to fill his cabinet. Reagan had wanted a strong-willed, no-nonsense secretary of state, a man who would not blink when it came to high-stakes diplomacy with the Soviets.

Humphries had been that man. A lifelong friend and confidante of the former actor, California governor, and now United States president, J. Robert Humphries had projected the image of toughness and hard-nosed diplomacy abroad that former president Jimmy Carter's administration had lacked, particularly following the disastrous rescue attempt of the American hostages in Iran.

J.R. Humphries wondered where that strong, tough ex-marine had gone. Lack of sleep, nonstop stress, fear, and the relentless throbbing in his hand where his little finger had been sheared off just below the knuckle had reduced him to a shell of his former self. For a while, he had attempted to keep rough track of the time since he had been taken. But he was so disoriented he really had no idea. It might be a couple of days, might be a week. Time had lost all meaning.

Now, as the door to his room crashed open, J.R. realized his restless doze was being interrupted by one of his captors.

It was the man who had cut off his finger. He entered the room carrying what looked like a small tray table and a pad of paper.

J.R. cringed involuntarily, blinking hard and wishing he could wipe the sleep from his eyes but was unable to get his shackled hands anywhere near his face. He tried to control his rising panic in the face of the knowledge that he might be about to lose another body part. "What now?" he asked quietly, impressed by the relative steadiness of his voice.

The man smiled broadly, making clear to J.R. that he could see right through his captive's forced nonchalance. "It is time to keep the pressure on your boss," he said.

"What is that supposed to mean?"

The man slid a chair across the dirty floor and positioned it directly in front of J.R. Then he sat. "It means you are going to compose a letter to President Ronald Reagan."

"And why would I do that?"

"Because if you don't you will soon discover that you are two fingers short of a full complement, rather than one."

J.R. sighed, and this time his nerves betrayed him. The shaking sound came through loud and clear, and he saw the man's smile grow wider. "I don't suppose I'll be writing down my own thoughts," he said.

"You are correct," the man answered. "You are to be strictly the middle man." He turned the small tray table over in his hands and unfolded two sets of wire legs, clicking them into place. Then he spun the table around and set it across J.R.'s lap. He placed a blank sheet of paper on top of the table and removed a pen from his breast pocket. He clicked the pen and held it in front of J.R.

"What am I supposed to do with that?" J.R. said bitterly. "You cut off my finger, remember? I'd be lucky to even *hold* a pen in this bandaged mess of a hand, never mind write anything!"

"You *can* write, and you *will*," insisted his captor, who

leaned over and inserted a key into the handcuff securing J.R.'s right hand to the chair. Sweat stains pitted the man's shirt, arcing in big semicircles under each armpit. The sour smell of body odor assaulted J.R.'s senses, and he wrinkled his nose in disgust. The man turned the key and the bracelet fell off of J.R.'s wrist.

He reached up and tentatively took hold of the pen. It felt awkward and foreign in his heavily bandaged hand. He lowered the pen to the paper and blew out a breath in frustration. "What do you want me to write?"

"'Dear President Reagan,'" the man began.

J.R. scrawled the words along the top left side of the page and grunted. "It's barely legible," he said, fighting the urge to collapse into tears as he contemplated the missing finger on his right hand and his near-inability to do something as simple as transcribe a few words onto a piece of paper. With an exertion of will as great as any he had ever expended, J.R forced himself to keep his emotions under control, refusing to give this barbarian the satisfaction of seeing him break down.

"Just keep writing," the man spat, and continued to dictate a letter to the most powerful man in the world.

Dear President Reagan,

I write to assure you that I am still alive. The finger you received yesterday as a demonstration of my new friends' seriousness was, indeed, my own, as you undoubtedly are by now aware. The injury is painful, but I am receiving medical attention. Aside from that issue, I am not being harmed and, in fact, am being treated well.

By now you have had time to review the evidence my friends sent to the State Department. You have certainly reached the same conclusion I did a couple of nights ago: the people holding me are devoted to their mission. They are serious about their achieving their goals and will not stop until these goals have been met.

Now, to the point of this correspondence.

You already received one letter detailing the demands of my hosts. These demands are simple and unyielding: begin the immediate dismantling of all allied missile defense systems in Western Europe.

Thus far, these demands have been ignored.

We all know the demand is a simple one, and once complied with will allow my hosts the opportunity to reciprocate, to begin the process of removing their own systems. But the United States must go first. My friends chose this rather unconventional method of breaking the stalemate between the world's two great superpowers because they recognize what both sides have long understood but have lacked the courage to say: neither side wants to be the first to blink in this dangerous nuclear stalemate.

Mr. President, you must understand that my friends have eyes everywhere. Your sluggishness in responding to their simple and most logical request has been observed and noted. Be aware that if no evidence is immediately forthcoming of your willingness to take the specified actions, my friends will be forced to remove another of my fingers, and another, and will continue to do so until their simple demands have been met.

J.R. was by now shaking so badly he could barely write. The words on the page were spidery and erratic, as if written by a seven year old, and it was becoming harder and harder for him to concentrate as the man sitting across from him calmly dictated his intention to continue J.R.'s dismemberment.

"Please . . ." J.R. said, with absolutely no idea what he was going to say next.

"KEEP WRITING!" his captor shouted, causing J.R. to jump. "We are almost finished," he said, more quietly.

Do not doubt the resolve of my friends to achieve what decades of useless diplomacy have failed to accomplish. Once disarmament has been finalized, both great superpowers will realize how worthwhile the process was, if painful at the time.

I look forward to meeting, in person, to discuss our greatest achievement. But understand responsibility for progress on this issue lies with you. If my friends see no indication within the next twenty-four hours that you are acting on their simple demands, you will receive another of my fingers shortly thereafter.

Sincerely,
J. Robert Humphries

The butcher who had snipped J.R.'s finger off his hand like a twig now snatched up the paper and examined it critically. He scowled, as if J.R. must have attempted to insert some kind of secret message into the text. Finally, apparently satisfied, he thrust it at J.R.

By now, the exhausted secretary of state had a pretty good idea what was to come next. He held the letter chin-level, just below his face, and waited while his captor stood and fished an instant camera out of his pocket.

The man snapped a picture and then retrieved the letter. He placed both items on his seat. Bent and secured J.R.'s right wrist to the arm of his chair. Then, without another word, he turned and strode out of the room, slamming the door shut behind him.

Humphries's head slumped onto his chest. The effort of holding it upright suddenly seemed too much to bear. He had never before felt as physically exhausted and emotionally drained as he did right now.

He tried to imagine, for perhaps the one-hundredth time over the last couple of days, exactly who these lunatics were that had kidnapped him. They claimed to represent the Soviet Union, and the content of the letter just dictated would indicate they were Russian. But J.R. Humphries had dealt with the Soviet Union extensively during his tenure on the president's cabinet, and he was as certain as he had ever been about anything in his life that these people were not Russians.

He found his thoughts beginning to wander and forced himself to concentrate. Their demands were ludicrous. They couldn't possibly believe that President Ronald Reagan would ever consider dismantling Western Europe's missile defense systems.

They could send his *head* in a box to the White House and it wouldn't change that fact. The action might start a third World War—probably would, in fact, given J.R.'s close relationship with Reagan and the requirement the United States would then have to show the rest of the world that kidnapping and murdering a high-ranking U.S. diplomat would not stand—but it would not force Reagan even to consider leaving America's European allies at risk.

Their demand was a non-starter, and the Soviets—or whoever these people were—had to know that.

But something else was going on here, something totally apart from a fringe element within the Soviet Union attempting to accomplish by hostage-taking what they could not accomplish through diplomacy. J.R. wished he wasn't so goddamned tired. If only he could think clearly, he might be able to puzzle through the issue.

But he could barely think at all, never mind clearly.

He was exhausted. Afraid. The contents of the letter were terrifying, especially the section that spelled out what would happen when—not if, but when, J.R. knew—the president ignored the deadline for action regarding the missile defense systems.

He would lose another finger.

And then another.

And perhaps other body parts.

Despite his best efforts at forcing himself not to think about the man returning to this room with his bucket, and his bandages, and his goddamn hedge clippers, it was all J.R. Humphries *could* think about.

He began to shake uncontrollably as the terror overwhelmed him. He knew there had to be at least one camera mounted somewhere in this room, even though he could not see any, and for that reason he had tried to be strong at all times, even when alone.

But now, the effort of maintaining his composure was just too great. He was too tired and too afraid. And if he was being honest with himself, the situation was too hopeless. It was obvious no one had a clue where he was being held; if anyone had been able to figure it out, he would have been rescued by now.

Despite himself he began to cry silently, tears rolling down his cheeks as he sat alone and dirty inside this room. He sniffled for a little while, grateful the president could not see his weakness, and then he fell into an uneasy sleep.

22

Wednesday, September 9, 1987
2:15 a.m.
Washington, D.C.

The big Lincoln Town Car wound its way around the slumbering D.C. metropolis, driving in a seemingly aimless pattern. For one awful moment Tracie thought she had been made, that the Lincoln's driver had seen her turn the corner onto Massachusetts Avenue and would continue driving to nowhere until she got tired of following and gave up.

Then she realized the situation was just the opposite. The driver of the car she was tailing *didn't* know he was being followed, rather, he was doing what anyone involved in illicit activity would do—*checking* for a tail.

This realization caused a spike in Tracie's pulse. Whoever was inside the car, the people who had left the Iraqi embassy under cover of darkness, were going to great lengths to keep their destination a secret. There was no guarantee, of course, that any of this was related to the Humphries kidnapping, but at least she knew that it *could* be. That in itself represented progress.

She had been careful to leave plenty of room between herself and the Town Car and now she backed off a little more. The roads at this time of night were practically deserted, which made it easier for the occupants of the Lincoln to spot the tail, but also made it easier for Tracie to track her prey.

The Town Car followed Massachusetts Avenue into Bethesda, Maryland, eventually turning onto Goldsboro and then making another immediate right turn onto River Road and reversing course back into D.C.

Once Tracie realized what the driver was up to, she relaxed a bit and allowed the Iraqis to dictate the pace. As long as she exercised appropriate caution and didn't allow herself to be spotted, eventually the driver would turn toward his ultimate destination. When the Lincoln turned north onto Georgia Avenue, Tracie paralleled its course, utilizing Thirteenth Street for a few blocks and eventually hooking a right on Longfellow to once again fall in behind the target.

Ten minutes turned into fifteen, and then twenty. Tracie was becoming more and more intrigued. Unless the passenger inside the vehicle ahead was suffering from a severe case of insomnia and had directed his driver to take a random course around the city, something big was happening. It was just not typical for a driver to put this much time and effort into losing a tail, no matter the time of day.

A few more lefts and rights and soon Tracie began to realize Act One of this strange drama being played out in the middle of the night to an audience of zero was approaching its end. The Washington surroundings had gradually became bleaker the longer the Lincoln drove. Now it was prowling through a neighborhood that would never adorn a tourist's postcard.

Urban blight was everywhere. The devastation was easy to see even at this time in the early morning. Brightly colored graffiti was scrawled across brick-sided abandoned buildings like an anarchist's wet dream. Windows not boarded over had long-since been smashed out. Poorly maintained sidewalks crumbled, the cement pocked with potholes big enough to snap an ankle. Scraggly looking men whose dreams had disappeared decades ago crowded around rusted trash barrels inside which flames burned brightly, licking their way toward the darkened sky.

Far ahead, brake lights flared as the Town Car pulled to the curb. Tracie immediately hung a right, drove down a trash-littered alley, and then pulled a quick K-turn.

She killed her headlights and eased back to the intersection.

Peered right.

Saw the Lincoln's doors swing open and two men climb out of the back.

Bingo.

She kept the lights off and turned the corner, parking at the curb far behind the Town Car in a location that would afford her a clear view of the car.

She reached into the backseat and grabbed her binoculars, lifting them to her eyes and expertly spinning the focusing knob. In seconds she had a razor-sharp view of the activity taking place several hundred feet north of her position.

The men glanced left and right. Once again, Tracie had to resist the urge to slide down in her seat. She had parked far enough away that there was no chance the men could see through her windshield. Their body language and the casual way they looked up and down the street made it clear they did not suspect they had been followed.

To Tracie it looked like they were putting on a show, feigning vigilance. Was someone besides the driver still inside the car? Someone important?

After a moment, the men put their backs to Tracie and began walking. One of them had a backpack slung over his shoulder, and while neither was openly displaying a weapon, she had no doubt they were both armed. They moved to the corner and turned right, walking along the side of a building and disappearing from view.

Tracie immediately opened her door. She had disabled the interior dome light before leaving her apartment, so there was no telltale flash that might have alerted any occupants still inside the Town Car to her presence. She slid out of her car and eased the door shut, then hurried along the sidewalk in the opposite direction, keeping to the shadows of the decrepit buildings lining the street.

The area seemed to be deserted. It struck Tracie as odd that the homeless derelicts, so prevalent in the blocks leading up to this area, were nowhere to be seen. She wondered if the men inside the Town Car had something to do with that.

Had they sterilized the area?

She made a mental note to return in the light of day and do a little unobtrusive reconnaissance. Right now, though, she had to move fast or she stood the chance of losing the men she was trying to follow. She turned at the first corner and hugged the side of the building, breaking into a full-fledged sprint the moment she was out of sight of anyone still inside the Town Car.

She raced along the narrow alleyway until arriving at the cross street located one block east. She slowed to a fast walk as she reached the corner of the building, which appeared to be a long-abandoned three-story tenement house. Peering left, she spotted the two men just before they disappeared again behind another building.

Based on the angle at which they had crossed the street Tracie guessed they were not planning to continue another full block, so she turned left and moved as quickly as she dared in their direction. If the men doubled-back in an effort to ensure they weren't being followed—a distinct possibility and something Tracie herself would have done—she risked running right into them.

That kind of risk was unavoidable in a one-person op. There was no partner to cover her back and no one to help if she got into trouble. But Tracie wasn't concerned. She barely noticed. She was used to working alone.

When she reached the corner where she had lost sight of her quarry, she slowed and peered left. The neighborhood had been constructed in such a way that the streets, rather than being placed at ninety-degree angles, were slightly asymmetrical. This meant that she was not visible to the driver and any other occupants of the Lincoln Town Car, presumably still idling in the darkness one block to the west.

"Small favors," she muttered, and again turned her attention to locating her two targets. They were easy to spot. Certain they had not been followed, arrogant almost to the point of irrationality, the men marched straight toward another abandoned structure, this one an old, faded, two-story brick building that would be recognizable to anyone who had grown up in the United States.

A school.

Carved into a granite slab above the front entrance was what undoubtedly had once been the school's name, but in the 2:50 a.m. darkness and the shadows of the surrounding buildings it was impossible to read.

Without so much as a glance behind them, the men climbed the wide stairway. They knocked at the big wooden double-doors and waited. Then one of the doors swung open and they disappeared into the building. No lights went on behind the few windows that had not been boarded up providing further indication—as if Tracie needed any by now—that whatever was happening inside that ancient building was not legitimate.

Curiouser and curiouser.

She retreated a few steps, pressing her back against the side of an empty building—the entire neighborhood appeared to have been abandoned like an afterthought—and considered how to proceed.

She was dressed in dark clothing, her vibrant red hair stuffed up under a black Oakland Raiders baseball cap. She had unrolled the neck portion of her black turtleneck sweater so that the lower half of her face was covered. Between the bill of the cap and the cotton material covering her jaw and mouth, only a thin slash of her pearl-white skin would be visible to anyone keeping watch out the old school building.

Still, she hesitated, not sure how far she should push her luck. Not a single soul knew she was here. To her knowledge, no one in the U.S. intelligence community was even aware of this building, let alone whatever was going on inside it.

If she were to be caught by the men in the Lincoln Town Car, no one would come to save her. Now that she had been relieved of her CIA duties, no one would even know she was missing for days. Weeks, maybe. It wasn't like she had so many friends that people would become suspicious when she stopped showing up.

Tracie sighed and checked her watch and wondered how soon the men who had entered the building would return. Could they simply be relieving two other men who had been standing guard duty? Or were they here for something else, something that would take more time?

There was nothing to gain by standing in the shadows waiting for the men to return. She knew where they had come from, and had a pretty good idea where they would go when they left. Of much greater importance was conducting surveillance of the school's exterior. She had to learn more about this mysterious abandoned building.

23

It was still dark as Tracie drove back to her apartment, but the sky was beginning to brighten on the horizon. Skies had mostly cleared overnight and before long day would break on a beautiful fall morning in the nation's capital.

She yawned and rubbed her eyes with one hand as she turned into the parking lot, considering her next move. The accumulation of evidence, taken separately, proved nothing. But when viewed as a whole, Tracie believed there was at least a chance J. Robert Humphries was being held inside that abandoned brick and concrete structure not far from the White House: Professor Brickley's belief that the ransom note and proof-of-life newspaper had been written by someone with a Middle Eastern background, most likely an Iraqi. Saddam Hussein's strange Middle Eastern troop movements. The furtive nature of the men Tracie had followed from the Iraqi Embassy. Her conviction that Humphries was likely being held in the area.

It all added up to at least a glimmer of hope.

But one thing was clear. Time was of the essence. The longer Humphries was gone, the less chance there was of him ever coming home alive, and the greater the chance the United States would find itself at war with the Soviet Union. And if the secretary of state was *not* being held in that abandoned D.C. school, if Tracie's hunch was wrong, she needed to know immediately so she could begin looking elsewhere in the haystack for the needle that was J. Robert Humphries.

Where else that might be, she had no idea.

But for now, that was irrelevant. Her immediate priority was to get inside that school building and find out what it contained that was of such paramount importance the Iraqis needed to enter and exit under cover of darkness.

Her reconnaissance had revealed no exterior mounted surveillance cameras, which came as a relief. Security cameras could be circumvented, but the process could be time-consuming and risky, especially without backup, and their absence would make a fast entry much easier.

There was always the possibility cameras were installed inside the building, making them impossible to detect from Tracie's outside vantage point, but she doubted that was the case. For one thing, the vast majority of the old school's windows had long since been smashed out and boarded up, meaning that interior-mounted cameras would not provide three-hundred-sixty degree coverage. And for another, the resolution of cameras mounted inside the building and pointed through windows would be lower, making them much less useful.

No, Tracie felt confident there were no cameras. Which left only one possibility: the Iraqis had decided to rely on the presence of patrolling guards to provide security.

She rubbed her eyes again, shifting her little Toyota into neutral and shutting down the engine. Any further planning would have to wait until she had grabbed a few hours of sleep. She was exhausted.

She climbed out of the car and was walking toward her apartment when a massive figure moved up next to her, approaching from her blind spot. The figure was walking fast, looming into her personal space, and she reacted instinctively, based on training that had been ingrained into her consciousness from her earliest days in the agency.

She ducked and spun left, kicking out at the figure's left kneecap, barely managing to stop herself before shattering the fragile bone when she recognized the arrival at the last possible moment.

It was Marshall Fulton.

He stumbled back, eyes wide open in half-shock, half-confusion.

"Jesus, Marshall," Tracie said, exasperated. "Didn't your mother ever teach you not to sneak up on people?"

He shrugged, regaining a little of his poise. "I was always too big to sneak up on anyone. I guess she figured it would never be an issue."

Tracie laughed, her exhaustion tempered by the adrenaline shooting through her system. "Ah, don't worry about it. It's my fault, anyway. I should never have been so unaware of my surroundings that you were able to do it. If we had been in Russia, that never would have happened, no matter how tired I was. Actually, I should thank you. This was a great wake-up call, both literally and figuratively."

"You're welcome, then," Marshall answered, his faltering smile making it clear he wasn't quite sure what she was talking about but was glad that he no longer seemed to be in imminent danger of a trip to the emergency room.

By now they had arrived at Tracie's apartment door, and she turned to him with a frown. "What are you doing here, anyway? How did you happen to arrive at my place just as I was driving in at," she looked at her watch, "six a.m.?"

"I didn't just get here. I've been waiting in my car for you."

"Waiting in your car? For how long?"

It was Marshall's turn to glance at his watch. "Close to three hours."

Tracie shook her head. "Why in the world would you do that?"

"Because I was worried about you," he answered as if it should have been obvious.

"I feel like we're going around in circles here. But why would you be worried about me?"

"Let's see," Marshall said, ticking things off on his fingers. "You lost your job yesterday, and then you went out in the middle of the night, all by yourself, to follow God knows who while they were doing God knows what, and then when I showed up at your home at three o'clock in the morning you were nowhere to be found. How could I *not* be worried?"

Trace slid her key into the lock and turned the knob. "Jeez, Marshall, that's very sweet, but what I did last night was no different than what I've been doing for the last seven years, with the possible exception that I was on my home turf instead of in some foreign land. What I did last night is my job!"

"Not anymore," he said quietly. "What you did last night *used* to be your job, remember? And it bothered me that you were out there, alone, probably in danger, possibly getting hurt, doing something based on information I gave you that I had no right sharing."

Tracie had taken two steps into her living room, and now she turned and gazed into Marshall Fulton's face. His chestnut-brown eyes were big and soft and concerned, and just like that she felt a lump forming in her throat and her eyes beginning to tear up. With the notable exception of Shane Rowley a few months ago, not a single living soul besides her mother and father had shown the kind of caring and concern for her well-being over the last seven years that this man, practically a stranger, was exhibiting right now.

She realized her lower lip had started to quiver and clamped her jaw shut angrily. You didn't work for long in CIA covert ops without developing the ability to compartmentalize, and now Tracie compartmentalized like never before, forcing those feelings of loss and sadness and regret deep down inside her. She could break down later.

She cleared her throat. ""That was so...thoughtful of you." She knew how ridiculous the statement sounded but couldn't think of anything else to say. "What about work?"

"I have about an hour before I have to leave."

"You were up half the night, sitting in your car in my parking lot, and now you're going to go to work?"

He shrugged. "I wasn't up half the night. I was up all night. I'll survive."

"Come on in, I'll make you a cup of coffee. It's the least I can do."

* * *

"Your intel was right on," Tracie said. The pair was seated at her tiny kitchen table that was wedged into a corner of her tiny studio apartment, a cup of coffee in front of each of them. Drinking coffee was a mistake, given that she intended to try to get some sleep as soon as Marshall left. But she did it anyway.

"Somebody inside the Iraqi embassy is going to great lengths to hide something," she said. She outlined the night's events and then continued, "The two guys that entered the school weren't out for a nighttime stroll."

"Did you follow them when they left?"

"Didn't need to. I know where they went."

"So, what's the verdict? Is Humphries being held there?"

Tracie shrugged. "No way of knowing until I can get inside."

"How are you going to manage that?"

She smiled. "It's what I do."

Marshall shook his head. "With no backup."

"I don't have a choice. I no longer work for the people who have the resources to provide backup, as you so thoughtfully reminded me a few minutes ago."

She was trying to lighten the mood, but Marshall was having none of it. "What can I do to help?" he asked, his face grim.

"Try again to bring the information about the Iraqi troop movements to the attention of the big shots at Langley. Something's not right about that, even if it's completely unrelated to Humphries's kidnapping. Who moves men and equipment *away* from the fighting when they're in the middle of a war?"

"It sure seems like a radical new theory on warfare."

"Yeah. And everybody they're moving seems to be headed toward one of the most strategically important countries in the region."

"Saudi Arabia."

"Exactly."

"You don't think Saddam Hussein's considering attacking Saudi Arabia…" Marshall's voice drifted off as he considered the possibility.

"I don't know what to think," she said. "But there's nothing else down there, and we *are* talking about Saddam Hussein. You're the expert on Middle Eastern affairs, what do you think of the guy?"

He considered the question for a moment. A very short moment. "He's a wild card," he admitted.

"Exactly. And one thing I've learned in the field is that coincidences are rare."

"They don't happen."

"Oh, they happen. Sometimes. But it's a rare enough

occurrence that when I see two significant events that seem unrelated, it makes me look for a connection."

"The Humphries kidnapping and the bizarre Iraqi troop movements?"

"That's right. Something doesn't smell right."

"It might just be me. I've been sitting in your parking lot most of the night."

Tracie laughed as Marshall yawned and finished his coffee. "Holy shit," he said. "I don't know how you do this clandestine stuff. One night without sleep and I feel like I'm about a hundred years old. You, on the other hand," he eyed her up and down appreciatively, "look like you're ready for a night on the town."

"I'm ready for a few hours of sleep. The town will have to wait."

The pair rose from the table and Marshall stretched and yawned once again. "You look exhausted," she said. "Let me make you a coffee for the road."

24

Marshall was surprised when his request for a meeting with Middle Eastern Analysis Branch Director Sean Rafferty was approved almost immediately. Face-to-face meetings with a branch director inside Langley just didn't happen, at least not with lowly analysts and not without good reason.

He thought back to his two conversations with Tracie inside the building yesterday, one before her firing and one after. Both had been conducted in plain view of agency surveillance equipment, which was ubiquitous around the Langley complex, for obvious reasons. Had that played any part in the swiftness with which his request had been approved? He would never know the answer to that question, and supposed it didn't matter anyway. At least he was getting the opportunity to do what Tracie had asked of him.

He stifled a yawn as he sat uncomfortably in a hard-backed wooden chair in the anteroom outside Rafferty's office. A young woman paid him no attention, typing industriously until a console telephone buzzed on her desk. She picked up the handset, listened for a moment, and then turned to Marshall with a patently fake smile that she did little to disguise. "Mr. Rafferty is ready for you," she said, turning in her chair and resuming her typing before she had finished the statement.

Marshall crossed the room and knocked on the closed door

147

before entering. He had never been inside Sean Rafferty's office and took the opportunity to check it out as he crossed to Rafferty's desk. The floor was institutional tile, the desk government-issue steel. A set of gunmetal-grey filing cabinets that looked as though they had been beaten with a baseball bat took up most of the wall behind Rafferty's desk. A couple of pictures hung on the side wall: one of Rafferty with a harried-looking woman Marshall assumed was the man's wife, and a second showing a youngish Rafferty romping in a park with two children.

"Have a seat," the director said without lifting his gaze from a report he was studying on his desk. Marshall eased into a chair that was just as uncomfortable as the one in the outer office and waited for Rafferty to finish reading. After a moment, the man looked up in apparent annoyance. "Well?" he said. "What can I do for you, Marshall?"

"Sir, it's about the intel regarding the unexplained movement of Iraqi troops toward the Saudi border."

"Okay. What about it? Has the situation changed?"

"No, sir. At least, not that I'm aware."

"Then why are we having this discussion?"

"Sir, I'm just wondering. It seems quite significant. Is any action being taken to follow up on this intel?"

"Excuse me?"

"Is anything being done about the apparent massing of troops close to the Saudi Arabian border?"

"Marshall, the same thing was done with that information that is done with everything that's flagged. It's reviewed further and then passed up the line. What you're asking is not something I can readily answer, nor is it any of your concern." He stared hard at Marshall. "Is there anything else?"

"I just...no sir, there's nothing else."

"Then I suggest you get back to work."

25

After the coffee, and with adrenaline from her nocturnal activities still pounding through her system, Tracie was certain she would not be able to sleep. She was wrong. Within five minutes of her head hitting the pillow, she had dropped into a deep slumber, and seven hours later—an inconceivable interval for a covert ops specialist running a mission—she awoke feeling refreshed and ready to go.

She showered and ate and tried to pass the time. It was too early to go back to the abandoned school building; that would have to be done under cover of darkness. And until she knew exactly what was inside it that was so important to the Iraqis, she would not know how to proceed.

She sipped coffee and picked at junk food as afternoon turned into early evening. The sun was low in the Washington sky when she rose from her kitchen table, rinsed out her mug, and dropped it into the sink. Then she fished a backpack out of her bedroom closet—it looked similar in style and color to the one the two Iraqis had carried last night—and moved around her apartment, filling it with items while she ticked them off a mental checklist.

By the time she finished, dusk had long since given way to night, and it was time to get to work.

* * *

Thursday, September 10, 1987
12:40 a.m.
Washington, D.C.

This time, when Marshall Fulton approached her in the parking lot, Tracie's senses weren't dulled from lack of sleep. She scanned the area as she walked, and she spotted him almost the moment he stepped out of his car, a 1979 Buick Regal. When he got close, she smiled and said, "Don't tell me you've been sitting in my parking lot again, like some lovesick teenager or deranged stalker!"

Marshall grinned, taking the teasing like a man, and said, "Nah. This time it's coincidence. I had just driven up when your front door opened and out you came."

"Why aren't you sleeping?" Tracie asked. "You must be exhausted."

"Not as much as you might think. I went home sick after my meeting with Rafferty. Spent the afternoon in bed. I still feel a little logy, but I'm fresh as a daisy compared to when you saw me this morning."

"Huh," Tracie said, eying him up and down. He was a very large man, muscular and fit. "More like a mountain of daisies."

This time Marshall laughed out loud. Tracie said, "So, what are you doing here, besides making my neighbors afraid to come out of their apartments?"

"Thought you'd want to know about my meeting with Rafferty."

"I do have a phone, you know. You could have called me."

"Didn't want to wake you up if you were still asleep."

Though Tracie guessed that the real reason was something else, she didn't argue. She shrugged and said, "I was an agency employee long enough to have a pretty good idea already, but since you went to the trouble of coming all the way over here, why don't you fill me in?"

"You want the complete rundown or the Cliff's Notes version?"

"Well, as you can see, I'm heading out for a night on the town, so why don't you just hit the high points?"

"They don't give a shit about Saddam Hussein moving his

troops around."

Tracie raised her eyebrows. "Those are the high points?"

"Basically. Rafferty told me to mind my own business, said the intel had been moved up the chain just like procedure says to do."

"Where it will disappear into someone's filing cabinet or desk drawer until it's too late. *Then* it'll be resurrected, just so the bureaucrats can figure out who to blame."

Marshall raised his hands in a *What can you do?* gesture. "You had to know it was a long shot. The powers-that-be aren't interested in taking policy advice from a lowly data analyst."

"I know," Tracie said. "Like I said, I already had a pretty good idea what you were going to say before you even started talking. I just wouldn't have felt right if we hadn't at least given it a shot. Thanks for trying."

"Not a problem. If I won't put my career on the line for a friend, what kind of man would I be?"

Tracie laughed. "Don't go getting yourself fired on my account, Marshall. I don't know where I'm going to find the money to feed *myself*, let alone anyone else."

They shared a moment's awkward silence, and then Tracie said, "Well, I don't want to keep my date waiting, so I really should be going."

"Date, huh?" Marshall took in her faded jeans, frayed at the bottom, and her ancient Washington Redskins T-shirt and said, "Isn't it kind of late? And who's the lucky guy, a skid row bum?"

Tracie winked at him. "You never know what the night will bring, my observant friend." Then she unlocked her car, tossed her backpack into the front passenger seat, and slid in next to it.

She closed the door and rolled down the window. "Seriously, Marshall, thanks for the help. You're a sweetheart and it's nice to know someone cares. Now, go home and get a good night's sleep and forget about all of this. Don't put your career at risk on my account."

* * *

Tracie drove to a liquor store she knew stayed open until two a.m. She stepped out of her car and waved to Marshall, who was rolling slowly down the street a hundred yards back, trying unsuccessfully to tail her without being seen.

He pulled to the curb and rolled down his window, looking abashed. "Marshall, what are you doing?" she said. "I thought I told you to go home."

"I know," he said, refusing to look her in the eye. He gazed at the empty sidewalk like it was the most fascinating thing he had ever seen. "I'm just worried about you, that's all. You're all alone, trying to do God only knows what, and—"

She lifted a hand to cut him off. "This is what I'm trained to do, remember? It's my job, or at least it used to be. You don't have to worry about me. And there's nothing you can do to help me in any event. Just go home. It'll be better for everyone, trust me."

"I understand," he said. "Sorry about that."

"You don't have to apologize," she said. "I appreciate your concern. It's very sweet, but it's unnecessary."

"Okay," he said, still refusing to meet her eye. "Got it. See ya later." He rolled the window up and accelerated away.

Tracie watched his car until the taillights flashed briefly and he hooked a left at a cross street a couple of blocks down. She wondered whether he would actually listen to her this time. Then she put Marshall Fulton and his sweet gesture of concern out of her mind and walked into the liquor store.

Three minutes later she was back in her car, a fifth of Jack Daniel's nestled inside a plain brown bag on the passenger seat. She sat for a moment and considered her next move.

It was dangerous.

Foolhardy.

She was going to do it anyway.

She pulled away from the curb and retraced as much of the path the Town Car had taken last night as she could remember, purposely approaching the abandoned school using the same route. One thing that had struck her at the time was how little activity there had been within the couple of blocks immediately surrounding the school.

The District of Columbia contained a significant homeless population, much of it confined to a ten- or twelve-block zone in and around this neighborhood, so although it had been the middle of the night when she drove through yesterday, there should have been plenty of evidence of that population.

Indeed, she had seen men huddled around burning trashcans and sleeping in doorways, but once she got close to the school all evidence of the homeless had disappeared.

Almost as though the indigent population had been driven off.

By the Iraqis.

Because they had something to hide.

Once again as she drove, Tracie observed the clumps of dirty men and even the occasional woman, drinking from bottles hidden inside paper bags, some of them watching her drive past with the vacant expressions of people with nowhere to go and no expectation that their lives were ever going to improve.

Tonight was busier than last night. But still, as she motored through the trash-strewn streets of a section of D.C. the tourists never visited unless they were hopelessly lost, Tracie noticed that all activity ceased as she got close to the school building. She continued past it and discovered that an identical sector north of the building had been sanitized as well.

There was no way this could be a coincidence.

For a moment Tracie wondered why the car from the Iraqi embassy stopped so far from the school, subjecting their people to the added risk of detection as they walked to and from it.

Then the answer occurred to her, so simple she was embarrassed not to have thought of it immediately. Deniability. If the men were apprehended, any remaining occupants in the Town Car could simply drive away and no one would be the wiser. And from a distance, even if the car were to be seen it would be much more difficult to prove a connection between it and whatever was happening inside the abandoned school.

Tracie returned to where she had parked last night. She eased to the curb in the same spot. Shut down the engine and sat quietly in the darkness, allowing her senses to adjust. She could hear the ambient noise of any large city at night—a siren wailing, a dog barking—but it was all muted by distance; the immediate area was as still as an empty church.

After ten minutes, during which time Tracie maintained a continuous scan and saw nothing unusual, she picked up her backpack and bottle of whiskey and eased out of the car. She locked the vehicle and slung the backpack over one shoulder. Then she started walking.

Half a block from the school, she melted into a darkened doorway and broke the seal on the whiskey bottle. She swished some around in her mouth and then spit it out. Poured some over both forearms, letting the amber liquid run over her hands and splash to the ground. She splattered some liberally over her Redskins T-shirt.

Within seconds, Tracie Tanner had transformed herself from a beautiful twenty-something woman into a wasted skid row drunk. She had purposely left her normally lustrous red hair unwashed and unbrushed, and now she stumbled out of the doorway, holding the bottle of JD by its stubby neck.

She turned a corner and the big brick school building loomed in the distance, silent and alien-looking in the near-total darkness. She weaved along the deserted road, pretending to pay no more attention to the school than to any other structure, all of which were abandoned and still.

She affected a drunkard's warble and started singing a verse from Joan Jett's *I Love Rock and Roll*, her voice low but clear: "I love rock and roll, so put another dime in the jukebox, baby. I love rock and roll, so come and take your time and dance with me…"

Tracie was certain that at least one person was inside the big building providing security. The paranoid route the driver of the Lincoln had taken last night in order to avoid detection suggested the Iraqis considered whatever was inside the school to be of extreme importance.

She was probably being watched right now.

At least she hoped so.

The idea was to draw the attention of the guard, to lure him outside. Tracie had every confidence her ploy would work. If the Iraqis had gone to the considerable trouble of sterilizing the area of the homeless population—which she was sure they had—they would not hesitate to drive away an intruder, especially a drunk, defenseless woman.

She stumbled and weaved down the street, still singing, pretending to stop and drink from the bottle every few steps. She passed the school's entrance, keeping as close a watch on it as she could in her peripheral vision.

Bingo.

She had no sooner crossed in front of the big double-doors

than one of them opened, just a bit, and a lone figure slipped out. Tracie started moving a little faster. She was still weaving, still singing, but she needed to get around the corner of the building, out of sight of a second guard, if there was one, before her pursuer caught up to her.

The man didn't shout at her, didn't make his presence known. Had Tracie really been drunk, she would never have known he was even there. He closed the distance between them rapidly. But not rapidly enough.

She angled off the road, crossing the crumbling sidewalk and a small patch of weed-strewn brown grass, disappearing from the man's view around the corner of the school. By now he was no more than ten feet behind her. He still had not said a word, and the moment he rounded the corner, she would once again be in his sights.

She hoped she would have enough time.

She darted to the side of the building and tossed her backpack to the ground. Then she bent over, hands on her knees, like she was about to vomit. She waited, counting down the seconds in her head. When she reached three, she started dry-heaving, knowing her pursuer would now be right behind her.

She was right. The man finally spoke, saying in a gruff, heavily accented voice, "What are you doing? You cannot be here."

Tracie ignored him. She sank to one knee, still with her back to the man, and pretended to puke onto the grass. The sound was deep and convincing, as she coughed and sputtered.

The man spoke again, more sharply this time. "I *said* you cannot be here. You must leave, now!" He stepped right up next to Tracie's kneeling body and reached for her shoulders to haul her to her feet.

Exactly what she was waiting for.

In an instant she spun sideways and shot to her feet, extending her right arm, palm out, forcing it up and under the man's exposed jaw. Between the drive from her leg muscles and her arm extending at the same time, the amount of torque was tremendous. His mouth slammed closed, teeth clattering together, as his head bounced violently backward.

He stumbled, stunned, but stayed on his feet. In his hand was a pistol, which he somehow managed to hold onto despite the suddenness and ferocity of Tracie's attack. She grabbed his wrist with both hands and slammed it against the bricks once, twice, then the gun dropped to the ground with a soft thud.

The man swayed and stumbled but tried to fight back. He took a wild roundhouse swipe at Tracie's head, which she slipped easily. Then she stepped forward and hit the bigger man in the side of the face with a closed left fist. His head connected with the side of the brick building with a muffled wet smack. He staggered sideways, dropped to his knees, then sank face-first to the ground where he lay still.

One down.

Tracie nudged him in the side of the head with her foot, ready to defend herself if he was playing possum. It didn't seem likely, given how hard his head had struck the bricks. What *did* seem likely was that he would be down and out for several minutes and would awaken with a headache the likes of which he had probably never experienced before.

But Tracie hadn't stayed alive in some of the most dangerous locations on earth by making assumptions. So she played it safe. She nudged the man and he didn't move.

She wedged a foot under his shoulder and rolled him over onto his back. He still didn't move.

Out cold. A thin line of blood ran from under his hairline across his face. Tracie took a quick look around to be sure they were still unseen. The buildings loomed over them like ghosts, silent and accusing. If anyone was watching, he was keeping to the shadows.

She quickly retrieved the man's weapon, checked the safety to be sure it was engaged, then shoved it into the waistband of her jeans at the small of her back, next to her own personal Glock 19. Then she pulled her long T-shirt back down, covering both guns.

She had to get her attacker out of here. Leaving him unconscious in the schoolyard was unacceptable. Moving him would be risky and dangerous, but there was no other option.

Tracie positioned herself behind the unmoving man's head and knelt, threading her arms under his shoulders at the armpits. Then she lifted with her legs and dragged the much bigger man's unresponsive body across the schoolyard and the empty road, to another of the dozens of abandoned tenement buildings littering the neighborhood.

A dilapidated door providing access to what had once been a triple-decker apartment building, or perhaps a boarding house, swung in the light breeze. The wooden door was partially rotted, and a padlock meant to keep out vandals had long since been destroyed.

Tracie kicked the door fully open and dragged the still-unconscious guard inside. The air felt stagnant despite the partially open front door close behind her. Four feet past the entryway the darkness was nearly complete. It surrounded her, stifling her, pressing down on her like a heavy blanket.

She turned left, dragging the man into what may have once been some kind of sitting room or common area. A furtive scrabbling noise from somewhere off her right side told her the rats that had claimed the space were abandoning ship. For now.

She eased the man's upper body to the floor. His head struck the dirty hardwood with a crack. Then she straightened and considered her next move.

She had forgotten her backpack.

Dammit.

Tracie turned and sprinted outside and across the street. She had to balance the need for stealth with a recognition that speed was of the essence. There was no way of knowing how many men were guarding this mysterious location. If there was more than one, it wouldn't be long before he became concerned about how long his partner had been gone.

If it hadn't already happened.

Seconds later she was at the school's side wall. The backpack lay undisturbed in the dusty schoolyard. She grabbed it and slung it over her shoulder, then ran back across the deserted street to the building where she had left the guard.

She stopped at the doorway. Flattened herself against the wall. Unzipped her backpack as quietly as she could. Rummaged inside until finding a small flashlight and a roll of duct tape. Then she re-zipped the bag and placed it on the ground.

She crouched just outside the doorway to present as small a target as possible in the unlikely event the man inside had regained consciousness and was waiting to ambush her. Then she pivoted and swung into the building.

She covered most of the flashlight's lens with her hand,

leaving only an opening the size of a quarter for the light to shine through. Then she flicked it on, ready to defend herself.

The unconscious man lay on the floor exactly where she had left him. His eyes were closed and he was unmoving. Tracie shined the thin beam of light around the room, examining it quickly. It was big and empty, the once-shiny hardwood floor now littered with trash and the detritus of drug use and homelessness: a used needle here, an unopened condom there. A pair of men's underwear lay in the far corner of the room.

Tracie returned her attention to the man on the floor. He moaned softly and his arms and legs twitched before falling still again. She knelt and frisked him, paying special attention to his pockets, unsurprised to find no wallet and no form of identification. The only item in his possession was a set of three keys. She pocketed them.

She rolled him onto his belly and then began ripping strips of duct tape, first sealing his mouth and then binding his arms behind his back at the wrists and elbows. After that, she repeated the procedure on his legs, taping them together at the ankles and then just below the knees.

Then she went back over what she had done, repeating the process for added security. She hated using up more valuable time but could not afford to take the chance that the man would be able to free himself after waking.

Tracie counted in her head while she worked. She estimated the entire process, from stumbling down the street singing Joan Jett in an off-key voice to trussing up her attacker like a Thanksgiving turkey, had taken no more than six or seven minutes.

It was too long.

The man still had not awakened, but he had begun to stir, and Tracie knew it would only be a matter of minutes before he regained consciousness.

She slapped him on the back companionably and whispered, "Thanks for the workout." Then she picked up the flashlight and switched it off, sliding it into her pocket. She grabbed the duct tape and made her way back outside, where she picked up her backpack and returned to the school grounds across the street.

26

Date unknown
Time unknown
Location unknown

This time, when the man who had cut off his finger entered the room, J. Robert Humphries was surprised to see that he was not alone. A second man trailed behind then took up a position next to hedge-clipper man as they approached, taking their time, strutting arrogantly across the room.

J.R. was tired.

He was hungry.

He needed to use the bathroom.

But mostly, he was afraid. More afraid than usual. He was terrified. This departure from the norm—two men entering his prison cell instead of one—signaled a change in the status quo, and that could not be good news.

The two men stopped in front of him and stood silently, looking him straight in the eyes. Their faces were impassive, their postures relaxed and confident. He knew they were playing with him, more of the mind games they'd been subjecting him to from the moment he had heard the piece of glass hit the floor in his Georgetown study.

He told himself not to react, tried not to react, but couldn't manage it. The panic built steadily, and soon he was panting, hyperventilating, as he recalled the sound of his little finger falling with a barely audible plop into the bucket. He thought he might be sick.

159

The man who had severed his finger spoke. "It is time," he said.

J.R. cleared his throat and tried to keep his voice steady. "Time for what?" He was marginally calmer now that he had something, anything, to concentrate on, rather than allowing his imagination to run wild.

"Time for you to begin the long trip to your new home." The man smiled, and the sense of relief J.R. felt was almost overwhelming. Moving him meant they weren't going to kill him, at least not yet, and calling it his "new home" implied their intention was to keep him alive for the foreseeable future.

His sense of relief at the sudden realization that he was not going to be murdered, not yet and not the near future, was so strong it was almost overwhelming. The feeling washed over him like an ocean wave, cool and refreshing, and for a moment he wanted to leap up and shake the two men's hands, to hug them and slap them on the back, maybe buy them a drink.

J.R. tried to keep his facial expression neutral, but doubted he was successful. The sensation was too strong. He said, "New home? What new home?"

"Never mind that. Right now, the question you must consider is whether you wish to do this the easy way or the hard way."

"What do you mean?"

"Doing it the easy way means you will come quietly, make no attempt to escape or to alert anyone to your presence. Your mouth will be sealed and your hands will be secured behind your back, but you will be conscious, and with our assistance, will walk to the vehicle in which you will begin your journey."

"What is the alternative?" J.R. spoke without thinking. The words escaped almost before he was even aware of opening his mouth, and his fear and horror returned with a vengeance. Why had he said anything?

The man smiled. The effect was ghastly. His eyes remained cold and blank and emotionless. "The alternative is that we carry your unconscious body to the vehicle. You do not want to choose this alternative. We have no drugs with which to render you unconscious, so we will be forced to do it the old-fashioned way. With this." He reached behind his back and lifted up a short length of common rubber garden hose, which hung from a piece of twine tied to his belt. J.R. could tell the hose had been filled with something, he guessed sand, rendering it heavy and lethal but still somewhat pliable.

Hedge-trimmer man held the length of hose in front of J.R.'s face and then let it drop. It swung back and forth beside him in ever-decreasing arcs. "I suggest you choose the first option, but the decision is, of course, entirely yours."

"I choose the first option. I won't give you any trouble." J.R. hated himself for the lack of hesitation in his response. But, like before, the words came out before he was even aware he had spoken.

The man smiled again. It was no warmer this time than it had been the first. "I thought you might. But you should know that if you make one move we find threatening, just one, or attempt any kind of escape, or simply look at either of us in a way we do not like, your fate will be sealed, and we will do what we must."

J.R. shook his head violently. A headache had been forming at the base of his skull and now it flared like a lit match, but he didn't care. He wanted to reassure these lunatics, to do whatever was necessary to avoid being beaten unconscious with a rubber hose. "Don't worry," he said firmly. "As I told you before, I won't give you any trouble."

The man nodded, and then the two of them began unlocking the cuffs binding J.R. Humphries to the chair.

27

Thursday, September 10, 1987
2:00 a.m.
Washington, D.C.

Marshall Fulton wiped his sweaty palms on the legs of his jeans and checked his watch.

Again.

Three minutes had elapsed since the last time he looked.

After Tracie had dismissed him outside the liquor store parking lot, he had driven away and then circled back, making a left and another immediate left, driving four blocks before repeating the process. He had wound up two blocks north of Tracie, certain she would be long gone.

But to his surprise, no sooner had he turned the corner onto Seventh Street than Tracie's battered Toyota pulled away from the liquor store and turned south.

And Marshall followed, much more carefully this time, reminded by his last attempt that, until getting fired earlier today, Tracie Tanner did this sort of thing for a living and he did not. Unless he focused one hundred percent of his attention on staying out of sight, she would spot him again. And send him home again.

It might happen anyway. Probably would, in fact.

He tried to figure out why in the world he was doing this, skulking around in the middle of the night following someone who had made it clear she didn't want his help, but he couldn't come up with a good answer. Tracie was little more than a work acquaintance, someone with whom he had shared good conversation at one party years ago.

And it wasn't like she needed his protecting. *She* was the covert ops specialist. *She* had risked her life dozens of times in locations spanning the globe, where one slip-up would have resulted in imprisonment or worse. *She* had been involved in fistfights, knife fights, gunfights, and more.

He, on the other hand, was nothing more than a data analyst, sifting through reports, video and voice recordings, and other minutiae in search of intel with national security implications. His work was important, Marshall knew, but nothing about it qualified him in any way to assume he could protect a seasoned CIA field operative from the scary bad guys.

It was silly. Pointless. He should be home in bed, getting a good night's sleep in preparation for another long day sifting through foreign telecommunications data in the never-ending quest to keep America safe and secure.

And yet here he was, maintaining a reasonable distance from Tracie's car while still—more or less—keeping it in sight. He knew she must be distracted by the events of the last few days, or she likely would have made him within five blocks, extra precautions or no extra precautions.

The fact that she hadn't seen him yet told him he was doing the right thing. Tracie Tanner was truly alone. Even more alone than she had been on the most dangerous mission she had ever undertaken inside the borders of the Soviet Union. She had no job. No backup. No official sanction. No one else was even aware of what she was doing.

She continued to drive and Marshall continued to follow in a seemingly random pattern that somehow felt not so random, and it occurred to Marshall with the force of a ton of bricks why he was out here in the middle of the night doing a job for which he was utterly unprepared. It was more than just the fact that she was working on a high wire with no safety net.

She was on to something. She knew it and so did he.

Everyone else would recognize it as well, eventually. But for now, Washington officialdom was lurching along as it always did—with a slavish devotion to geopolitical narratives that were often alarmingly out of date but that survived unquestioned until some watershed event occurred, significant enough to shake the blinders off of the bureaucrats and the politicians.

Tracie was convinced that the kidnapping of Secretary of State Humphries was such an event, and Marshall wanted to help her. He needed to help her.

And then another realization struck him with a crystal clarity he had never before experienced. He was infatuated with her. He might even be falling in love with her, despite the fact such a notion was patently ridiculous. Was it even possible to love someone when the sum total of your personal interaction with that person could be counted on the fingers of one hand? When the only thing you have in common is a national security emergency?

Marshall Fulton was a muscular bear of a black man, raised in Louisiana by parents who had nothing much to offer their children but unconditional love and boundless optimism. He had escaped the grinding poverty of a New Orleans Eighth Ward housing project and against all odds carved out a life and a career for himself. He was proud to know he made a difference; that every day when he went to work he was contributing to the security of his country.

Tracie Tanner, on the other hand, was a petite redheaded white woman with porcelain skin who had been raised among the D.C. elite. He didn't know much about her background, but what difference did it make, really? He was a large black man and she, a tiny white woman. To contemplate a relationship would be silly. Even if it was 1987 Washington and not 1963 Alabama, the hurdles facing them as a couple would be enormous.

And she had made it perfectly clear she was not interested.

Romance-wise or any-other-kind-of-wise.

Yet here he was, acting for all the world like a love-struck teenager trailing along behind his crush, wide-eyed and stupid, after being dismissed in no uncertain terms.

He followed anyway.

Eventually Tracie pulled her little Toyota to a stop in one of the grubbiest sections of D.C., a roughly ten-square-block underbelly of poverty and despair that was deceptively close to the White House and the Capitol building, but at the same time seemed light-years away.

He crept along a couple of blocks behind her, driving with his lights off. Traffic was almost nonexistent thanks to the neighborhood's sheer devastation, and he was sure she would have noticed him had he not done so.

The moment she parked, Marshall drove into a trash-littered alleyway between two darkened three-story tenement buildings. He turned around—the space just barely wide enough—then nosed forward to the intersection and stopped, double-checking to be sure his doors were locked. The area seemed deserted, but Marshall had no desire to be pulled from his vehicle and beaten for cash because he was so focused on what was taking place up the block that he neglected to maintain awareness of his surroundings.

He peered to his right, eying the deserted sidewalk. Dozens of apparently abandoned, junked cars sat between his position and Tracie's, their rusting hulks stripped of any items of value and left to rot. The junkers obscured his view of Tracie's car, but he could clearly see the area immediately surrounding it on both sides, and knew he would be able to spot her the moment she climbed out.

And he did.

She got out and shrugged a backpack onto her right shoulder, looking like a young college girl setting off to a class that was being held in a war zone. She took a moment to scan in all directions before setting off along a cross street to Marshall's right. She disappeared in seconds and he was faced with his first tough decision: follow her or stay where he was?

He reached for the door handle and then changed his mind. He would wait where he was. For a while.

28

Tracie moved carefully but quickly. She had briefly considered trying the keys she had secured to enter the school through the front door—time was of the essence, after all—but immediately discarded the idea as reckless. If more than one man had been stationed inside the old building, and she was almost certain that was the case, she could be walking right into his arms by using the main entrance.

Instead, using the building for cover, she melted into the shadows and moved directly to the rear corner. On each side wall of the schoolhouse was an old-fashioned cast-iron fire escape bolted to the bricks. It was the type with a small landing outside an oversized second-story window, where children and teachers could exit through the window onto the landing, and then lower the iron ladder to the ground and descend to safety.

The ladder had been folded into two long sections and stored on the second-floor landing. It had been padlocked in place years ago, probably decades ago, to prevent vandals from lowering it and climbing into the building. Even from the ground, in the darkness and shadows, Tracie could see the lock was rusted and corroded so badly it would never open, even if she had a key.

But she didn't care. She wasn't going to use the ladder.

She knelt and uncoiled a length of light mountain climbing

rope from her backpack, then closed the pack and tucked it neatly against the wall on the ground. She hated to leave it but couldn't afford the extra weight. The length of rope featured a carabiner on one end and was longer than what she needed, but that was a hell of a lot better than the alternative.

Tracie knew she had to hurry. She would be completely unprotected during this process, an easy target should a second guard come to check on the whereabouts of the first.

She grasped the carabiner end of the rope in her hand and stepped backward to get a better angle. Then she tossed it up and over the iron railing ringing the landing. It dropped through the grates in the landing's floor and fell to the ground. She quickly picked it up, gripping both ends of the now-secured rope in her hands.

Looked around carefully, alert for any signs of the presence of another human being.

Saw none.

And began climbing, hand over hand, lifting her entire one-hundred-ten-pound frame solely with her arms and shoulders. If anyone came around the front corner of the building now and saw her, she would be a sitting duck, hanging in the air, totally exposed, her Glock and the gun she had taken off the Iraqi guard tucked away in the rear waistband of her jeans.

She climbed rapidly, her deceptively strong upper body allowing her to reach the iron landing after just a few seconds. Long experience and training had taught Tracie Tanner that survival in the field of covert ops almost always depended upon the operative's ability to outmaneuver and outthink her enemies, and her near-obsessive focus on an exhaustive training regimen favored by elite Delta Force operators had more than once enabled her to fight—and/or run—her way out of tight situations.

But that was before she had been shot in both shoulders and though doctors told her the healing process was progressing well, the strain of climbing was testing those weakened shoulders to their very limit.

She shifted her grip from the rope to the iron bars of the landing's railing, first her left hand and then her right, and tried to pull herself up. The bars were cool and slick with condensation from the autumn dew, and for a moment she struggled to maintain her grip. One hand slid down the railing, smashing the iron floor and bruising her hand.

She cursed silently and tried again.

Slipped again.

It wasn't going to work. The bars were too slick.

She hung for a moment, considering her options. There was only one, short of admitting defeat and accessing the school some other way. She transferred her grip from the vertical bars of the railing to the horizontal grillwork of the landing's iron floor. Then she lifted her feet, pushing them through the gaps between the railing bars, hooking them as tightly as she could. She tightened her stomach muscles and lifted her torso upward, straining to reach the top of the railing with her right hand.

An inch short.

She was sweating despite the cool temperatures, and her muscles were beginning to burn from the exertion of fighting gravity to keep her body suspended in the air. She could feel the iron bars bruising her ankles where they were jammed into the muscle and bone. Her calves felt as though they were being blasted from the inside with a flamethrower.

She panted out a deep breath and tried again, this time straining for the extra inch, feeling the iron dig into her ribs as she thrust her arm upward.

Her open left palm impacted the upper portion of the railing. She wrapped her fingers around the iron, withstanding the pain in her ribs for a moment longer to ensure she had the best possible grip. Then she unthreaded her feet from the bars. Her body swung away from the railing and then back, slamming into the iron and taking her breath away.

She held on doggedly. Gasped. Reached up with her right hand and gripped the iron, taking some of the strain off her left hand and aching shoulder. And then drew herself up until she could hook her armpits over the railing. She swung her legs over the top and dropped soundlessly to the floor of the fire escape.

The entire process took less than a minute.

* * *

The second floor window was closed and locked, but almost all of the ancient glass panels had been broken away over time, and

Tracie simply reached through one of the panes, moving carefully to avoid slicing her arm on a jagged shard of broken glass, and unlatched the brass locking mechanism from the inside.

She struggled to push up the big casement window, to break the seal that time, weather, and lack of use had created on the moisture-swollen wood. After a moment the window slid sluggishly upward on its frame, and she was in.

She slipped through the opening and then turned and pulled the window closed behind her. Tracie quickly walked to a wide stairway adjacent to the end of the hallway. Now that she was inside, she had to discover what the hell was so important in here that armed members of the Iraqi mission to the United States were protecting it while other members visited in official vehicles at all hours of the night.

Before searching the school, though, it was critical she determine whether another guard was stationed at the front entrance or roaming the building. She removed her Glock and crept down the stairs, alert for anyone who might appear around the corner.

No one did.

At the bottom of the stairs, Tracie went methodically from room to room, clearing them and finding nothing—and no one—of interest. The long-abandoned classrooms were all identical and all mostly empty, except for the occasional desk or chair that had for whatever reason never been removed.

She checked every classroom closet and each restroom, approaching with extreme caution, fully aware that behind every toilet stall might be a man with a weapon.

Nothing.

At the far end of the apparently deserted first floor was a suite of offices, some with windows that looked out on the front yard, offering a clear view of the main entrance. It was in one of these offices that Tracie assumed the guard who had stalked her earlier must have been stationed. The view of the empty street was as clear as the view of the front door.

But no one was here, either.

Why would the Iraqis go to such great lengths to keep secret whatever was happening inside this building, and leave just one man to guard the place, especially in the middle of the night? Were they that confident their activities would remain undetected? It was giving Tracie a bad feeling.

She shook her head in frustration. She must be missing something; what was it? She rolled her shoulders in a vain attempt to loosen them—they continued to ache badly after the strain of climbing the fire escape—and moved to the janitor's stairway leading to the school's basement.

It was almost completely dark, and as she descended the stairs, Tracie became aware of the sound of a running engine, muffled but identifiable. She waited at the bottom, giving her eyes time to adjust to the darkness and listening intently for any sign that she might not be alone.

A minute passed. Two. The only sound was the engine.

Acutely aware of the time passing—the risk of being discovered increased with each passing minute—Tracie removed the flashlight from the pocket of her jeans. She covered the lens as she had done across the street, leaving just a pinprick opening for the light to penetrate, then crouched and flicked the switch.

She rotated three hundred-sixty degrees, moving quickly. The basement was almost completely empty. It was a cavernous storage area from which all supplies, heating equipment, and whatever else had once occupied the space had long since been removed.

Except for a small generator that had been placed in one corner. Orange power cords snaked from it and ran up the concrete wall, where they continued through a hole in the ceiling. A crude exhaust system had been fashioned out of aluminum tubes, venting gases through a small window.

The generator chugged contentedly, the accompanying engine noise minimal thanks to generous amounts of acoustical padding that had been stuffed around the unit. The result was a small supply of power for whoever was using this building that would be undetectable to anyone who hadn't done what Tracie did—break in.

She examined the generator assembly for a moment and then flicked off her flashlight and dropped it back into her pocket. The discovery of the generator helped confirm her suspicions about the Iraqis and J. Robert Humphries. They needed power because they were keeping the secretary of state prisoner right here in this building, just blocks from the White House.

But so far she had found no concrete answers as to *why*, just more uncertainty, more unanswered questions. Maybe the answers were on the second floor. Unless she had missed something, the basement and the entire first floor were empty. Something was here. Something had to be here. There was no way members of the Iraqi embassy were driving out here in the wee hours of the morning just to avail themselves of the fine D.C. late-summer air, and certainly no way they were employing one or more armed guards to protect an abandoned hulk of a building in which they should have no legitimate interest.

She thought about J. Robert Humphries and climbed the stairs. It was time to check out the second floor.

29

Thursday, September 10, 1987
2:35 a.m.
Washington, D.C.

Tracie flattened herself against the wall and strained to hear. The moment she had reached the top of the stairway leading to the long central hallway bisecting the second floor, she had seen what she was looking for: an open doorway with artificial light spilling out of it far down the hallway on the left.

The hallway itself had appeared deserted, and Tracie moved toward the light, knowing that any of the darkened rooms she passed on her way could contain some form of security prepared to put a bullet in her head. She cleared the rooms as quickly as possible as she went. None of them were occupied.

Glock in hand, Tracie flitted silently along the hallway, keeping as close to the ancient metal lockers ringing the concrete-block construction as she could, until she reached the doorway. It had been left ajar, and an open padlock hung in a hasp, ready to be snapped closed to keep anyone from entering.

Or exiting.

Tracie inched forward and then stopped in her tracks, halted by the sound of voices floating through the open door. The people inside the room were speaking quietly, but after a few seconds she recognized J. Robert Humphries's voice. She had never met him in person, but had seen him on television and heard him speak on the radio many times.

It was definitely the missing man.

He was here.

And he was alive.

Tracie knew she should retreat immediately and get to a phone. Call Director Stallings and alert him to the secretary's location. Keep the school building under surveillance and wait for the cavalry to arrive.

But there was one problem with that plan. Whoever was holding Humphries was getting ready to move him.

Right now.

His captors—as near as Tracie could tell, there were two men inside the room with Humphries—were talking about taking him on a long ride to his new home, and warning him that his fate would be dire if he attempted to escape.

She had to risk a look inside. She eased her head around the doorjamb and was surprised to see that the classroom had been partially renovated. The corner opposite the door where she was standing had been constructed to look like the interior of a house. Like a bedroom.

A pair of floor lamps mounted on spindly aluminum stands provided lighting. A chair had been placed at an angle facing the door, positioned roughly equidistant from the two faux walls. It was obvious Humphries's kidnappers had planned to provide proof-of-life photos to the authorities and had wanted it to appear that the secretary of state was being held inside a private home. All of the classroom's windows had been sealed with plywood, ensuring none of the light would escape the building and alert any passersby—not that there were likely to be any—to the possibility that the supposedly abandoned building was inhabited.

As Tracie watched, two men worked on removing four sets of handcuffs, their backs to her. A set of cuffs bound each of their prisoner's hands to the arms of the heavy wooden chair, and another two secured his ankles to the chair legs. The chair itself didn't appear to have been bolted to the floor, but she supposed that step hadn't been necessary. With the door padlocked from the outside and Humphries shackled to the chair, what difference would it make? It wasn't like he could go anywhere.

Humphries looked pale and exhausted, and a bloody bandage covered most of his right hand. Otherwise he appeared uninjured. His captors opened the cuffs and one by one the steel bracelets dropped to the floor.

When the last handcuff had been unlocked, the men helped Humphries to his feet, standing on either side of him and bracing his elbows in their hands. He rose and then his knees buckled. He would have fallen to the floor if not for the support of his captors.

"Easy," one of them said. "We will take this nice and slow, but remember the consequences of doing anything to draw attention to yourself once we leave this building."

"I remember," Humphries said tiredly. "May I just stand here for a moment to get my legs under me?"

The man on the left glanced at his watch and said, "Fine. But just for a moment."

"Thank you," Humphries said, swaying on his feet like a delicate tree in a strong wind. "I don't suppose you'll tell me where it is you're planning on taking me." His face looked even whiter than it had when Tracie first peered into the room and she hoped the older man wasn't on the verge of suffering a heart attack.

The kidnapper on the right hadn't said a word. The one on the left seemed to be in charge. He paused for a moment, considering the question, and then surprised her, and probably Humphries, when he shrugged and said, "I don't suppose telling you could do any harm."

He seemed to straighten proudly and then said, "From here, we will walk you to a waiting car, where you will be driven to a secret location not far from Ocean City, Maryland. You will be loaded onto a waiting helicopter, where you will fly low-level to a private landing strip in the North Carolina countryside. There you will be transferred to a private Learjet leased by an American businessman sympathetic to our interests. The Lear will depart immediately for my country, where your sole purpose in life from the moment of your arrival will be to convince your meddling president to keep his nose out of our affairs."

"And what country would that be?"

"Iraq."

A second's silence stretched into two, and then five, as the U.S. secretary of state absorbed the man's words. His confusion was obvious. "Iraq? But...we've supported you monetarily and strategically in your war against Iran. Why . . . why would you . .

.?" His voice trailed off.

The man chopped at the air with his hand, as if swatting away a pesky mosquito. "You are allies of convenience for us, no more and no less. We have nothing in common with your decadent country, and to a man we long for the day when you are ground into dust under our heels. As our influence in the world rises, so will yours fall. And as far as the conflict with our much bigger neighbor to the northeast is concerned, the war with Iran will be over soon. We already have our sights set on a much bigger prize."

A little of the color seemed to be returning to Humphries's face, and it looked to Tracie as though he had regained a little of his footing. For his part, the kidnapper seemed to be enjoying himself. He made no move to hurry Humphries out of the room. Humphries asked the logical next question: "What prize is that?"

"We have already begun moving troops—including thousands of our elite Republican Guard soldiers—toward our common border with Saudi Arabia. Soon, we will annex the country, by force if necessary, and absorb it into Iraq. By doing so, we will gain control of one of the most strategically important regions in the world."

Humphries shook his head. "But that's madness! You can't hope to succeed. You will find yourselves at war with the United States within hours of attempting it."

The man smiled. Tracie knew it without even being able to see his face. She could hear the amusement in his voice when he spoke. "But it is already succeeding," he said. "We have been moving forces quietly for some time. Has anyone attempted to stop us? No. Has anyone even noticed? No."

Humphries decided to try a different tack. "What does any of this have to do with kidnapping me? All you'll accomplish with this foolishness is to force a United States response before you've even made a move into Saudi Arabia."

"Not true. In fact, the reality is just the opposite. You see, as far as your government is concerned, you have been taken prisoner by the Soviet Union. That is what we wanted President Reagan to think, and that is what he thinks. Your country's attention is fixated on an enemy you've been fighting for decades in a 'Cold War' that cannot be won, and you will soon be fighting the same enemy militarily. At that time we will act and thus position ourselves to become the first great superpower of the twenty-first century and beyond!"

"The Soviet Union? Why would the president think I've been taken by the Soviet Union?"

"Because that is what the evidence tells him. Evidence *we* have manipulated. Meanwhile, we continue to move our plan forward. A plan that has been months, even years, in the making. We have considered everything. For example, this entire setup," he gestured at the crudely constructed sham bedroom, "was built to hold you for only a few days, while we directed your country's attention where we wanted it. Then, after convincing your leadership the Russians had committed an act of war that must inevitably require a response, we move to Phase Two."

"Which involves transporting me to Iraq."

"Correct. Now that we have waited out the most intense portion of your manhunt, all the while stashing you within a few short miles of the White House, we will transport you to Baghdad. There, you will become our most significant bargaining chip in convincing your country not to interfere in Iraq's destiny. By that time they will realize we have played them for fools, but will most likely be so busy fighting a nuclear war with the Soviet Union that they will not be able to concern themselves with what is happening on the sacred ground of our ancestors."

Humphries looked stunned. The small amount of color that had returned to his face was gone. He said, "Saudi Arabia is not your homeland."

"It is *all* our homeland!" the man barked angrily. The terrorist jerked Humphries forward, pulling on his elbow, and the exhausted secretary of state tripped over his own feet and nearly tumbled to the floor.

"Enough talking," the man said. He took half a step backward, forcing Humphries to move an equal distance toward the door.

Where Tracie was standing, her body mostly shielded by the doorframe.

"We will waste no more time. We must go now," he said, and turned toward the door, his hand still on Humphries's arm.

Tracie took a deep breath and then pivoted around the doorframe, raising her Glock in a two-handed grip, training it dead-center on the talkative man holding J. Robert Humphries.

30

Thursday, September 10, 1987
2:35 a.m.
The White House Situation Room

Aaron Stallings stifled a yawn and tried to keep his growing irritation in check. A late-night briefing of the president by his top national security advisers was not unusual and, given the current situation, certainly not unexpected. But Aaron was facing a full schedule starting at daybreak, and the leisurely pace at which some of the participants entered the White House Situation Room annoyed the hell out of him.

The way Ronald Reagan drummed his fingers impatiently on the surface of the long walnut table suggested the president felt the same way.

After what felt like forever, everyone had filed into the briefing area and taken a seat. Glum expressions adorned haggard faces. Mugs of coffee stood in front of each man, with cream and sugar in silver serving dishes placed in the center of the table. Some ignored the coffee, others downed it greedily.

"Everyone's here, finally?" the president asked his chief of staff pointedly.

"Yes, sir," a clearly exhausted Chester Moore answered.

"All right, then. You called this meeting so let's get the show on the road. What do you have for me?"

Moore hesitated, then plunged ahead. "Mr. President, rumblings are beginning to circulate among the press corps concerning Secretary of State Humphries's absence."

Reagan shook his head. "Rumblings? What is that supposed to mean?"

"Sir, it means there's likely been a leak somewhere. In the last few hours I've been asked point-blank by more than one journalist about the possibility that Secretary Humphries has been kidnaped."

"Is that so? And what did you tell them?"

"I've stuck to the narrative: that the secretary of state is suffering from a minor illness and will be back to work soon. But the cat is climbing out of the bag, sir, and while no one has yet gone on record to report the kidnapping angle, experience tells me it's only a matter of time before that happens, and probably not very much of it. Once the first news outlet runs with the story, everyone will follow. In mere hours, certainly less than a day, this thing is going to explode in our faces."

FBI Director Matt Steinman spoke up. "This sounds like a strategic political discussion to me," he said, his words dripping with annoyance. "Would you mind telling me why *we* all have to be here?" Aaron Stallings noted with a touch of amusement that the deference customarily afforded the president was missing from Steinman's question to Reagan's chief of staff. Steinman made a vague gesture at the rest of the room, Aaron assumed in an effort to ensure they were on his side. "We have work to do."

Chet Moore was rail-thin and balding, with gold wire-rimmed glasses and a perpetually rumpled suit that made him look like an overworked accountant during tax season. But Stallings knew the chief of staff's meek, mild image could not be further from the truth, and the FBI director should have known it as well. Moore had a mind like a steel trap and was as competent at his job as every other man in the room was at theirs, including the president.

Reagan's chief of staff had been with him since before his days as governor of California, and Aaron knew the rumpled little man had the president's full faith.

Moore slid his glasses down his nose and peered over the top of them at Steinman. "*You* all have to be here," he said quietly, like a teacher reprimanding a recalcitrant student, "because this news affects every one of you. *You* all have to be here, because presumably you'd like to come to agreement on how to get out in front of this bombshell. *You* all have to be here because once it's reported that the U.S. secretary of state has been missing for over two days *and nothing has been done*, that we've begun taking delivery of the secretary of state's body parts *and nothing has been done*, this administration will appear in the eyes of the world to be nothing more than an impotent joke. *You* all have to be here—"

"All right, that's enough," the president interrupted. "You've made your point, Chet, quite effectively. And I have to say I agree with you. The time has come for a response. In fact, that time might well be past, but there's nothing we can do about that now. All we can do is move forward."

Moore nodded once and said, "So the question is simple: what will our response to this outrage be? To answer that question, every one of you must be here and must participate."

Reagan cast a withering glance in Steinman's direction and only then did Chief of Staff Chester Moore push his glasses back up onto the bridge of his nose and look away from the FBI director.

The room was totally silent.

After a moment, Reagan fixed his gaze on Secretary of Defense Mark Carmichael. Carmichael cleared his throat—Stallings guessed to buy a little time—and then said, "Mr. President, given the Soviet Union's involvement, my suggestion would be a targeted strike on their interests. We need to get their attention and let them know in no uncertain terms that this barbarism will not stand."

"Wait a minute," Reagan said, raising a hand. "Do we now have concrete proof that the Soviets have taken J.R.? Because my understanding is that none of the evidence is conclusive. And in every single conversation I've had with Secretary Gorbachev—four in the last two days—he has steadfastly and vehemently denied any knowledge of J.R.'s whereabouts—"

"Well, sir," Steinman interrupted. Aaron Stallings smiled inside. He had long believed that his FBI counterpart was overmatched in his position, and Steinman was proving it now. It was like watching a slow-motion car accident.

"Yes?" Reagan said, no small amount of irritation in his voice.

Steinman didn't seem to notice. He continued blithely on. "Mr. President, when you consider the totality of the evidence, from the Makarov recovered inside Secretary Humphries's home, to the Russian newspapers used to provide proof of life, to the specifics of the demands required to ensure the secretary's safe return, it seems absurd in the extreme to believe anyone else *could* be responsible."

"I'm aware of the evidence, Director Steinman, none of which is new since our last meeting, I might add. But if we're talking about military strikes, I want to know with certainty that we're not striking the wrong target and provoking the wrong enemy!" Reagan's face had begun coloring the moment he started to speak and had turned a dark red by the time he finished his sentence. His eyebrows were knitted together and his face resembled a thundercloud as he stared at Matt Steinman like he might launch a targeted strike on *him*.

"Mr. President, if I may?" General Jack Matheson was chairman of the Joint Chiefs of Staff, and he spoke calmly, steadfastly ignoring the chastened FBI director.

"Please, Jack, go ahead," Reagan said.

"Thank you, sir. We've prepared a list of potential targets for a limited strategic strike that would demonstrate our resolve not to allow the secretary of state's kidnapping to go unanswered while at the same time minimizing the risk of all-out war with the Soviets. We'll forward the entire list to you, of course. But all of us, including Secretary Carmichael, agree that the optimum response would be an F-16 strike on the Soviet destroyer *Smetlivy*, currently operating in the eastern Mediterranean."

"Explain to me what you mean when you say 'minimizing the risk of all-out war.'" For the moment, Reagan seemed to ignore the chairman's specific suggestion of targets, focusing instead on something else.

"Well, sir, the Soviets understand we cannot allow Secretary Humphries's kidnapping to go unanswered. They must. This strike would permit us to demonstrate the seriousness with which we're taking his disappearance, while limiting the Soviets' loss to a single military asset, which is currently operating in an area without any significant Soviet presence. Given that they provoked the encounter, it seems unlikely they would respond with a full military assault unless their aim all along has been to provoke war."

Reagan was silent for a moment as he absorbed the general's

words. Then he murmured, almost as if to himself, "Unless, of course, the Soviets *don't* have our secretary of state, and never did."

Matt Steinman rolled his eyes and for just a moment Aaron thought he was going to interrupt again, but he seemed to decide against it and kept his thoughts to himself.

The president sighed and spoke to General Matheson. "All right, Jack, how would this assault take place?"

31

Tracie stepped clear of the doorway and said, "Everybody freeze. Stay right where you are."

She didn't know if the terrorists were wearing body armor, but Tracie assumed that they were not. As far as the Iraqis knew, their plan was working to perfection, and their involvement in the kidnapping of J. Robert Humphries was taking place completely below the radar of United States officialdom.

Besides, what choice did she have other than to interfere? After coming this far, there was no way she was going to allow the terrorists to waltz out of here and disappear again, whisking the secretary of state off to become a pawn in a high-stakes geopolitical game of chicken.

Humphries gasped at Tracie's sudden appearance, but the two men supporting him looked less surprised. A red flag went up in the back of Tracie's mind but there was nothing she could do now. She was committed.

For a long moment nothing happened, and then the silent terrorist's eyes widened briefly and an oily smile slid across the talker's face. Then Tracie felt the cold, unyielding steel of a gun barrel placed against her temple.

A voice behind her said, "Lower your weapon. Do it now."

The words were barely louder than a whisper, but the menace behind them was unmistakable.

Tracie hesitated just a moment. With a grunt of frustration, she slowly pivoted her wrist until her Glock was pointing at the floor.

"Good decision," the voice said. "Now hold your gun out to the side, gripping the handle with two fingers."

For a brief moment, Tracie considered spinning and lashing out, pistol-whipping her as-yet unseen captor with the butt of the gun. But although she could sense his bulk in her peripheral vision, there was no depth-perception attached, and thus no way of knowing whether she would strike him in the head or simply miss him entirely and flail at the air.

And she would only get one chance.

Presumably the men holding Humphries were also armed and could take down the secretary in an instant if they chose to do so.

The risk was unacceptable.

She did as she was told. And said a silent prayer that the terrorist would not discover the second gun, currently wedged into her jeans at the small of her back.

The weapon was taken from her hand. The barrel of her assailant's gun remained pressed to her skull. The voice said, "How fortunate is your timing, Miss..."

Silence.

"No matter," the voice said after a short pause. "As I was saying, your timing is exquisite. Secretary Humphries no longer requires his chair, so we will use it to secure you until you are killed."

Tracie worked at keeping her expression placid, but beneath it her anger simmered, directed almost entirely at herself. She had *known* the Iraqis would have posted more than one guard. She had somehow missed the second one and now, thanks to her negligence, not only was Humphries going to disappear, she would pay for her mistake with her life.

She allowed herself to be shoved forward. "Where were you?" she muttered through clenched teeth.

"What do you mean?" the man behind her replied mockingly.

"I searched this entire building. I knew you had to be here. Where were you? You're going to kill me anyway, the least you can do is tell me where I went wrong."

"We owe you *nothing*," the voice said. "But, just to drive home the point that you are not as intelligent as you think you are, and that a woman should always know her place, I'll tell you. I waited at the front entrance while Muhammad tracked you. You make a very convincing drunk, by the way, not that you'll ever get the opportunity to repeat the deception."

"Thank you. I figured any girl would have to be shit-faced to hang out with the likes of you," Tracie taunted.

The man either didn't understand her comment or chose to ignore it. "I waited a few minutes, and when Muhammad did not return, I exited the building through the front door and circled behind it in the opposite direction."

Tracie shook her head, kicking herself mentally. She should have known. "You were behind me, watching me, the entire time."

"You are fairly intelligent. For a woman. When I reached the rear corner of the school, you were just making your very impressive assault on the fire escape. I simply returned the way I had come and waited in the stairwell, out of sight, until you entered through the second story window. Then I followed you. The rest of the story, well, it is self-explanatory."

"Goddammit," Tracie muttered as the man urged her past Humphries, who was watching the proceedings with wide, hopeless eyes.

"I am curious about one thing, though," the man said. He took her roughly by the shoulders and turned her around. Tracie could see him now. He was average height, stocky, with olive skin and thick black wavy hair. And a long white scar running up his right forearm. "What did you do to Muhammad?"

Tracie looked up at him a she was pushed into the chair. "The same thing I'm going to do to you in about three minutes."

This time the man laughed, his contempt clear. "It doesn't matter. My job after Secretary Humphries is taken away is to stay behind and clean all evidence from this building. It will take all day, but by the time I am done, your FBI can search the school with magnifying glasses and they will find nothing. While I am completing that chore, I will seek out Muhammad and find him. He is obviously somewhere close by. When I find him I will kill him. It is no more than he deserves after his carelessness."

"You'll never get out of here," Tracie said. "This entire block is cordoned off. The building is surrounded by federal agents. You won't make it fifty feet when you try to leave. I know there was at least one person—a driver—sitting inside your Lincoln Town car a couple of blocks over, and maybe more. Those guys are already in custody."

A momentary shadow of concern passed behind the man's eyes and then his cocky demeanor returned. "I don't think so. If agents were out there, as you claim, we would already have been swarmed under. I don't know how you found this place or what you're doing here all by yourself, but you *are* alone, aren't you?"

Tracie shrugged, determined keep her features impassive. "Think what you want," she said. "You'll see."

Her assailant began cuffing her arms to the chair. "What do you want me to do with her?" he asked the talkative terrorist, the man who had bragged to Humphries about using him to start a war between the United States and the Soviet Union.

The man fished two sets of keys out of his pocket and tossed them to his accomplice. "Secure her here until we have made our escape, and then kill her. After you've found and killed Muhammad, take one of the cleanup team's cars and weight the bodies down with concrete, then dump both bodies off a bridge into the Potomac River. By the time their corpses surface, we will be long gone."

The man nodded. By now, he had cuffed both of Tracie's wrists to the blocky wooden chair. He stood and stretched. The man in charge said, "Be thorough cleaning the building and be careful disposing of the bodies."

"I understand," the man with the scar on his arm said.

The leader turned his attention away from Tracie, dismissing her as if he hadn't a care in the world. He began half-dragging, half-supporting Secretary of State Humphries toward the classroom entrance.

Scar-arm walked them to the door and Tracie could see the three Iraqis talking quietly among themselves, probably in Arabic. The secretary of state was the picture of hopelessness, his head hanging. He stared resolutely at the floor. After a moment, the men rounded the corner and were gone.

32

Thursday, September 10, 1987
2:50 a.m.
Washington, D.C.

Within seconds, the Iraqi who had gotten the jump on Tracie returned. He swaggered through the door with the look of an eight year old on Christmas morning.

Tracie eyed him suspiciously.

"Good news," he said as he entered, "although perhaps more for me than for you. As a reward for the alertness and skill I displayed in following and capturing you, I've been given permission to...*enjoy* you...before killing you. I am only permitted ten minutes, but still, it is ten minutes I suspect I will long treasure."

Tracie chuckled, trying to keep the overwhelming sense of revulsion she felt out of her voice. "Ten minutes? That's probably nine-and-a-half more than *you'll* need, am I right, big boy?"

The man scowled. "What did you say?" He walked faster. He was now halfway across the room.

"You heard me," Tracie answered breezily. "In fact, I'll be surprised if you even last thirty seconds."

The man frowned, his hooded eyes darkening. He rushed forward, cocking a fist. He reached her chair and unloaded a roundhouse right at Tracie's jaw.

She ignored the incoming blow, twisting in her chair and snapping off a karate side-kick aimed at her assailant's left leg, the leg he had just planted to halt his forward motion. She connected

189

solidly and felt—as well as heard—the man's kneecap shatter. The force of the blow drove her body backward in the chair and the man's fist whistled harmlessly past her nose.

He dropped to the floor, gasping in pain, and reached into the waistband of his pants. "Infidel bitch!" he wheezed, half in agony, half in fury. He plucked a gun from under his shirt.

Tracie planted her feet and tucked her head, burying her chin in her breastbone. Then she leaped upward, driving with her powerful legs, executing a forward half-somersault. The heavy wooden chair spun through the air, Tracie still handcuffed to its arms, and landed on its back directly on top of the furious Iraqi.

The combination of Tracie's weight and the force of gravity generated tremendous torque, and she could hear and feel the man's bones breaking as the chair shattered against the resistance of his body, crushing him against the floor.

The back of Tracie's head struck the chair and rebounded violently, and a lightning bolt of pain flared. She ignored it.

The Iraqi screamed and lost his grip on the gun.

Tracie rolled and kicked it away.

He lashed out with his good leg but connected only with air, as Tracie was already moving again. She rolled to her side and pushed off with her right knee against the floor, lifting her body enough to allow her to drop her left knee squarely on the man's throat, cutting off his air supply.

Then she reached into the front pocket of the Iraqi's trousers with her left hand, dragging the wooden chair along and stretching her right arm behind her back until she felt as though the muscles in her shoulder would pull away from the bone. There should be two sets of handcuff keys.

She reached to the bottom of the pocket.

There.

Keys.

She wrapped her fingers around them and ripped them from the man's pocket. Then she dropped them into his hand and said, "Uncuff me."

His face was bright red, his eyes bulging out of his head from lack of oxygen, but his response was to swing a fist wildly at her ribs.

The blow was harmless—the angle was all wrong for him to generate any power, and the lack of oxygen was already beginning to weaken him badly—but she felt the gesture indicated a fundamental lack of understanding of his new reality.

She leaned forward, increasing the pressure on his windpipe. "Maybe you didn't hear me," she said. "Unlock these cuffs or you won't take one..."

She leaned forward. "More..."

She added weight. "Breath."

The man's head whipped back and forth. No matter his determination to hold out, his body's natural instinct for self-preservation was kicking in and he needed to breathe. It was like a drowning man trying to hold his breath. Eventually his brain would force him to breathe in, even if it meant filling his lungs with water.

The man was now at that point. He began nodding enthusiastically, flailing his arms and his uninjured leg. Tracie eased off his throat and he sucked in a deep breath, coughing and gagging.

"Unlock these cuffs," she repeated, and after a half-second's non-response, she eased back down, again cutting off the now-desperate man's air supply.

The hand with the keys shot forward, smashing into the chair just above Tracie's manacled wrist. She took that as a sign of compliance and once again lessened the pressure on the terrorist's throat.

After repeating the coughing and gagging routine, the man forced himself to concentrate, clearly not wishing to have his windpipe crushed a third time. His shaking hand struggled to force the key into the tiny locking mechanism, the difficulty compounded by the fact that he could not lift his head to see what he was doing.

Tracie waited impatiently.

Finally the key slid home. The man twisted it and the cuffs sprang open.

Tracie grabbed the keys with her now-free hand. She maintained just enough weight on the Iraqi's throat to demonstrate in no uncertain terms who was still in charge. She crossed her left arm in front of her body and unlocked her right wrist.

The mangled chair fell away and crashed to the floor. Tracie shook some feeling back into her hands and rubbed her aching shoulders. She unlocked each bracelet still attached to the chair and then slapped one pair around the man's wrists. With the other, she cuffed his good ankle to the chair.

Not ideal, but it would have to do. The man wouldn't be going anywhere with a shattered kneecap, and she was running out of time.

Maybe she was already out.

She tried to estimate how long it had taken to overcome her Iraqi captor and guessed maybe three minutes. Would that have been enough time for the other two men to assist a weakened J. Robert Humphries to their car and then disappear?

Probably not. If they had parked a block-and-a-half away, as they did last night, she might have time to catch up with them and follow.

She leapt to her feet. Bent and retrieved the Iraqi's weapon—another Makarov semi-auto. *They definitely stocked up on Russian weapons.* She returned to the terrorist, now sweating heavily, likely going into shock from his injury, and felt around the waistband of his trousers until retrieving her Glock.

Then she turned and bolted for the classroom door. Before she had taken two steps she was sprinting at top speed.

She prayed it would be enough.

33

Tracie had been gone more than forty-five minutes. Marshall's concern had long since transformed into worry and he was by now near panic. He checked his watch, not knowing why. He knew exactly what time it was. What he *didn't* know was what to do.

The last twenty-five minutes had been the worst. That was when a dark-colored Lincoln Town Car had rumbled up the street, crossing slowly left to right in front of Marshall's Buick Regal like something out of a presidential motorcade. Marshall ducked below the dashboard until the car had passed, for the first time in his life grateful that his eight-year-old Buick was beaten and rusted to the point where it looked right at home in one of the worst sections of D.C.

He didn't know the significance of the Lincoln's sudden appearance, but guessed it wasn't good. He wracked his brain and could come up with no legitimate reason in the world why this shiny, fancy automobile would be prowling one of the most devastated sections of D.C. at this time of night.

There weren't even any hookers on the street corners, so it wasn't a pimp or a rich guy looking to get laid. In fact, there didn't seem to be *any* activity on the street corners.

The Town Car slowed and then stopped, pulling to the curb on the opposite side of the road not fifty feet from where Tracie had left her Toyota. A pair of men climbed out of the back seat, scanned the area much as Tracie had done less than an hour ago, and then set off in the same direction she had gone.

That was when his palms had begun to sweat non-stop and he had instantly developed the habit of glancing at his watch almost often enough to observe the second hand make its three hundred sixty degree journey each minute.

Furtive movement in the semi-darkness along one of the buildings a hundred or so feet away caught Marshall's attention. It was in the direction Tracie had gone nearly an hour ago and the men from the Lincoln twenty-five minutes later. He squinted, cursing the lack of working streetlights.

People.

Three of them, moving through the shadows. As they approached, they stepped out from the shadows cast by the decrepit buildings and Marshall could see that two of them were the men who had walked away from the Town Car a little while ago. They lurched and stumbled, struggling to support a third man, who was being half-carried, half-pushed toward the still-idling Lincoln.

The strange-looking group reached the empty street and began to cross, and Marshall gasped in surprise. The weak light cast by a waning moon and the proximity of the group to his position allowed Marshall to identify the third man, the one being forced along obviously against his will.

It was U.S. Secretary of State J. Robert Humphries.

34

Tracie raced out the abandoned school building's front entrance. The Iraqis had left the double doors unlocked, either accidentally in their haste to get Humphries safely to the waiting car as quickly as possible, or intentionally to make life easier for the terrorist staying behind to eliminate all evidence that the building had served as a makeshift prison.

Tracie didn't know which it was and didn't care. She had been prepared to smash out one of the few remaining windows, but instead barely had to slow, barreling out the door at full speed and taking the wide granite staircase three steps at a time. She leapt to the crumbling walkway and sprinted along the empty road in the direction the Iraqis had parked their Town Car last night.

She hoped they had used the same staging area for their thugs tonight. If they had changed things up and parked in another direction she would lose them for sure.

Before he had been taken away, J. Robert Humphries had appeared basically uninjured—with the exception of the impromptu surgery the terrorists had performed on his hand, of course—but he was not a young man, and the stress of his situation would likely have slowed him down even more than usual. She prayed she had escaped her horny captor quickly enough to catch up to them before they shoved Humphries into their car and disappeared.

They were taking him to rendezvous with a helicopter somewhere along the Maryland seacoast in the vicinity of Ocean City, that much she knew, but it wasn't nearly enough information to be useful. Even if she could find a phone immediately—an impossibility in this devastated neighborhood—and convinced Aaron Stallings that she hadn't gone stark raving mad, there wouldn't be enough time for the CIA to mobilize law enforcement and the military to search every nook and cranny along the east coast. The Iraqis would vanish without a trace.

She cut south one block and pounded along the pavement, making only a minimal effort to conceal herself from view, willing to sacrifice stealth for speed. By now she knew there was no one here to see her.

Moments later, Tracie burst from behind the abandoned tenement buildings not far from her Toyota, her Glock held ready in two hands. She searched desperately for an idling Lincoln Town Car or similar vehicle.

She was too late. Either the Iraqis had parked somewhere else or they had managed to hustle the prisoner into their car and take off before she could get here. Now they were gone and she had no way of knowing where.

She had lost Secretary of State Humphries.

"Dammit!" She slapped her hands together in frustration and turned toward her car. She would have to find a phone and alert Stallings to the situation. There was now no alternative.

After that, she didn't know what she was going to do. She had been fired, after all, and she was quite sure Aaron Stallings wasn't about to let her tag along in the search for the kidnapped secretary of state like some pathetic unpaid volunteer.

She reached her Toyota in seconds and had the door half open when the throaty growl of a revving engine caught her attention. She looked up in surprise as a pair of headlights flashed on and a familiar-looking Buick sedan barreled around a corner half a block down. The beat-up car accelerated straight at her and then squealed to a stop.

She had her Glock trained on the closed passenger side window, certain she recognized the car but unable to recall from where. The weak moonlight and reflection off the glass made it impossible to see inside.

The window rolled down and Marshall Fulton said, "Get in, they just left! If we hurry we can catch them!"

Tracie froze for half a second, flabbergasted at Marshall's arrival. Then she ripped open the door and flung herself inside. "Go!" she said, slamming the door closed and tumbling sideways onto the seat. She immediately had questions for Marshall, but they would have to wait.

He punched the gas and the Buick surged forward. Tracie's momentum carried her across the bench seat, where she slammed into the bulk of the man's much bigger body. He barely flinched and didn't slow.

"How long have they been gone?" she asked, pushing herself upright and buckling her seat belt.

"You missed them literally by seconds. I was trying to decide what to do when you came charging around the corner."

"Was Humphries walking on his own?"

"Depends what you mean by 'walking.' He was upright, but he didn't look too steady. I think the guys who took him were mostly carrying him."

"Thank God," Tracie said fervently. "If not for that, they would have been long gone before I was able to escape."

"Escape?" Marshall took his eyes off the road for half a second, glancing across the front seat before returning his attention to navigating the twists and turns of the run-down neighborhood. "What the hell was going on back there?"

"Never mind that. It's a story for another time. How do you know where to go?"

"I don't. I was waiting for you to give me some direction. All I know is that big, fancy car took off like a bat out of hell in this direction just a couple of seconds before you came along."

"So we're not far behind them."

"Not at all. At least not until we take a wrong turn."

Tracie was silent for a moment, thinking hard. "Okay. While I was listening, one of those goons let slip to Humphries that their plan was to rendezvous with a helicopter outside Ocean City for the first leg of a trip that will eventually take him to Iraq. It's been years since I spent much time in the D.C. area, but to my recollection, there's no easy way to get across the Chesapeake Bay than via the—"

"Chesapeake Bay Bridge," Marshall interrupted excitedly. He had slowed the car when they had approached Malcom X Avenue, uncertain which direction to turn, but now he stomped on the gas again and the old Buick Regal leapt forward. He hooked a left and a half-mile later they were merging onto I-295 North.

Tracie stared out the windshield, paying no attention to Anacostia Park, which flashed past on the left. "They're not going to want to take the chance of being pulled over with the missing U.S. secretary of state in the backseat, so they'll drive like Grandma on her way to church. But they also aren't likely to stop anywhere between here and their rendezvous point, either, and for exactly the same reason—it's too risky with Humphries in the car."

She looked over at Marshall. "I haven't been to Ocean City since I was a kid. I'm guessing the trip takes about two and a half hours. Does that sound right to you?"

She waited patiently while he considered the question. "Two and a half hours," he agreed. "Give or take."

She was silent for a moment and Marshall said, "Well? What do you think, should I speed up, try to catch them?"

Tracie shook her head. "Not yet. Drive the speed limit for now. If they actually took off just a few seconds before I showed up—"

"They did."

Tracie smiled. "I wasn't doubting you, Marshall. I'm just trying to figure out what might be my best play."

"You mean *our* best play."

She opened her mouth to argue, to tell him that it was too dangerous, that there was no way in the world she was letting him get involved, that she would handle it herself. Then she glanced over and saw the hard set of his jaw and the determined look in his eyes and realized, for better or for worse, that he was already involved, that he had been from the moment he put his job and his freedom on the line by sharing classified information with her.

"Okay," she agreed, "*our* best play."

He grinned triumphantly, like a little boy celebrating a successful practical joke, and she laughed in spite of the stress.

"Anyway," she continued. "We know where they're heading,

approximately, and we know the only reasonable route they can take to get there. We know they're probably not going to stop. Since they left just before I arrived at the car, we can't be more than a minute behind them. Maybe less. Maybe a lot less."

She looked over at Marshall again. "Will you recognize the car again when you see it?"

"Hell, yeah, I'll recognize it. A big, dark Lincoln Town Car with diplomatic plates. Pretty tough to miss."

"That's the same car they used last night," Tracie said. "Or at least a similar one. In that case I'll recognize it, too. I say let's keep to the speed limit, which we can be sure they're doing as well, and maintain our distance. The last thing we want is for them to know they're being followed. As we get closer to Ocean City, we'll pick up the pace until spotting the car, because by then we'll have to tail them to their rendezvous spot."

"So for now we just drive?"

"Looks that way," Tracie agreed. "Please tell me you're not going to have to stop for gas. Do you have enough to make it the hundred-thirty miles or so from here to Ocean City?"

Marshall grinned again, his white teeth highlighted against his black skin in the darkness of the car's interior. "I was never a Boy Scout," he said. "But I could have been."

* * *

Thursday, September 10, 1987
4:20 a.m.
Central Maryland

After taking I-295 through northeast Washington along the Anacostia River, they merged onto U.S. Route 50 toward Annapolis and the Chesapeake Bay Bridge. Tracie was mostly silent, watching the landscape roll past as Marshall maintained a steady speed.

At last, he said, "So it's the Iraqis."

She nodded. "It's the Iraqis. None of this has anything to do with the Soviet Union. Saddam Hussein is using the Soviets as a distraction. He wants to take over Saudi Arabia in order to gain control of their oil fields. Once he does that, he figures he'll have the West right where he wants us."

Marshall whistled softly. "Jesus. The Russians and the

Americans start blowing each other up, meanwhile he grabs the means with which to destroy our economy whenever the mood strikes him."

"That's about the size of it."

"It's a pretty good plan," Marshall said, "from a strategic standpoint."

"If you don't mind the idea of two nations lobbing nuclear devices at each other."

"I don't think Hussein minds that one bit," Marshall said drily. "In fact, he'd probably like nothing better."

They were silent again for a while, but as the rusty old Buick approached the Chesapeake Bay Bridge, Marshall said, "I've been wondering something."

"Why we haven't called in the cavalry?"

"Exactly. If we know where they're going and what their plan is, why don't we just stop and find a phone, let our bosses know what's going on, and wait for help to arrive?"

"Excellent question. To be honest, I'm not entirely sure Aaron Stallings would even talk to me. And if he did, there wouldn't be enough time for the CIA to mobilize the manpower required to have a reasonable chance of finding the Iraqi helicopter, especially at night if it's flying low-level with no lights. They'd barely get started and the Iraqis would be long gone. We can't afford to take the chance of losing them in order to make a call that would likely not help."

Marshall pursed his lips in frustration. "There must be something we can do. What about calling the state police? We know their car is on this highway, not very far in front of us; we could describe it and tell the cops there's a kidnap victim inside. Then they'd have to stop it."

Tracie shook her head stubbornly. "It's not worth the risk, Marshall. The diplomatic plates on their vehicle would ensure the Iraqis would be handled much differently than you or I would be."

"But if there's a reported kidnapping, they'd *have* to do something!"

"Sure they would. But that's the problem: we don't know *what* they would do. And more to the point, we don't know what the *Iraqis* would do if they get pulled over. If they feel cornered, they might very well pump Humphries full of holes.

The idea is to get him back alive, not zipped into a body bag."

Marshall took a long look across the seat at her, his brown eyes boring into her blue ones. It was obvious he disagreed with her, but he said nothing. After a moment, he returned his focus to the highway and the sparse early morning traffic. The Buick Regal droned along, the speedometer pegged on the speed limit.

"So, how do you plan to stop them?"

"I'm still working on that," Tracie admitted. "But I do know this: it's about time we moved up on them and got a visual. Now that we've crossed the bridge I don't have a whole lot of confidence in where they might decide to get off the highway."

"But we've still got a ways to go before we get to Ocean City, and this is still the only route that makes sense."

"True," Tracie said. "But when I overheard them talking to Humphries, the exact words they used when they referred to their helicopter rendezvous point were, 'not far from Ocean City.' There's no way to know exactly what that means. It could be anything from 'just outside downtown' to 'fifty miles from the city,' and in any direction. I don't want to lose them, so it's time to make our move."

"Makes sense to me," Marshall said, and eased down on the gas. The Regal surged forward, its speedometer needle creeping past fifty-five and hovering around sixty.

Tracie shook her head. "No, don't speed up. In fact, I need you to pull off at the next exit. It's time I took the wheel. You've done a great job, Marshall, but I have a little more experience at field operations than you do. No offense."

He laughed. "None taken. In fact, the only way you have a *little* more experience in field ops is if you only have a little experience. Otherwise, you have a *lot* more. I've been waiting for you to take the wheel ever since we left D.C., to be honest."

A roadside sign appeared in the headlights, indicating an exit a mile ahead. "Get off there," Tracie said.

"Why don't I just pull onto the shoulder and we can switch positions? It would save time, and obviously you don't want to fall any farther behind the Iraqis."

"It would save time, but I'm not worried about falling farther behind. Their car is big and recognizable, and barring this beast suffering a mechanical issue, I have plenty of time to make up the distance I'll lose by taking the exit."

Marshall glanced over, his lips turned down in a frown. "I can't help but notice you using the word 'I,' rather than 'we.'"

Tracie was impressed. This guy was sharp. "I'm sorry, Marshall, but we're going to have to split up. That's why we're getting off the highway. I'm going to drop you somewhere with a phone, and I want you to call Sean Rafferty. Get him out of bed and let him know what's going on. Tell him to alert Aaron Stallings and call out the cavalry."

"But you just said there's no point notifying the CIA."

"Not exactly. I said they would have virtually no chance of assembling enough help to find the chopper at night, and I still believe that. But maybe the Iraqis will get delayed, or for some reason won't depart until after daybreak. If that happens and if Rafferty and Stallings can coordinate the launch of a few Navy P3 sub-hunter aircraft, maybe they'll get lucky and locate the chopper before it ever reaches the Learjet they have waiting to depart for Baghdad. It's a long shot but it's worth a try.

"Also, Stallings can work with the FBI to mobilize the FAA and local law enforcement. Lock down as many uncontrolled airports in North Carolina as possible that are large enough to handle a Lear. Establish surveillance and maybe nab the Iraqis as they transfer Humphries from the helicopter to the jet.

"But most importantly," she said, "they need to know what's really going on here. Everyone except us still thinks the Soviet Union is behind this kidnapping. The country could be mobilizing for war even as we speak."

* * *

Marshall pulled under the covered portico outside a Holiday Inn located less than a quarter mile off the highway. The old Buick Regal rocked on its springs, squeaking and squealing in protest as they slid to a stop. He had driven as fast as he dared after exiting the highway, risking getting pulled over in order to cost Tracie as little time as possible with the detour.

"I'm not happy about you going off on your own," he said. He felt silly saying it—she was a longtime, experienced field operative; it wasn't like she needed a career desk jockey to keep her safe—but felt compelled to say it anyway. He needed to let her know he was worried about her. She could laugh at him if she wanted; he didn't care.

Tracie flashed a smile. She was beautiful. Even with her hair a rumpled mess, her t-shirt and jeans torn and dirty and stinking to high heaven of old whiskey, his heart skipped a beat as she trained her high-wattage smile and impossibly bright blue eyes up at him. "I'll be fine, Marshall, thank you," she said quietly. He appreciated that she didn't ridicule him or minimize his concern.

He opened the door and prepared to climb out. "Wait a second," she said.

He looked at her quizzically and she continued. "I think you missed your calling by taking a data analyst position," she said. "You're a natural at covert ops. You've handled yourself like a real pro, and except maybe for that first try at tailing me, everything you've done tonight has been just about perfect."

He smiled, touched. "Beginner's luck," he said.

"I don't think so. But in any event, thank you. You've done so much more than I can ever repay you for."

"When this is over, let me take you out for a drink and we'll call it even." It was out before he could stop himself. It was out before he even really thought about what he was saying.

Tracie froze, her body half in and half out of the idling Buick's passenger side. She ducked her head and looked across the front seat at him, her face an unreadable mask. Then she said, "I'd love that. You're on, and thank you." Marshall thought he saw tears in her eyes, but it was dark and he couldn't be sure.

Then she got out, slammed the door, and sprinted around the front of the car. He heaved himself out of the driver's side and she barreled into him, squeezed him tightly in a bear hug that was about as fine a thing as he ever felt, then slipped past him and behind the wheel. "Remember," she told him one last time. "Do whatever you have to do to convince Rafferty to drag Stallings's fat ass out of bed. The White House needs to know what's happening, and the military has to get some birds in the air and find that helicopter before it's too late!"

"Got it," Marshall said. Then she was gone, leaving a trail of parallel black marks on the pavement and the acrid smell of burnt rubber in the air.

35

Thursday, September 10, 1987
4:30 a.m.
The White House - Situation Room

Aaron Stallings had long since reached the conclusion that he would not be getting any sleep tonight. The initial details of the proposed United States attack on the Soviet destroyer *Smetlivy*, currently cruising the Mediterranean Sea, had taken a couple of hours to hammer out, and General Matheson only now seemed to be running out of steam.

Debate had been spirited, and Aaron could sense the president's extreme reluctance to undertake military action against the regime he had once famously termed "The Evil Empire" without further—and indisputable—proof of their culpability in J. Robert Humphries's kidnapping.

Aaron had had plenty of time for reflection during the interminable meeting, and had spent most of it thinking about Tracie Tanner. About her insistence that responsibility for the crime was being fixed in the wrong place, that all of the evidence implicating the Russians was nothing more than very clever misdirection. He considered the bizarre Iraqi troop movements and Tanner's theory that Saddam Hussein had engineered the disappearance of the U.S. secretary of state—as if they could actually pull off such a complicated operation inside the boundaries of the United States—for some as-yet unknown purpose.

He thought about his own misgivings regarding the

evidence, while Matheson droned on at the head of the table, seemingly gaining a second wind. Right after Humphries's disappearance Aaron Stallings himself had been nagged by the sense that something was not as it seemed. It all came down to that Makarov discovered on the floor near Humphries's desk. As Tanner had pointed out, the idea that an elite Soviet covert ops team would make such an obvious mistake while otherwise running their op to perfection made no sense.

Aaron's long career in U.S. intelligence made that discovery just not smell right. But then the evidence had started to mount, all of it pointing in one direction: Moscow. He wondered whether he had fallen victim to "group think," unconsciously allowing himself to go along with a flawed theory simply because everyone around him was so convinced of its truth.

Could Tanner have been right? Was it really possible that Mikhail Gorbachev was *not* lying when he claimed the Soviets knew nothing about J. Robert Humphries's disappearance?

If there was any chance that Tanner's theory was correct, now would be the time to stand up and be counted. Military action was about to be undertaken against the Soviets. Aaron Stallings had been around long enough to know that once an attack was launched, targeted or not, it would no longer matter who was holding Humphries. The Soviets would respond in kind, and the United States would respond to the response, and soon the world would erupt in another war. One that perhaps no one would survive.

So now was the time.

Before it was too late.

But if he was wrong . . .

* * *

U.S. Army General Jack Matheson's presentation had finally ended. All of the questions had petered out, and the debate seemed to have ground to a halt. President Reagan ran a hand over his unshaven jaw and reluctantly said, "Very well, General, when can this assault be launched?"

"Mr. President, we can have the F-16s airborne out of Aviano Air Base in Italy within the hour. The strike itself can be completed before daybreak here."

The president sighed. "Give the order. We simply cannot afford to wait any longer given the investigation's lack of progress. I'd like continuous updates, from this moment on until our fighters are back on the ground at Aviano."

"Yes, sir," General Matheson said. "If you'll excuse me, sir."

"Of course," Reagan replied. "Do what you have to do. And make this operation a success."

"Consider it done, sir." The general double-timed it out of the room, followed immediately by the rest of the joint chiefs.

When the door had closed, Reagan focused his attention on Chief of Staff Chester Moore. "Chet, how would you suggest we handle the media?"

"Sir, we need to do nothing until the attack on the *Smetlivy* has been completed successfully. Then we should request network television airtime, interrupt daytime programming and make the announcement. We'll lead with the news that Secretary Humphries has been missing for two days, and follow that with our assertion that the Soviet Union is responsible. We should indicate that we have overwhelming evidence to support this charge, but that we're unable to release all of the evidence at this time. Then we should immediately announce that we have launched a tactical assault on a Soviet target in response, and finish by announcing we await the secretary's release by the Soviets before determining our next move."

"But, Chet—"

There was a curt knock on the door, and then it was flung open. A Situation Room duty officer stood in the doorway, his suit perfectly tailored even at this hour of the night. His necktie was drawn up in a tight Windsor knot and his impeccably ironed dress shirt shone with the brilliant white of newly fallen snow. His face was flushed with excitement.

Before he could speak, Matt Steinman barked, "What the hell? Don't you know we're in a meeting here?"

"I'm sorry, sir," the man replied, perfectly unruffled by the FBI director's outburst.

Then the man turned to Aaron Stallings. "Director Stallings," he said, "Analysis Director Rafferty is on a secure line at the Watch Desk. He says he needs to speak with you immediately regarding the Secretary of State Humphries situation."

Aaron frowned. Sean Rafferty's area of expertise was Middle

Eastern affairs. There was that pesky Middle Eastern connection again. He raised his eyes to the young duty officer. "Did you tell him I'm in a meeting with the president?"

"Of course, sir, but he said the information was critical and simply could not wait."

Aaron rose from his seat. "Excuse me, Mr. President," he said, ignoring the rest of the room. Then he followed the duty officer to a secure bank of phones inside the control room adjacent to the Situation Room.

The young officer handed a telephone handset to Aaron and then stepped a discreet distance away, although not, Aaron noted, out of the control room entirely. "Yes, Sean, what is it?"

"Director Stallings, I've just heard from one of my analysts, Marshall Fulton. He says he's in southeastern Maryland with Tracie Tanner and that they've been tailing the kidnappers of Secretary of State Humphries."

"Tracie Tanner no longer works for the agency. What is one of your data analysts doing in southeastern Maryland with her?"

"I don't have all the details, sir. All I know is that Fulton said the kidnappers plan to move the secretary out of the country today, and that they need help immediately."

He shook his head. What the hell had Tanner gotten into now? "How confident are you in this information?"

"Sir, Marshall Fulton is one of my best analysts, and he claims to have seen the secretary firsthand. He says he is one hundred percent certain it was Humphries. I believe him."

Aaron pursed his lips "Okay, tell me what she needs and we'll get it for her. But first, how are the Russians planning to get Humphries out of the country?"

"It's not the Russians, sir. It's the Iraqis."

* * *

Aaron returned to the Situation Room as the national security team was discussing contingencies. What would the next step be if the Soviet Union still refused to release Humphries even after the strike on the *Smetlivy*? What if they *did* agree and released the secretary without a military response? How would they go about restoring diplomatic relations, and should they even try after such a heinous act as kidnapping a sitting U.S. secretary of state?

The CIA director stood silently in the open doorway, waiting for the buzz of voices to die down.

Eventually it did.

Again ignoring the rest of the national security team, Aaron spoke directly to Reagan. "Mr. President, the situation's changed. We need to talk. Immediately."

"Well, that's why everyone's here, Aaron. Say your piece."

At that moment, Aaron Stallings was reminded why he disliked Ronald Reagan so much. The man had come to Washington as an outsider, winning the White House twice while running on a platform of fiscal responsibility and limited government, concepts that Beltway insiders detested, both Republican and Democrat alike.

To the seasoned Washington pro, of which CIA Director Aaron Stallings was one, a Reagan presidency meant one thing: budget cuts. Making do with less.

For the time being, though, he would be forced to put aside his personal dislike for the man in the interest of stopping World War III. If that was even still possible. "I'm afraid I can't 'say my piece' here, sir. We need to talk in private."

Understanding dawned in the president's eyes and he nodded once. "I see. All right, then. Would everyone be kind enough to leave Director Stallings and me alone for a couple of minutes? Refresh your coffee, grab a smoke, whatever. We'll call you all back in shortly."

A chorus of angry voices greeted the president's words. "Whatever Stallings has to say he should say to everyone!" "This is outrageous!" "We're your national security advisors, for Christ's sake!"

Reagan stared down each man in turn until the voices died away. Assistant Secretary of State Joe Malone was the first to leave. He silently pushed his chair back from the long table and strode out of the room, refusing to meet Aaron's—or the president's—eyes. One by one, the rest of the team followed, until moments later only Aaron, Ronald Reagan, and Chief of Staff Chester Moore were present. "You too, Chet," Reagan said, not unkindly.

"Mr. President, I'm by your side for everything. I should stay."

"I take a crap every morning without your assistance, Chet. I'll be fine."

The veteran political operative opened his mouth as if to argue, then clamped it shut and huffed angrily as he turned on his heel and marched out of the room. He was muttering under his breath as he pulled the door closed behind him. He knew better than to slam it.

"Okay, Aaron," Reagan said without preamble. "What's going on?"

"Sir, Agent Tanner has located Secretary Humphries and is in pursuit of the men who are even now attempting to smuggle him out of the country."

"Tanner? I thought you fired her. You told me she was incompetent and had wasted two days chasing shadows when she should have been looking for J.R.!"

"Yes sir...uh...yes I did. I...uh...I changed my mind about Tanner and took her back, giving her specific direction that led to her discovery of the kidnappers and the location they had been keeping the secretary of state."

"Specific direction? What specific direction?"

"Sir, that's not important now. What matters is that Agent Tanner has learned the Soviet Union is not, in fact, involved in the Humphries kidnapping and never was."

"No Soviet involvement?"

"No sir."

"You're certain of this?"

Aaron hesitated. It was time for the rubber to meet the road. Time to shit or get off the pot, as the saying went. His next words would likely cement a sterling career in the intelligence community or leave it in a shambles. He went with his gut. "Yes, Mr. President, I'm certain."

"Then we've got a problem. Because we're about to drop a bomb on Moscow's head."

36

Thursday, September 10, 1987
4:55 a.m.
The White House - Situation Room

Aaron Stallings had known Ronald Reagan since before his first inauguration nearly seven years ago, and he thought the president looked less like a man nearing eighty years of age than he had ever seen as the rest of the national security team filed back into the room. Reagan stood ramrod-straight behind the table, steely eyed and impatient, waiting until everyone had settled into their seats before taking charge of the meeting in a way he had not done before.

"Everything's changed," he said without preamble. "We have strong and credible evidence that suggests the Soviet Union is *not* involved in Secretary Humphries's disappearance. J.R. was taken by Iraq."

The room erupted in chaos, all of the men shouting questions and demanding to know what had happened to change the assessment of the situation so dramatically.

Reagan ignored them all. He raised his hands and barked, "That's enough, people," and after another moment, the buzz of chatter died away.

The president turned to Secretary of Defense Mark Carmichael. "Mark, I want you to get on the horn to General Matheson immediately and rescind the order for an aerial strike on the *Smetlivy*."

"But sir, what—"

211

"Immediately means *now*, Mark," Reagan interrupted. "I'll explain as much as I can as soon as I can to everyone who needs to know, but right now, the priority absolutely must be to put a stop to the unprovoked attack on the Soviets that will likely start a third world war. So get moving."

Reagan waited silently while Carmichael gathered his things and rushed toward the door. As he was leaving, Reagan said, "Mark?"

The secretary of defense looked back. "Yes, sir?"

"This might be the most important thing you'll ever do in service to your country. Stop that attack and let me know immediately when the order has been acknowledged by General Matheson."

"Of course, sir," Carmichael said. Then he turned and was gone.

Reagan turned his focus to Secretary of the Navy Admiral James Shoop. "Jim, brand-new intelligence indicates J.R. was held right here in D.C. until just a few hours ago, and that the Iraqis' plan is to smuggle him out of the country via low-level helicopter flight from Ocean City to an unknown airstrip in North Carolina, where they'll then fly him out to Iraq on a small business jet."

The room was deathly silent. All eyes focused on the president. Admiral Shoop said, "So we need to get birds in the air immediately."

"Exactly. I want every P3 sub hunter available fueled and in the air ASAP, and I want them to stay airborne until that helicopter is located. I have no registration number to give you, no description of the helo's type or color. But they'll likely be flying low-level, probably a short distance off the shoreline as they move south from Ocean City in order to minimize the likelihood of being observed by witnesses on the ground. If they get airborne before daybreak, they'll fly with running lights off, making them nearly invisible. I don't care what you have to do. Get those P3s in the air and find that chopper."

"I'll get right on it, Mr. President. Every available P3 from New England to Georgia will be in the air within thirty minutes, you have my word." Shoop pushed his chair away from the table and hurried out, exactly as Mark Carmichael had done moments earlier.

Next, the president addressed Assistant Secretary of State Joseph Malone. "Joe, prepare to contact the Soviets immediately. Once we receive verification that the strike on the *Smetlivy* has successfully been aborted, I want you to offer our official apologies for misreading the situation. Let them know we look forward to a continuation of the improved relations we've experienced over the last few years, blah, blah, blah. You know what they need to hear."

"Yes, sir, will do."

"But don't take any action until we know there's been no attack."

"Of course, sir." Malone rose and exited.

"Chet," Reagan said to his chief of staff, "you and I can huddle privately to determine how we want to manage the media on this. We have to give them something since the secretary of state's disappearance is about to become public knowledge, but obviously *no* specific details that might endanger the operation until Secretary Humphries is safely recovered."

Chester Moore was furiously scribbling notes on a stenographer's pad that Aaron had never seen him without. He nodded as he wrote and then said, "Yes sir. I'll nail everything down in your office, but for now I'll get started on the outline of a press release." He looked up. "You'll probably want to make a television appearance as well."

Reagan nodded. "Of course, but not until this thing is over." He looked around the nearly empty room and said, "Everyone else, I'm sure you understand that the intelligence this sudden operation is based upon is classified and will remain so. Say nothing to anyone without a need to know."

The president glanced at the clock hanging on the wall behind the table. "We'll reconvene later today to discuss the operation and where we go from here."

With that, the president turned and strode out of the Situation Room, Chester Moore right on his heels.

37

Tracie ditched Marshall's Buick along the thick underbrush several hundred feet north of an unmarked trail leading off a narrow, poorly maintained road southeast of Ocean City.

Once Tracie had visually acquired the Iraqis' Lincoln, following it without being spotted after the kidnappers left Route 50 had been a nightmare. Under normal circumstances, darkness was the ally of the tracker, but given the almost total lack of traffic, Tracie had been forced to back off a greater distance than she was comfortable with.

She didn't dare keep the Lincoln in sight, fearing that if she followed closely enough to keep eyes on her prey, the Iraqis would become suspicious later on when she would be forced to creep closer to them so she wouldn't miss their turnoff when they left the road.

She had taken the Route 50 off-ramp more than a quarter-mile behind the Town Car, allowing it to pull away and disappear, betting everything that the vehicle would turn east toward the Atlantic. She reasoned that their helicopter pilot would want to stay out over the ocean for most of the flight to North Carolina in an effort to avoid detection, and that they thus would have chosen a rendezvous point as close to the water as possible.

After leaving the highway, Tracie had pushed Marshall's

215

Buick hard, driving the two-lane Maryland country road much faster than was sensible. She was anxious to reacquire the target before too much distance had elapsed.

A half-mile passed.

Nothing. Tracie thought she should have caught up to the vehicle by now.

When a mile passed with still no sign of the Town Car, she began to doubt herself. Maybe the Iraqis had made her. She couldn't imagine how, she had been very careful to keep Marshall well behind the target, but the proof was in the pudding, and the big vehicle was nowhere to be found. But still she continued.

Finally, nearly a mile and a half after leaving the highway, Tracie spotted the distinctive Lincoln taillights far ahead along a straight and open stretch of backcountry road. She breathed a sigh of relief and immediately turned off at the next intersection, flipping on her turn signal far in advance to maximize the likelihood of it being seen by the vehicle ahead.

Then she had doused her headlights, waited a moment, and pulled a U-turn and reentered the road behind the Lincoln.

The rest of the trip went the same way. Tracie varied her distance behind the Iraqis, never getting close enough for any sharp-eyed passenger ahead to identify her vehicle. For a short time, driving through a heavily wooded area, she followed with her lights off, counting on the lack of horizon behind her to make the Buick invisible to the kidnappers.

Eventually, the Town Car's brake lights flashed and it made a sharp left, leaving the road and disappearing. It was as if the car had vanished into thin air a thousand feet in front of Tracie. She had been approaching a four-way junction, the road still and deserted, and she immediately signaled for a right turn and drove onto the crossroad at a ninety-degree angle to her prey.

She continued a hundred feet and felt confident she had gone far enough to be invisible to any sentry posted where the Lincoln had exited the road. Tracie had caught glimpses of the Atlantic Ocean through the trees to her left for the past several miles, vast and dark and empty, and if the car carrying J. Robert Humphries had turned onto an access road in that direction, she knew it couldn't have gone far before reaching the water's edge.

She drove off the road and parked. It was time to continue on foot.

She set the emergency brake and prepared to leave the car behind, wondering how long it would take for it to be discovered and towed as an abandoned vehicle.

She wished she still had her backpack filled with goodies. She cursed herself for not taking the time to retrieve it before leaving the abandoned school back in D.C. There was nothing in it that could be used to identify her, but still, it had contained some things that might have come in handy.

As it was, she was a little light on supplies. She had her Glock 19 and two Makarovs: the one she had taken off "Muhammad" after knocking him unconscious outside the school building, and the one she had removed from her unnamed Iraqi captor back inside the school.

Three handguns would be too unwieldy without any way to carry them, so she stashed one of the Makarovs in the glove box and while doing so, found a small flashlight, which she grabbed. It might come in handy.

She cupped a hand over the flashlight's lens and thumbed the on-off switch. A weak beam of light struggled out. Tracie shook her head in frustration.

Thought for a moment.

Then she stepped out of Marshall's car and knelt on the damp ground next to the front door. Directed the flickering beam beneath the dashboard under the steering wheel.

There. Running out from under the plastic steering-column housing was a series of a half-dozen different colored electrical wires. Two of them would be the ignition wires. What function the rest might have, Tracie didn't know or care. The wires were held together with a plastic clip and ran in a neat line out of the housing and along the underside of the dashboard, where they snaked under the frayed seven-year-old carpeting and disappeared into the engine compartment.

Tracie mumbled, "Sorry, Marshall," and wriggled her fingers under the edge of the carpeting. She struggled for several seconds before getting a solid grip. Then she yanked hard. The carpeting pulled away from the firewall accompanied by the sound of dried glue ripping and plastic anchors popping. When she had finished, the carpeting hung folded onto the floor under the foot pedals, exposing several feet of wiring.

She wrapped her fist around the wiring and began pulling.

After a moment's resistance, the wires pulled free, trailing out of the engine compartment like tiny snakes where they had broken from their connectors. Then she reached as far up under the steering column housing as she could and performed the same maneuver.

The result was a roughly six-foot length of electrical wiring. Not ideal, but the best she was going to do, considering her time constraints. The clock was ticking and she really had to move. But, she felt better having the wiring. There were plenty of potential uses for it. She just hoped she hadn't wasted too much time getting it.

She also hoped she hadn't made a serious tactical error in disabling Marshall's Buick. If she was successful in rescuing Humphries, she now had no car and no way of escaping the area. But rescuing the secretary of state meant neutralizing the men holding him, and if she could do that, she should be able to use their Lincoln to escape.

Tracie wound the wires into a loose ball and shoved it into the right front pocket of her jeans. The small flashlight went into her left front pocket. Then she closed and locked the car and began trotting along the edge of the road. At the intersection, she slowed and peered cautiously into the darkness in the direction the Lincoln had disappeared maybe three minutes ago.

It was quiet. Apparently deserted.

She crossed the road thankful for her dark clothing, and disappeared into the woods on the far side. Ten feet in, Tracie veered right ninety degrees and hiked south as quickly as she was able, stealthy and silent, keeping the dark mass of the Atlantic Ocean on her left and the deserted strip of pavement off to her right.

One hundred feet turned into two hundred and then the distinctive smell of cigarette smoke alerted Tracie to the presence of another human being. The Iraqis had posted a sentry after all, albeit a careless one.

She slowed and moved even more cautiously, flitting from tree to tree, careful not to step on a dead twig or tree branch and alert the guard to her presence.

Ten feet later she saw it. The flare of a lit cigarette as its owner took a deep drag. She paused and watched, alert for the possibility of a second sentry. The man leaned on a large boulder next to the rough trail. He wasn't quite sitting, but wasn't standing at attention, either, and he didn't seem too interested in keeping watch.

He finished his cigarette.

Flicked it away, yawned and stretched.

Tracie assumed he was wearing a holstered pistol but couldn't tell for sure. What she *could* see was that he wasn't holding a weapon in either hand.

She shrank back, carefully retracing her steps for at least twenty feet into the cover of the forest. Then she circled behind the sentry, crossing the trail between his position and the shoreline, where by now the Iraqis must have begun loading Humphries into their helicopter. She couldn't hear the whine of the chopper's engine or the distinctive *whup-whup-whupping* of the rotors biting at the air, but still, she knew she had to hurry.

She considered ignoring the sentry entirely now that she had gotten past him. It was tempting, and she almost did exactly that. But she had no real plan for retrieving Humphries, and whatever action she had to take would likely involve a significant amount of noise, probably including gunfire. She simply couldn't take the chance of the sentry hearing the commotion and coming running, shooting her in the back as she traded fire with the men in the helicopter.

So she would have to take the time to eliminate him. She lowered herself to the cold ground and combat-crawled across the trail, Glock held securely in her right hand. She held her breath and waited for the shout of alarm to come from off her right side that would tell her she had been spotted.

Or worse, for a bullet in the back.

Nothing.

Seconds later she was back under the reassuring cover of the woods. Tracie picked a fist-sized rock up off the trail and got to her feet. She weaved from tree to tree, steadily moving toward the sentry's last known position.

Then she was there. Behind him.

Incredibly, the man still hadn't moved. He leaned against the boulder, the picture of boredom. His attention was directed at the empty roadway, but he hadn't exhibited the slightest bit of initiative since she had first spotted him. *Jeez, no wonder the Iraqis gave this guy the simplest job.*

She crept as close as she dared, knowing he was unlikely to turn around unless a noise gave her away. Less than five feet behind him she stopped. She could hear him breathe, his respiration slow and steady.

Holding the Glock in her right hand, she hefted the rock with her left. She lobbed it silently, grenade style, over the sentry's head in the direction of the road. A second later it struck the pavement, bouncing once and then skittering onto the shoulder.

Instantly, he jolted, fully alert. He shoved off the boulder and spread his feet, dropping into a shooter's crouch as he lifted his weapon and peered in the direction of the noise.

Perfect.

Tracie used the sound of the man's movements to mask her own. She sprang forward, lifting her right hand and pistol-whipping the guard. The butt of her Glock smashed into his skull just above the right ear and he crumpled noiselessly to the ground, dropping his weapon at his feet as he landed face-first on the forest floor.

Tracie bent and hefted it. Another Makarov. Of course. *The Iraqis must have purchased or stolen the damned things by the truckload.* She had no room to carry it, so she ejected the magazine and scattered the rounds on the forest floor as far from the unconscious sentry as she was able without making too much noise. Then she tossed the now-useless pistol into the woods in the opposite direction.

She turned back to the man and leaned over him. He was bleeding heavily from the head wound, but his breathing was regular and his pulse was strong. He would live.

The man had been wearing a light windbreaker against the overnight chill, and Tracie slipped it off his back. She rolled up one sleeve and stuffed it into his mouth and then fished the bundle of electrical wires out of her pocket. She unwound the ball, moving quickly, wondering why she had still not heard the sound of the helicopter preparing for departure.

When the wires were separated, she took one strand and used it to secure the improvised gag in the sentry's mouth, winding it around his skull twice and then twisting the stiff wire into a knot behind his head.

Then she took two more strands and fashioned them into a

makeshift rope. She bound his wrists together behind his back, lashing them to a six-inch-thick young maple tree that had grown thankfully close to the boulder where the man had been standing. When he awoke, he would be unable to cry out for help and, unless he was the Middle Eastern descendant of Harry Houdini, unable to escape.

It was the best she could do.

She turned, cursing at herself for wasting valuable time, and sprinted along the trail toward the shoreline. As she ran, she could hear the sound of an engine firing up. But it wasn't a helicopter engine; the sound of their rotors turning was unique and instantly recognizable.

This sounded more like a car's engine turning over.

Had the Iraqis changed their mind? Had their plan changed for some reason? Would a set of automobile headlights suddenly flash on, bathing her in their light and rendering her helpless?

Tracie had no idea. All she knew was that she had come too far to stop. She said a silent prayer and sprinted on.

38

Thursday, September 10, 1987
5:50 a.m.
Near Ocean City, Maryland

I t was a boat.

After running no more than two hundred feet along the rutted dirt trail that passed for a road, concerned that at any moment she would step in a pothole and break an ankle, Tracie suddenly found herself approaching a clearing. Parked in the clearing was the Lincoln Town Car she had tailed.

But it sat empty and silent.

And there was no helicopter anywhere in sight.

Instead, there was a boat. It looked to Tracie to be about a twenty-five footer and it had been tied to an ancient wooden dock that threatened to fall apart and crash into the water at any moment. As she looked on in confusion, Tracie could see two men, one of whom was forcing the other into the boat.

The grey early-morning light of an overcast day made it hard to see, but undoubtedly the reluctant boater was J. Robert Humphries, and undoubtedly he was being prodded at gunpoint. His head hung and his shoulders slumped, and the man on the dock pushed him into the boat. Then the man untied a rope line from the dock and leapt aboard.

The engine, which had been idling patiently, instantly roared as the second Iraqi hit the throttle. The boat lunged forward and turned into the small inlet, heading for the Atlantic Ocean beyond.

Tracie drew her weapon and brought it to bear on the boat, knowing immediately she was too late. She was unlikely to hit anything from this distance, with the craft moving rapidly away, and even if she did, she was just as likely to strike Humphries as a kidnapper.

"Goddammit!" she muttered, lowering her weapon and staring in shock at the retreating boat. What the hell had just happened?

She shook her head to clear the confusion and realized she would just have to treat the scenario like she would any overseas operation that had just gone to shit. She would improvise.

She picked a direction at random—north—and began sprinting along the shoreline. The inlet was heavily wooded and the open Atlantic was just beyond its mouth, and yet the water here was docile and calm, perfect for vacationing and camping and pleasure boating.

There would have to be cabins constructed in the immediate area. Maybe she would get lucky and find a boat she could "borrow" to follow the Iraqis. The kidnappers' speeding craft was growing steadily smaller as it raced toward the ocean, but she could still see it, barely, fading away into the darkness.

The boat was heading directly toward the northern end of the inlet's mouth. This meant that not only were the Iraqis not transporting Humphries via helicopter, they weren't heading toward North Carolina, either. Everything she had overheard just before the confrontation with the Iraqis in the abandoned school building was false. Everything.

And then it struck her. It was so obvious she should have thought of it before.

The kidnappers had planted false information regarding their plans because they *knew* Tracie had been listening at the door! The man she had eventually overcome to escape the schoolhouse had been following her from the time she climbed into the school building until the moment he stuck his gun in her ear, so they had had plenty of time to improvise the misinformation.

They had *wanted* Tracie to overhear the dramatic intel about the helicopter, just in case she was in contact with anyone else. It was a kind of failsafe. They had never intended to transport Humphries south out of Ocean City in a helicopter; had never intended to fly him out of North Carolina in a Learjet, either.

She had been played for a dupe and had fallen for it, hook, line and sinker.

Anger flared inside her—directed mostly at herself—as well as a grudging respect for her opponent. She had underestimated the Iraqis, had been doing so all along, because they weren't the vaunted Soviets who the United States had been trading covert operations with for decades.

The Iraqis were new to the world of international espionage, and so she had not taken them as seriously as she should have. And now, J. Robert Humphries was paying for her poor judgment.

She pushed herself harder, leaping over fallen branches and dodging trees and underbrush as she charged along the water's edge. Night's blackness was giving way to daylight, but the steel-grey skies were surrendering light reluctantly, and the Iraqis' boat had disappeared into the darkness. She could still hear the scream of its engine as it raced toward the open ocean, but soon even that would be gone.

She rounded a bend in the rocky shoreline and saw what she had been hoping for. A powerboat tied to a rickety dock was bobbing gently in the distance. A small cabin set back roughly forty feet from the shoreline made clear to whom the boat belonged, but a quick glance to the rear of the building confirmed that no car was parked in the small driveway.

The cabin appeared deserted.

If true, that was good news, but Tracie couldn't afford to lose the time it would take to ensure the cabin was empty. Once the Iraqis made it to the Atlantic, they would disappear, swallowed up by the watery expanse, with Tracie no closer to rescuing Humphries than she had been two days ago.

She had to risk it. If the boat's owner was inside, hopefully he was still asleep. He would never be able to react quickly enough to interfere once Tracie fired up the engine and pointed the craft away from the shore.

She moved directly to the dock, padding down it quickly but quietly. The boat looked to be about a twenty-three footer, roughly the same size as the one the kidnappers were using, with a crisp white paint job and a small enclosed cabin. The name *Tequila Sunset* was stenciled proudly on the stern.

Tracie clambered aboard, breathing heavily. Her uncle was an avid weekend boater and had once told her that most recreational mariners kept a spare key hidden somewhere inside their boat. They often lived a fair distance from where they moored their craft and didn't want to have to turn around and go home in the event they forgot their key. He had shown her where his spare key was stored, and had suggested that many other boat owners utilized the same location.

She headed directly to the rear outboard engine and decided to test his theory. If he was right, and the key was where she hoped it would be, she would save a little time. If not, she would abandon the search and immediately begin working on hot-wiring the engine.

She knelt between two gas cans lashed to the deck at the stern and couldn't help glancing toward the mouth of the inlet. The Iraqis' boat was gone. Their engine noise was now just a thin whine, soft on the early-morning air like the buzz of a mosquito.

Dammit.

With a renewed intensity, Tracie got to work. She clawed a long combination cushion/flotation device off the bench seat running along the port side. The seat was hinged at the rear, as she had suspected it would be. She lifted from the front and the seat cover swiveled upward, revealing a storage locker underneath.

Picking through it quickly, Tracie found life vests, some fishing equipment and other assorted vacation necessities, but nothing that looked like what she was hoping to find.

She lowered the seat and replaced the cushions and turned to the other side, repeating the procedure. This time she hit pay dirt. A metal toolbox had been fitted snugly into the bottom of the storage space, crammed between more faded orange life vests and a pile of plastic fishing bobbers.

Tracie lifted the box out and placed it on the deck.

Opened it and began pawing through it.

She was making more noise than she would have liked, clanking the metal tools together and against the sides of the toolbox, but was acutely aware that her window for catching up with the Iraqis was closing fast. It might already have slammed shut.

After a few seconds, she smiled. At the bottom of the

toolbox, covered by a greasy set of adjustable wrenches, screwdrivers, pliers, hammers, and other tools, was a magnetized key case. Just large enough to hold a single key.

Tracie plucked the case out of the toolbox and slid it open. Inside was a brass key that looked exactly like a car key. She pumped her fist in silent triumph and closed the toolbox, dropping it back inside the storage area and lowering the bench seat. Now all she had to do was make sure it wasn't the owner's spare house key.

She crossed the deck and climbed down inside the boat's small cabin. Slid the key into the ignition. Perfect fit.

She left the key in the ignition and climbed out of the boat's cabin. Stepped off the boat and onto the dock to untie the mooring. Looked up at the small building built into a slight incline in the distance.

And froze.

Walking out the door in mid-stretch, travel mug in hand, was a middle-aged man.

She had been wrong. The cabin wasn't empty. Maybe the man's car was parked somewhere else, or maybe he had been dropped off by a wife or a girlfriend or a buddy. Her assumption that the lack of a car in the driveway meant the cabin was unoccupied had been off the mark.

After a split-second of indecision, Tracie kept moving. The man hadn't noticed her yet and was walking slowly, his attention on the murky sky, apparently trying to decipher the upcoming day's weather conditions. With luck, she might be able to fire up the boat and accelerate away from the dock before he could react. She had no doubt she could disable the man, but doing so would take valuable time—time she simply could not afford.

She bent and lifted the mooring line off a dock post, tossing the rope onto the boat. It landed with a soft thud that went unnoticed by the owner, who was still too far away to have heard it.

Tracie bent as low as she could and hurried along the dock, watching the man the entire time. He had covered almost half the distance to the dock.

She stepped quietly down onto the *Tequila Sunset*'s deck.

And slipped.

She crashed down in a heap and heard a startled, "Hey!"

from the direction of the cabin.

Scrambling to her feet, Tracie ducked into the cabin. The man had dropped his coffee mug and was now running toward the dock. In another five seconds he would be on it, and maybe two seconds after that he would be able to leap into the boat.

She cursed her untimely slip and turned the ignition key. The engine fired on the first try, sputtering and coughing for a moment and then settling into a throaty burble. Tracie cut the wheel away from the dock and shoved the throttle forward, hoping the engine wouldn't die because it hadn't warmed up properly.

The throaty burble became a throaty roar and the *Tequila Sunset* reared up like a wild stallion. It began moving away from the dock, slowly at first and then faster as the outboard engine churned the water.

Tracie glanced back and her eyes widened in surprise. The boat's owner hadn't slowed. He was sprinting along the dock and when he reached the end, he launched himself in an all-out dive at the left rear corner of his boat.

For one horrible second, she thought he might fall short, dropping into the water at the stern and getting chewed to pieces by the relentlessly churning propeller. But then he crashed into the side, half in and half out of the boat, and tumbled forward, landing on the deck in a misshapen heap.

Tracie straightened the wheel, aiming as best she could at the mouth of the inlet. Then she exited the cabin to deal with the boat owner. He was lifting himself heavily off the deck, apparently not seriously injured but definitely bruised and battered. He was muttering curses as she climbed out of the cabin, and when he looked at her, his shock was evident. He had expected the boat thief to be a man, not a petite, beautiful young woman.

Tracie didn't hesitate. She took advantage of his surprise, moving forward quickly, closing the distance between them so he could not extend his arms, which were much longer—and more powerful—than her own. "Sorry about this," she said, "but I promise you'll get your boat back safely."

"You're damn right I will," he said, recovering from his surprise and beginning to stand. "Right now."

"Not yet," she said. "I need to borrow it. It's a matter of

national security."

"I don't think so," he said, and began shoving her backward, apparently planning to pin her against the enclosed cabin's exterior wall.

It was obvious he had no intention of listening to her excuses, not that she blamed him. She was sure she would have reacted the same way had the boat been hers. Still, she couldn't afford to waste any more time dealing with him.

She allowed herself to be pushed, backpedaling in a slight semicircle to avoid crashing into the cabin. When the man suddenly stopped pushing, she used his momentum against him, grabbing his forearms and tugging. His feet scrabbled on the deck. He was off-balance and now nearly defenseless.

At the side of the still-moving boat, Tracie ducked her head and pulled with her arms and flipped him over the side. He hit the water with a splash and sank out of sight. Seconds later he surfaced, sputtering and spitting salt water, but by now the boat had churned forward twenty feet and was out of reach.

The unfortunate man screamed in the direction of the receding boat, lifting one arm out of the water and shaking his fist. His words were drowned out by the engine's roar, but Tracie had a pretty good idea what he was saying. She promised herself that she would return his property to him in person, complete with an apology, when this was all over.

Assuming she survived.

39

The Iraqi boat cruised steadily northeast in the open ocean, gradually angling away from the shoreline until eventually the land disappeared entirely. Tracie had to fight the fear that the Iraqis' real plan was simply to motor far into the Atlantic and then weight Humphries's body down and toss him over the side.

After stealing the *Tequila Sunset* and leaving the secluded Maryland cove, she had pushed her stolen boat hard, assuming the kidnappers would have turned north to avoid the route their "helicopter" was supposedly taking. For several nerve-wracking miles there was no sign of the Iraqis—no sign of marine activity at all—but then, while scanning the vast expanse of ocean with a pair of binoculars she found stashed in the cabin, Tracie had spotted a tiny speck outlined against the clouds of the dirty grey horizon.

It was the Iraqis.

She throttled back to a more reasonable cruising speed and maintained a distance that would allow her to keep her prey in sight while minimizing the possibility of being spotted herself.

Tracie recalled her uncle telling her once, when she was eight years old and spending the day aboard his twenty foot Chris Craft, that people rarely did more than glance behind them while in a power boat. The tendency was to focus on what was ahead.

231

She hoped his theory was right, though she seriously doubted foreign nationals in the process of smuggling the world's highest-profile kidnapping victim out of the country would act like typical pleasure boaters. On the plus side, it was a struggle just to keep the Iraqis' boat in view even with binoculars, so she felt it was unlikely they would spot her trailing along far behind.

Unless they had marine radar.

That was her main concern. If their boat was equipped with it there was no way to avoid discovery, no matter how much distance she left between them. She tried to recall whether she had seen the distinctive rectangular radar sensor mounted atop their boat's cabin when she had burst out of the woods back in Ocean City.

She didn't think so but couldn't be sure. She had been in shock and had only seen the boat for a few seconds before it had sped away.

Ultimately it didn't matter. She wasn't giving up now.

Time passed slowly, exhaustingly, as the process of maintaining constant visual contact with the Iraqis required all of her concentration. If she looked away, even for a moment, reacquiring the boat in her binocs was maddeningly difficult. The still-healing bullet wounds in her shoulders throbbed and her eyes burned from strain and exhaustion.

To help ease the suffocating boredom, she tried to calculate how far the Iraqis might be able to take Humphries without refueling and what their ultimate plan might be. They clearly weren't taking a twenty-five-or-so-foot powerboat across the Atlantic, and if they wanted to kill the secretary of state and dump his body overboard, it seemed as though they had long ago gone far enough out to sea to accomplish that task.

* * *

Two hours passed, and then three, and Tracie began to eye her fuel gauge with concern. The Iraqi boat had followed an arrow-straight course virtually since leaving the inlet back in Ocean City, and she knew that if they continued for too much longer, she would be in danger of running out of gas. She wondered if their boat had been modified in some way, maybe with extra fuel tanks.

She glanced toward the stern of the *Tequila Sunset*, where two five-gallon gas cans had been lashed to the deck. Presumably they contained fuel. If necessary, she could hurry back there and add those ten gallons to her rapidly decreasing supply, but the fact of the matter was that if the situation didn't change soon, she was going to run out of gas.

And she would lose J. Robert Humphries again, probably for good.

She glanced at her radio. Considered calling for help. Decided against it, as she had dozens of times over the last few hours. If she called on a frequency the Iraqis were monitoring, she would seal the fate of J. Robert Humphries.

She cursed and scanned the horizon, sweeping her binoculars from side to side while keeping an eye on the tiny speck that represented the fleeing Iraqis. She had observed little other marine traffic during her pursuit, and the few times she had seen other boats they had been massive freighters far off in the distance, steaming their loads toward unknown destinations.

Tracie narrowed her eyes and focused her attention on what appeared through the glasses as little more than a faint smudge coloring the sky just above the horizon, a smear of dark color barely visible against the grey water and greyer skies.

The image blurred and she blinked her tired eyes in an effort to clear them. Looked again.

It was a tiny spit of land.

And the boat containing J. Robert Humphries and his captors was heading straight toward it.

Tracie knew they were now well clear of the U.S. coastline. The compass told her they had been moving steadily north-northeast, which meant that somewhere far behind would be Long Island, protruding jaggedly into the Atlantic. But by now they were dozens of miles out to sea, far from the coast.

She wracked her brain, trying to recall her knowledge of U.S. geography. Were there any inhabited islands this far out in the Atlantic Ocean east of the D.C./New York corridor?

She didn't think so.

She maintained her speed until she was absolutely certain the Iraqis were heading toward the island, which was gradually resolving from a barely-identifiable slash of color into a clearly recognizable outcropping of land. Tracie shook her head. The tiny tree-covered rock had seemingly sprouted from the ocean utterly at random.

Convinced the island was the Iraqis' destination, Tracie slowed the *Tequila Sunset*, her previous concern about fuel now forgotten. Within twenty minutes, the contours of the island became clear. The spit of land was lush and green and small and featured a rocky shoreline but an interior bristling with trees and vegetation.

She cut the power completely and examined the island's shoreline through the glasses. As she looked, the Iraqis' boat disappeared into a sheltered cove that appeared to provide access to a small cabin built atop the rocks right at water's edge.

She played the binoculars over the remainder of the island that was visible from her position and could find no evidence of inhabitation. No other homes, no activity, nothing that would indicate the presence of other people.

The small cabin, which had all of the characteristics of a makeshift lookout, had been the Iraqis' destination. But why? What was the plan from there?

Tracie thought hard, rolling her shoulders in an unsuccessful attempt to loosen them and stop the dull throb of pain that beat in time with her heart. The damp ocean air was wreaking havoc on the surgically repaired tissue. When the effort went unrewarded, she sighed. She would have to ignore the pain. She'd done it before, plenty of times.

The *Tequila Sunset* bobbed in the choppy water, drifting slowly away from the island as Tracie pondered her next move.

Were the Iraqis planning to kill Secretary of State Humphries on this nearly invisible speck of land? If so, would they do it immediately? If not, what was their endgame?

She had no ready answers, but she knew she could not afford to take the chance of sacrificing her only advantage—surprise. She was outnumbered and alone, armed with only two handguns and limited ammunition.

And she was running out of time. The minute the Iraqis entered their strange-looking little shack they would likely scan the empty ocean for pursuers. The *Tequila Sunset* couldn't be seen with the naked eye, she was too far away for that, but their hideaway was undoubtedly equipped with binoculars, if not a telescope, and once they accessed either of those she *would* be discovered.

She pictured the shack's location, built at the edge of the water, on top of the rocks on one of the highest elevations of the island, and knew immediately that an armed assault would be difficult even under ideal circumstances: plenty of assets, equipment, intel, and a carefully constructed plan.

Her current situation offered none of those advantages. And there was no margin for error. One wrong move would result in the death of J. Robert Humphries—and probably herself—on a remote, apparently uninhabited island miles out to sea. No one would ever know what had happened. Humphries's body would likely never be found.

She studied the interior of the powerboat, not sure what she was looking for. She needed something she could use to go on the offensive, she just didn't know what.

A moment later she saw it and smiled grimly. The seeds of a plan began to take shape.

Tracie applied power to the throttle and turned the wheel and the boat began moving slowly west, giving the island a wide berth. After ten minutes the cabin disappeared behind the dense island foliage. After fifteen more minutes she guessed she had traveled far enough that the Iraqis would not be able to detect the sound of the *Tequila Sunset*'s engine.

There was still no evidence of any other presence on the island.

She turned straight at the shoreline. It was time to take action.

40

Thursday, September 10, 1987
10:20 a.m.
Atlantic Ocean,
Somewhere off the U.S. East Coast

It only took a few minutes to find a small stretch of rocky sand on which to bring the *Tequila Sunset* ashore. The little strip of beach was about forty feet long, sandwiched between two massive, ancient stone ledges giving just enough room to access the island.

Once she had secured the boat, she unlashed one of the *Tequila Sunset*'s spare five-gallon gas cans, hefting it and hauling it off the boat. Then she began walking.

Tracie hiked counterclockwise along the little island's shoreline, being careful to stay hidden and move quietly—she had no way of knowing what sort of security the Iraqis might maintain—while working her way steadily to the shack she had seen from the boat.

For the better part of an hour she lugged the heavy container through the island's wooded interior, fighting her way through the trees and underbrush. During that time, Tracie saw no sign of any security presence—no patrolling guards, no cameras, no tripwires. Nothing.

Finally, she caught a glimpse through the trees of the small building and stopped moving, hunkering down in the brush and observing the shack for activity. Fifteen minutes turned into twenty, and then thirty, with no sign of movement around the shack.

After forty-five minutes of utter inactivity, Tracie concluded that the kidnappers must have decided to hole up inside, waiting for whatever was to come next. She knew they hadn't loaded Humphries back into their boat and headed out to sea while she was finding entry onto the island, because she could see the boat bobbing gently in the distance, tied up to a makeshift dock in the small cove roughly a hundred feet from the shack.

Without knowing what the Iraqis had planned for Humphries, she had no way of calculating how much prep time she had. She didn't want to act rashly, but if she waited too long to launch her assault, things could once again spiral out of control. When an hour had passed with no sign of life coming from the shack, Tracie reluctantly decided to break off her surveillance.

She needed to act decisively. She was sick and tired of being on the defensive.

She backtracked quietly until the weathered structure disappeared from sight. Then she angled behind the building in the general direction of the cove containing the Iraqis' boat. When she guessed she had traveled far enough, she turned sharply right and within minutes emerged from the trees almost directly in front of their moored boat.

Again she stopped and observed.

She was facing the cabin's only door, which was closed tightly. Still there was no sign of activity.

She broke cover, keeping the bulk of the boat between herself and the cabin windows, which had all been covered with what looked like ancient, unmatched curtains. She climbed aboard, crouching as low as possible, and slipped silently onto the deck. The boat the Iraqis had used to transport J. Robert Humphries was ironically named the *Freedom*. It appeared well maintained.

It was also now missing its ignition wires, which Tracie ripped out, as well as its spark plugs, for good measure. She tossed the plugs into the water as far from the boat as possible, and then stuffed the wires into her pocket. Then she climbed off the same way she had climbed on.

The Iraqis were now trapped on the island unless they had

another boat stashed somewhere or stumbled upon the *Tequila Sunrise*.

She retraced her steps and found herself back in the woods behind the building, satisfied that at last she could devote her full attention to the strange-looking cabin, which approximated the size and shape of a one-bedroom vacation cottage. It had clearly been constructed decades ago, by whom and for what purpose Tracie did not know, but its weathered pine siding testified to its age.

It had been built high above the water using the massive granite ledges as a rudimentary foundation. Despite the cabin's obvious age and its rickety appearance, closer inspection revealed that the Iraqis—or someone—had reinforced it. New two-by-four framing had been added in a number of locations, the newer wood lacking the distinctive weathered grey of the rest of the structure.

Tracie approached carefully, using the thick underbrush for cover, and tried to determine what the building might originally have been used for. Its primary purpose probably hadn't been as living quarters—the cabin was too small and too remote. It had the look of a sentry's post. Built on high ground right on the shoreline, the location offered an unobstructed view of two hundred-seventy degrees of ocean, barring poor visibility.

It was a lookout, or had been at some point in the distant past.

A clearing of perhaps fifteen feet separated the outpost from the thick woods behind it where she stood. There was a single window in the rear of the shack, which was currently covered with an ancient gingham curtain. It appeared to block the entire surface of the glass, but there was no way to tell for sure, and no way of knowing whether someone might be peeking through a small opening.

Tracie took a deep breath and started across the clearing. She was at the rear wall in seconds and flattened herself against it, moving silently, breathing easily. Through the thin construction she could hear the muffled sound of voices; two males speaking easily in the confident back-and-forth banter of athletes in a locker room. Or kidnappers convinced they were alone.

She didn't hear J. Robert Humphries's voice but doubted he would have much to add to the conversation at this point.

She sidled to the southwestern edge of the building and eased her head partially around the corner, her Glock held securely in two hands, the barrel aimed—for now—at the ground.

The area was deserted. The granite ledge acting as the building's foundation looked ancient. Tracie had no difficulty imagining this very ledge sitting in this very location—minus the cabin, of course—ten thousand years ago. A hundred thousand.

She continued moving, keeping her body pressed to the wall, creeping toward the front of the shack. At the corner she repeated the drill she had performed seconds before, easing her head around to peer along the front of the cabin, weapon at the ready. She saw no one.

Her objective was to reach the only decent-sized window in the building. It faced out on the endless grey-green ocean, and although it, too, had been covered, it represented her best chance to get any usable intel before launching her offensive.

Tracie rounded the corner and crept along the seaward-facing exterior. The footing was treacherous. The relentless pounding of waves on the island and the ever-present sea-spray had turned the granite's smooth surface into an ice-skating rink, and a slip on this narrow shelf would likely mean a broken neck and a tumble into the pounding surf ten feet below.

As she inched closer to the big picture window, Tracie realized she might actually be able to manage a look inside the cabin. A blanket had been used as a makeshift curtain here, and had been hung carelessly. Instead of hanging straight down, it had been placed at an angle, resulting in an inches-wide gap at the corner of the window closest to her.

Tracie took a deep breath and eased her eye against the salt-encrusted, weather-scoured glass. She saw a small, sparsely furnished living area, consisting of a rickety wooden table, two chairs and a moth-eaten couch lining the far wall. The two Iraqis who had taken Humphries out of the abandoned school in D.C. sat at the table playing some sort of card game.

Behind the Iraqis was a wall into which two doors had been constructed. Both doors were closed. Tracie guessed that one of them accessed a rudimentary lavatory, probably nothing more than a toilet seat opening onto the boulder under the cabin. The other door must lead into another small room. Based on the cabin's dimensions, Tracie guessed the room was no bigger than a walk-in closet.

That was where J. Robert Humphries was being held.

It had to be.

It was obvious the kidnappers' stay inside this cabin was intended to be short. There was no kitchen and no food that she could see aside from the contents of a single brown paper bag that had been placed against the side wall. Whatever they were planning to do next might happen at any moment, so she needed to get moving.

She retraced her steps, moving slowly along the slick surface. Turned the corner. When she reached the rear of the cabin, Tracie continued walking straight ahead, across the clearing and into the forest beyond.

It was time to smoke out the kidnappers.

41

All the effort it had taken to lug the five-gallon gasoline can across the island was worth it. Tracie would be able to execute her hastily conceived plan. As an added bonus, it might actually work.

She lumbered across the clearing behind the cabin, her usual quickness and grace sacrificed to the weight of the container filled with fuel. In her left hand was the gas can, in her right, her Glock. When she reached the back wall she paused and listened keenly, tense and alert for any indication that she had been seen.

The surf pounded and the wind whistled around the building, unimpeded by the open ocean surrounding the lonely little island. From inside the cabin, Tracie could hear the voices of the Iraqis, still apparently engrossed in their card game, blissfully certain miles of water separated them from any other human beings.

She unscrewed the cap and began splashing fuel along the side of the cabin, reaching as high on the wall as she could and allowing the liquid to run down the siding. When she had finished, the lower two to three feet was doused.

Tracie was surprised to see the liquid absorb quickly into the siding. Her assumption had been that the constant unrelenting moisture would have soaked the boards, but the opposite was true. Decades of salty air, briny biting wind, and brutal Atlantic Ocean weather had completely dried the untreated wood, making it a dangerously combustible tinderbox.

She hoped she hadn't miscalculated and used too much fuel, but it was too late to do anything about that possibility now. She was committed.

She set the can down. The saturated siding reeked of gasoline. She fished a lighter out of her pocket, grateful to the owner of the *Tequila Sunset* for stashing it away in his toolbox, and then knelt at the rear corner of the cabin and touched the flame to the lower portion of siding.

The wood caught immediately with a muffled *whump*, as flames leaped enthusiastically from the tiny lighter and raced along the structure in both directions. The fire danced and surged, and Tracie double-timed around the building, moving quickly to the side of the cabin facing the cove.

The side with the only exit.

42

Jamaal Hakim was bored. He was also anxious to finish this unpleasant business and finally get home to Baghdad, where he would be reunited with his family after six long months spent suffering in the belly of the beast. But most of all, Jamaal was sick to death of being saddled with his partner in this venture, Adil Ajam.

Ajam was a decent warrior, strong and committed, but Jamaal had long-since concluded the man possessed the intellectual capacity of a sand flea. He spoke in a rumbling monotone and had never indicated any evidence of possessing the ability for independent thought.

He was muscle, nothing more.

And that was fine, as far as it went. Some situations called for the kind of muscle Ajam represented and Jamaal knew this was one of them. He understood why they had been ordered to work together. Smuggling the sitting U.S. secretary of state out of his own country and transporting him successfully under guard to the homeland was not a job for the weak of heart or the undedicated. In that sense, Jamaal appreciated Ajam's presence.

But spending so much time in the company of such an incurious dullard had driven Jamaal nearly to the point of distraction. He vowed that the minute they set foot on the holy soil of Iraq, he would rid himself of Adil Ajam and with luck, never interact with the man again.

And the end was in sight. Finally.

Jamaal tossed a card on the table, almost at random, not caring which one he played because it didn't matter. He wasn't paying attention to the game. He was only playing because doing so gave Ajam something on which to focus his limited intellect.

"How long now?" Ajam asked in Iraqi Arabic.

Jamaal checked his watch, not that he needed to. His partner had asked the same question not two minutes before. "Three hours," he said in exasperation. "In three hours we will rendezvous with the freighter that will bring us home. It is the same amount of time as it was two minutes ago, when you last asked the question. Please, Adil, have patience."

Ajam grunted and tossed a card. "I am anxious to leave this country behind."

"As am I. My only regret is that Muhammed had to stay behind and clean the school building of evidence, and then must serve another four months at the embassy before returning home."

Ajam was unmoved. "That is his problem. Besides, he was rewarded with the girl we captured." He grinned. "I doubt Muhammad minded the sacrifice too much."

Jamaal said nothing, partly because he had come to expect such responses from his partner, but mostly because he was beginning to feel that something was wrong. He sat quietly in his chair, card game forgotten, ill at ease but uncertain why.

And then it came to him.

He smelled smoke.

He looked around the room suspiciously. Nothing appeared out of place. There wasn't much inside the little cabin that could *get* out of place. "Do you smell that?" he asked.

"What?"

"Smoke. It smells like something is burning."

Ajam shrugged, his focus still on the cards scattered across the table. "I smell nothing."

Jamaal turned his attention reluctantly back to his cards. He slid one out of his hand. Threw it onto the table. Sniffed the air again. "I'm telling you," he said forcefully, "I smell something. What in the name of Allah is that smell?"

"I don't know. I don't care. Can we please just finish the game?"

Jamaal pushed his chair away from the table and stood. "Something is wrong. I hope the island isn't burning down around us." He pointed a finger at Ajam and said, "Go take a look around outside. See if anything appears odd or out of place. See if there is smoke above the trees, perhaps off in the distance."

Ajam mumbled something Jamaal could not make out and then picked up his gun and shuffled slowly toward the door. Jamaal thanked Allah, as he had done every day since the beginning of this mission, that *he* had been placed in charge and not his unmotivated partner.

43

Tracie climbed the steps to the door and took a position next to it, knowing it would only be a matter of minutes, and not very many of them, before the occupants smelled smoke. Seconds after that, one or both would come to investigate.

She was right. The sound of footfalls approaching from inside was followed quickly by a muffled screech as the ancient door swung open and the bulky, heavily muscled Iraqi from the abandoned school stepped through, muttering something unintelligible under his breath in Arabic.

The man's eyes widened in surprise as he looked over and saw Tracie, the door blowing closed behind him. He opened his mouth to alert his partner to the intruder's presence and began raising his gun, which he had foolishly been holding by his side, but he was much too late. Tracie pivoted her raised wrist and swung her arm in a sideways arc, smashing the butt of her Glock against the Iraqi's temple.

She ignored the pain in her shoulders and drove with her legs, following through like a baseball pitcher firing a fastball toward home plate and was rewarded with a loud *crack*. The man dropped like a felled tree. He tumbled down the three steps and crumpled face first onto the rocky ground. A low moan escaped his lips, and his arms and legs twitched spastically and then fell still.

Tracie leaped off the landing. She had mere seconds before the other kidnapper came to investigate. She didn't know whether the sound of her attack had been loud enough to reach inside the tiny shack but she guessed it had.

She pulled the ignition wiring she had ripped out of the Iraqis' boat out of her pocket. Used two strands to secure the unconscious man's hands tightly behind his back.

Repeated the process with his ankles.

Then she flew back up the steps, intensely aware that although the entire incident had taken no more than thirty seconds, the unconscious kidnapper's partner might already be approaching the door.

She reached the landing and went on the offensive, abandoning all pretense of stealth. She yanked the door open and then ducked behind it, using the punky wood to shield as much of her body as possible. Holding the Glock in two hands, she crouched low and peered around the open side of the door.

Her concern about the second kidnapper had been right on target. He was already halfway across the cabin and was advancing rapidly, gun drawn, posture wary. The moment Tracie poked her head out, he unleashed a wild shot. She ducked behind the door as the shot whistled into the wood, ripping matchstick-sized slivers out of the frame.

Then she was up and moving

She cleared the door, squared up quickly, and returned fire before he could get off another round. The blast took the Iraqi in the upper body and he staggered backward two steps before falling to the worn linoleum floor. His weapon dropped from his hand and clattered away, sliding to a stop a few feet behind him.

Tracie heard a hoarse shout of panic. The gunshots had spooked Humphries and he was screaming for help. She ignored him.

The Iraqi scuttled backward, feet scrabbling on the filthy floor as he tried to reach his gun. One hand was clamped over his heavily bleeding shoulder and the other searched desperately for the weapon as he locked eyes with Tracie.

She squeezed off a second shot and the slug struck the floor inches from the man's face, blasting a small crater in the linoleum and kicking up a flurry of dust, tiny linoleum chips, and plywood subflooring. The man froze.

Tracie leapt forward. She crouched and jammed the barrel of her Glock under the man's chin. "How soon will your extraction team be here?" she said.

The man stared at her with smoldering dark eyes and said nothing. The smell of burning wood was becoming overwhelming. The shack was filling rapidly with black smoke as the blaze ate through the exterior walls and began devouring the interior.

Time was running out. Tracie needed to get Humphries to safety. She punched the man's injured shoulder with the butt of her gun and he responded with a quick, tight gasp of pain. "I asked you how much time we have!" she screamed into his face. "Answer now or die, it's all the same to me."

His face was ghostly white with pain and shock but he clamped his good hand more tightly onto his shoulder and again refused to answer. Refused to acknowledge Tracie in any way.

She cursed in frustration and turned to Plan B. She was out of time. She rolled the man onto his stomach and as she had done with the unconscious kidnapper outside yanked his hands behind his back. This man screamed in pain and kicked at her violently, but she was ready for him. She jammed one knee into his back just under his shoulder blades. As he wailed in agony, she pulled more of the electrical wiring out of her pocket.

She looped a strand around his wrists, twisting it just once. "Get up," she said, and pulled him roughly to his feet. He screamed again and staggered, nearly falling back to the floor. She was sweating now and the orange-yellow light from the still-building fire was intense, casting the scene in a surreal flickering glow.

Tracie steadied him and began pushing/pulling/dragging him to the door as the inferno raged. Humphries's screams had become more insistent. He was obviously secured to something behind the closed door and had come to the realization that he was minutes—maybe seconds—away from being burned alive.

The door had blown closed during the gun battle and now she kicked it open. Shoved the kidnapper down the steps and followed behind closely. The Iraqi stumbled over the prone body of his accomplice and staggered. Nearly fell. Tracie rammed her Glock into his ribs and forced the groaning man across the clearing to a small but stout-looking birch tree.

She shoved him against the tree and braced his body with her own.

Removed the wire from his wrists and stepped back.

Raised her gun until it was pointing into his face.

Said, "Place your hands around the tree trunk. Do it quickly."

The man scowled and spit forcefully onto the ground but did as he was told. Tracie re-secured him, tying the wire tightly this time until all mobility in his hands had disappeared. The wire bit painfully into his skin. She didn't care.

She stepped back and eyed her handiwork.

It would have to do. She was out of time. The cabin was now nearly engulfed in flames.

44

Thursday, September 10, 1987
1:35 p.m.
Atlantic Ocean,
Somewhere off the U.S. East Coast

Tracie turned and sprinted back to the burning structure. She burst through the door then skidded to a stop, stunned at how quickly the blaze had spread. Bright yellow and red flames licked their way up the far wall and a quarter of the way across the ceiling. Deadly black smoke roiled, filling the top two feet of the cabin, poisoning the air and turning it into a deadly toxic stew. Red-hot sparks showered from a support beam running the length of the ceiling.

From behind the closed door, Tracie could hear Secretary of State Humphries screaming, now in a state of full-fledged panic, his words tumbling over one another in a flood of desperation and terror.

"I'm coming," she shouted, screaming at the top of her lungs to make herself heard over the noise of the fire. It sounded like an onrushing freight train, roaring and wailing as it devoured the building.

The heat was intense, suffocating. Tracie kicked the closed door just below the knob. Its cheap latch provided almost no resistance and it whipped open, smashing into the far wall with a loud bang and rebounding violently.

And there was Humphries.

He had been shackled to a heavy iron U-bolt fastened to the

floor of the otherwise-empty room. Four feet of chain ran from the U-bolt to his wrists, leaving him room to stand but not to escape. His clothes were filthy and his skin soot-blackened.

He looked at her in a panic for a half-second before continuing to tug and yank insistently on his bindings. Tracie could see that all rational thought had left him. He was consumed by the need to escape the fire, but had succeeded only in bruising his wrists and rubbing the skin raw. He was bleeding freely from both hands but seemed not to notice.

Tracie stepped close and grabbed Humphries's shirt with both hands, forcing the panicked man to look into her eyes. "Mr. Secretary, I'll get you out of here, but you have to trust me!"

For a moment he stared at her in apparent incomprehension, then nodded wordlessly and stopped struggling.

She bent and examined the restraints. A set of handcuffs had been placed on Humphries's wrists and then the short steel links between the cuffs had been secured to a longer chain threaded through the iron ring. The man could pull on the cuffs until hell froze over and his efforts would be rewarded only with more pain.

She squatted over the ring, putting her body between it and the secretary of state. Then she placed the barrel of her weapon against the metal chain, angling it so the slug would not ricochet and strike either herself or Humphries.

She hoped.

Then she squeezed the trigger.

The Glock roared, the chain snapped and J. Robert Humphries was free. He stood over the U-bolt as if uncertain what to do next, swaying drunkenly from shock and fatigue.

The blaze continued to eat away at the little cabin. Smoke poured into the room through the open door. It gathered quickly at the ceiling, thick and black, and moved toward the floor as it accumulated. Out in the main living area, Tracie heard a loud crash as something structural gave way.

The building would soon be nothing more than a smoking pile of rubble.

Tracie took Humphries by the elbow and began leading him into the teeth of the raging fire. He resisted at first, unwilling to face the wall of flame, but there were no other options—the room's single window was much too small even for Tracie's petite frame to fit through, never mind the much larger, slightly overweight body of Secretary of State Humphries.

She tugged insistently, screaming, "This is the only way out! We have to go *now!*" and finally Humphries allowed himself to be pulled along.

They hit the door at a fast walk, Tracie stunned at how the fire had progressed. She estimated she had been inside Humphries's prison cell for no more than a minute, and in that time the blaze had exploded in intensity. The stifling heat struck her in the face like a closed fist. She felt her eyebrows singeing and smelled burning flesh and wondered abstractly whether it was her own.

Behind her, Humphries was repeating, "Goddammit, goddammit, goddammit," like a mantra, his incantation interrupted only by a hacking cough every few seconds as he tried to breathe the fetid, superheated air.

Tracie stepped behind the secretary of state and shoved him hard toward the cabin's only entrance. The smoke was so thick the door was invisible. "Hurry!" she screamed, and Humphries stumbled forward, moving marginally faster now than he had been before. Tracie followed behind, right on his heels.

She hoped neither of the Iraqis had been able to work themselves free of their jerry-rigged bindings, because if they had, she would be sending Humphries right back into their arms. But she needed to be behind him to ensure that she would be able to redirect him toward the door if he became disoriented navigating the ten feet of smoke-choked cabin.

They burst into the cool, fresh ocean air, coughing and gagging on the landing. Tracie stopped Humphries and stepped around him quickly, Glock at the ready, uncertain of what she would find. Her eyes were watering so badly she could barely see.

She held her weapon up, blinking madly, aware that they were both sitting ducks until her vision cleared. After a moment, she could see through the tears streaming down her face that both of the Iraqis were still exactly where she had left them. The one she had struck in the head was moaning softly, blood trickling out from under his hairline, conscious but still plainly confused. He wouldn't be attacking anyone for a while.

The other man glared at her from under hooded eyes. He was fully conscious but also fully neutralized.

She returned her attention to Humphries in an effort to assess his condition. The older man continued to cough and wheeze and his features glowed bright red under the soot covering every inch of exposed skin, but to Tracie he seemed already to be improving, if slowly. He was no longer hawking up gobs of blackened phlegm and his coughing fits lacked some of the wracking violence they had earlier inside the burning building.

The intensity of the heat radiating from the burning shack was indescribable. They had only minutes left before the tinderbox shack collapsed in on itself. Tracie eased the secretary of state down the steps and as she did a loud roar from directly behind them signaled the end for the doomed building.

Flames leapt toward the sky and red-hot embers billowed outward in all directions as the shack fell. Humphries screamed as a burning chunk of wood the size of a quarter landed on his arm. Instantly, the fabric of his shirt ignited and flames raced up his arm.

Tracie dragged the secretary of state to the rocky, sandy ground and fell on top of the much larger man, covering his arm with her body and smothering the fire. He lay panting for a moment and then said quietly, "Holy shit."

"Are you all right?"

He shrugged. "I guess so. I don't know at this point."

She flaked blackened cotton ash off his arm and rolled what was left of his shirtsleeve up to examine his burn. The skin was raw and pink, but under the circumstances, and considering the filthy bandage covering his injured hand, Tracie decided one skin burn was probably the least of his worries. Humphries barely seemed to notice it.

She pulled him to his feet and said, "Come on. I know you must be exhausted, sir, but I'm not sure how many people are meeting these guys or how long it will be before they arrive. Let's get out of here while we still can. That smoke will be visible for miles out on the water. If the Iraqis have reinforcements coming—and there's no question they do—we might be down to our last few minutes to escape."

Humphries began following Tracie, moving slowly. "What about them?" he said, indicating his captors with an incline of his head.

"They'll be safe. The fire will burn itself out on the rocky outcropping and they're far enough away from the remains of the building that they won't be in any serious danger."

"I don't give a damn how much *danger* they're in," Humphries growled. "That's not what I'm getting at. They have to come with us. They need to pay for what they've done."

Tracie grabbed a fistful of Humphries's shirt, as she had done inside the burning building. She tugged at it forcefully, almost dragging him along. "No way," she said. "We've got a pretty significant hike ahead of us, and keeping those guys under control would cost us more time than we probably have. My number one priority is to get you to safety. When we're in the boat and a safe distance from here I'll fire up the radio and call in the cavalry. They'll descend on this island en masse and will have those assholes in custody in a matter of an hour or two."

Humphries shook his head obstinately and Tracie thought he was going to argue further, but he surprised her. He sighed deeply and continued trudging behind, following her into the thick woods. "Where's everyone else?" he asked.

"What do you mean?"

"I mean, where's the rest of the rescue team?"

"There is no one else. I'm it."

"You're it? What is that supposed to mean?"

"It means I'm the only one who knows where you are, and nobody else knows where *I* am. The rest of the United States Armed Forces thinks you're in a helicopter flying low-level to North Carolina where you'll be transferred to a waiting private jet and whisked out of the country."

"You're it," Humphries repeated dubiously, eying her petite frame.

"I'm it," she agreed.

"My God," Humphries said, looking anxiously behind him before picking up the pace. "Let's get the hell out of here."

45

The driveway leading to Aaron Stallings's home was long and winding and immaculately maintained. The house itself stood well back from the road behind a grove of evergreens and was invisible to anyone driving past. Although Tracie knew the house had been constructed within the last decade, it had the look and feel of a Revolutionary War-era home, like something George Washington might have lived in. Mount Vernon a couple of centuries later.

She parked in the circular turn-around and climbed out of her Toyota. The home's front door swung open and the corpulent body of the CIA director filled the open space. He had clearly been waiting for her. He scowled, watching her approach, saying nothing.

When she reached the door, he said, "You're five minutes late." Then he stood aside and gestured at the interior of the house in what she interpreted as an invitation to enter.

"Your house isn't easy to find," she said. "It's a little off the beaten path. And besides, I'm unemployed, remember? I'm not used to having any place to be." Stallings's eyes narrowed in annoyance and she brushed past her former boss into a foyer featuring gleaming hardwood floors and elegant raised panel wainscoting on the walls. A cut-glass crystal lamp that Tracie guessed cost more than she made in a month hung over the entryway. In the back of her mind she wondered how a career civil servant could afford such high-end furnishings.

"Come with me," Stallings answered, pointedly ignoring her comment. He led her down the hallway into a massive study. Bookshelves filled nearly to overflowing with a collection of hardcover volumes, many leather-bound and very old, lined the walls. A television had been placed atop a walnut chest in one corner, angled to face a massive desk. Stallings squeezed behind it and eased into a leather chair.

He motioned Tracie to sit. It occurred to her that the only difference between this home library and Stallings's office at CIA headquarters was the added privacy it offered, and even that advantage was questionable. Her cursory examination upon entering the room revealed potential locations for surveillance devices too numerous to count.

They sat in silence for a moment. *The hell with it*, Tracie thought. *It's one thing to put up with this cloak and dagger bullshit when I'm getting paid for it, but this is ridiculous.* "Why am I here?" she asked bluntly.

Stallings stared, his eyes revealing nothing, and then said, "I felt we owed you a debt of gratitude. I gave you an assignment and you completed it satisfactorily, despite little official support. Thank you."

Tracie laughed bitterly. "If by 'little official support' you mean being harassed nonstop and subject to constant second-guessing, being badgered to approach the assignment from the wrong angle, and then being accused of malfeasance and summarily fired with no recourse, then, yes, I have to agree. There was 'little official support.'"

Stallings's face reddened and Tracie felt a stab of satisfaction. His jaw tightened and he said, "Has it ever occurred to you, Tanner, that sometimes you should just shut your mouth?"

"All the time. But I don't work for you anymore, remember? I wasn't particularly concerned about what you thought of me when I did, and I definitely don't care now."

He slammed a fist down on the desk and Tracie sat quietly. She refused to give him what he was looking for. "That's what I'm trying to tell you, goddammit; I want you back!" He sat ramrod-straight in his chair and stared in exasperation up at the ceiling.

Tracie gazed impassively at her former boss. She had considered the possibility that this meeting might be about an invitation to return to the agency. Discussing the issue here, away from Langley, would allow Stallings to speak freely while providing deniability to the director should Tracie refuse his offer.

"Nobody comes back after being terminated," she said evenly. "You know as well as I do that it just doesn't work that way."

"It's my agency, I'll run it the way I see fit," Stallings said. "Besides, you wouldn't be returning to the same position. You would, of course, remain in an operational status—that's where your strengths lie—but your duties would be a little more . . . shall we say . . . *undefined.*"

"More undefined than covert operations? What are you going to do, make me invisible?"

Stallings looked as though he had just bitten into rancid meat. "Your sole responsibility would be to take on assignments of a similar nature to the one you just completed. Your duties would be unofficial, off the books. You would report directly to me."

"A tightrope with no net."

"You could look at it that way."

"There *is* no other way to look at it."

Stallings shrugged. He held all the cards and he knew it. If Tracie wanted to resume her career in service to her country she would do so on the terms of a man she knew to be ruthless and amoral, a politician/intelligence official who combined the most distasteful aspects of each calling into one monumentally untrustworthy package.

And she would do it.

Her career was the only thing in her life she cared about.

Except...she flashed back to Marshall Fulton and his offer to buy her a drink when their search for Secretary of State J. Robert Humphries had ended. No one would ever replace Shane Rowley, but she had been flattered by his offer, and touched. She hadn't seen Marshall since that early-morning hug outside Ocean City, but the idea of sharing a drink with him seemed...intriguing.

But that was a possibility for another day. For now, she

needed to focus on Aaron Stallings and his proposal. She paused a moment for effect after his shrug and then said, "What action are we taking against the Iraqis?"

Stallings furrowed his brow and glared at her. "You haven't accepted my offer yet. You said it yourself: you're just an unemployed citizen. I'm not sharing classified information with an unmotivated layabout."

"If I come back into the fold, will you fill me in?"

Stallings shifted in his seat. "I'll share what I can," he said, his eyes shifting evasively.

"Fine," she said. "I'm in."

Stallings smiled. To Tracie he looked exactly like a used car salesman who had just closed a deal to move the rusted-out shitbox from the back of the lot. "Was there ever any doubt?"

"Actually, there was. I don't appreciate being hung out to dry and pushed in a particular direction solely due to political considerations."

Stallings snorted derisively. "Welcome to the world of twentieth-century intelligence gathering. Political considerations *always* play a part in *everything* we do. Wake up and smell the reality, Tanner."

Not to me they don't, she thought, but didn't say it. Instead, she opted for, "Okay, I told you I'm in. What action are we taking against the Iraqis?"

Stalling shrugged. "Nothing."

"Excuse me?"

"You heard me. We have no actionable evidence of a plot by the Iraqis to kidnap the secretary of state and frame the Soviets while using the distraction to overrun Saudi Arabia. There is no concrete action we *could* take."

Tracie was stunned. "No actionable evidence?" she said, her voice rising in anger. "I followed the kidnappers from the Iraqi embassy straight to the abandoned building where Humphries was being held! I listened as they spelled out the entire plot, and later I heard them speaking to each other in Arabic. What the hell is not actionable about that?"

Stallings waved his hand dismissively. "Those men you captured are in custody and are undergoing intensive interrogation even as we speak. They refuse to talk; refuse even to give us their names. And we've thus far been unable to establish any connection whatsoever between them and the Iraqi mission to the United States."

"And you won't, either! That's the whole point, remember? Plausible deniability? It's exactly how *we* operate. It's how *everyone* operates."

"Oh, for Christ's sake," the CIA director exploded. "Grow up, will you, Tanner? Of course we know the Iraqis were behind the kidnapping plot. But knowing it and acting on it are two entirely separate issues. President Reagan wanted to go after Saddam Hussein five minutes after the story was laid out to him. But he was talked out of it. You want to know by whom?"

Tracie stared at Stallings, her mouth clamped shut. She knew what he was going to say.

Didn't want to hear it.

Waited for him to continue.

"J. Robert Humphries, that's who. The man who lost a finger to those animals. *He* talked the president out of retaliating. And do you want to know why?"

Again Tracie refused to speak.

Again Stallings continued. "The Soviet Union is crumbling before our eyes. Four decades of fear and mistrust of our most significant enemy since the end of World War Two are coming to an end. The American people are not ready to face a new enemy, they're not ready to turn in an entirely new direction and see nothing but trouble on that horizon."

Finally, Tracie had heard enough. "But the trouble is still going to be there, whether we bury our heads in the sand or not! This Iraqi operation demonstrated a level of operational sophistication that should strike fear into every single American's heart."

"Thank you for your analysis," Stallings said drily. "And I said we weren't taking any action. I didn't say we didn't immediately convey to Baghdad our awareness of their treachery and their plan to annex Saudi Arabia. We made clear the consequences of such naked aggression, and our intelligence indicates that they've taken our warning seriously. They have already begun repositioning their assets away from their common border with the Saudis. The danger has passed."

"For now," Tracie said. "You can't truly believe Saddam Hussein is simply going to give up on the notion of annexing

Saudi Arabia and gaining control of the flow of oil so critical to the West. You can't possibly be that naïve!"

"See, this is what I'm talking about," Stallings said, his voice tight and his face flushed with fury. "You need to learn to keep your mouth shut."

He took a deep breath, making an obvious effort to get himself under control. Blew it out explosively. "You're operational, so you have no need for this perspective, but I'm going to share a dirty little secret with you. It's something your new pal J. Robert Humphries knows full well: there is *always* a threat on the horizon. There is *always* a nation looking to take by force that which it cannot gain legitimately.

"Will Iraq eventually make more trouble in the world? How the hell do I know? Probably they will. But a nation can only deal with so many life-and-death situations at once, and the official position of the United States at this time is that there is no proof of any wrongdoing by Saddam Hussein, and no reason to act against him."

The room fell silent. Tracie considered the director's words. Finally she shook her head. "That makes no sense to me whatsoever."

Stallings shrugged. "Spend enough time in Washington and it begins to make sense," he said.

"I'll pass."

"Look at it this way," Stallings said helpfully, the oily smile again plastered on his jowly face. "It's these sorts of situations that permit those of us in the intelligence community to enjoy long careers in gainful employment. Think of it as job security."

"Job security. Right. Until you decide to fire me again."

"Do your job properly and you'll have nothing to worry about."

Tracie felt suddenly exhausted. It was barely past noon and she wanted nothing more than to retreat to her apartment and soak in the bathtub, to scrub her skin clean and remove the stench of international relations. "Will there be anything else?" she asked.

Stalling shook his head. "Not at the moment. You'll be hearing from me soon with your next assignment. Stick close to your phone."

Tracie nodded tiredly. She stood and left the room. Walked

down the elegantly appointed hallway and out the front door without looking back.

Her shoulders were killing her.

The still-healing bullet wounds from last June ached and throbbed.

She climbed into her car and drove home, wondering when the phone would ring.

———

Tracie Tanner will return soon in her third thriller. To be the first to learn about new releases, and for the opportunity to win free ebooks, signed copies of print books, and other swag, take a moment to sign up for Allan Leverone's email newsletter at AllanLeverone.com!

Reader reviews are hugely important to authors looking to set their work apart from the competition. If you have a moment to spare, please consider taking a moment to leave a brief, honest review of *All Enemies* at Amazon, Goodreads, or your favorite review site, and thank you!

ACKNOWLEDGEMENTS

If you write enough books it starts to feel kind of repetitious to be constantly thanking the same people, but the fact of the matter is that the most important folks in my life remain pretty consistent. It all starts with my wife of more than three decades, Sue. She made me the happiest young man in America—in addition to the most surprised—when she agreed to be my wife, and has supported me unflinchingly, both in my writing and in every other way, ever since.

My three kids, Stefanie, Kristin and Craig, are grown now, but whenever I see or talk to them I'm reminded that no matter how helpless I often felt (feel) as a parent, I must have done something right. All three of them turned into wonderful young adults.

My granddaughter Arianna is my little pal, and hopefully always will be.

I worked with a new editor on *All Enemies*, and the partnership worked out so much better than I ever expected. Jessica Swift of Swift Ink Editorial Services is sharp, relentless and possesses the unerring ability to improve her client's work, which is, after all, what providing editorial support should be all about. Plus, she's friendly, accessible and professional. I look forward to many more collaborations if she'll have me.

Thanks to Robert Shane Wilson for designing and formatting the *All Enemies* print edition. Bob's work is beautiful and professional and, as with Jessica, I look forward to many more opportunities for collaboration.

Thanks to Dan Gravelle for answering not just my stupid emergency medical questions, but my stupid boating questions for this novel as well. Thanks to Joe Serafino for his willingness to share his knowledge of weapons. Thanks to Jerry Zavada for reading the manuscript prior to publication and for his sharp eyes.

Thanks to the other eleven talented members of The

Twelve, my fellow mystery/thriller writers on a mission to take over the world. The fact that you consider me worthy of hanging out with you is a source of continuing amazement to me. You guys are the best.

Special thanks to you, the reader who chose to pony up the cash to buy and read this book. *All Enemies* is my eighth full-length novel to be published, and I'm continually humbled and grateful when readers elect to give me the chance to entertain them. Thank you for that; I promise I will never take you for granted.

Finally, an interesting little aside: The tiny uninhabited island miles out in the Atlantic Ocean where the final showdown in *All Enemies* takes place is based on an actual island. No Man's Land Navy Airfield was operational for the U.S. Navy from 1943 to the 1950s. The tiny base supported propeller-driven aircraft, and in addition to having the small airfield, was used as a practice bombing range from 1943 all the way up to 1996.

The real No Man's Land is located a few miles south of Martha's Vineyard, off the Massachusetts coast. That location didn't work for my purposes, so through the magic of fiction, I dragged the island south until it ended up off the Maryland coast.

Don't get the idea of exploring the real No Man's Land, though. There is said to be unexploded ordnance still littering the island...

THRILLERS FROM ALLAN LEVERONE

Parallax View – A Tracie Tanner Thriller (Rock Bottom Books, 2013)
Final Vector (Medallion Press, 2011 - Rock Bottom Books, 2013)
The Lonely Mile (StoneHouse Ink, 2011)

HORROR/DARK THRILLERS FROM ALLAN LEVERONE

Mr. Midnight (DarkFuse, 2013)
Paskagankee (StoneHouse Ink, 2012)
Revenant (Rock Bottom Books, 2012)
Wellspring (Rock Bottom Books, 2013)

NOVELLAS FROM ALLAN LEVERONE

Darkness Falls (Delirium Books, 2011)
Heartless (Delirium Books, 2011)
The Becoming (Rock Bottom Books, 2012)

STORY COLLECTIONS FROM ALLAN LEVERONE

Postcards from the Apocalypse (Rock Bottom Books, 2010)
Uncle Brick and the Four Novelettes (Rock Bottom Books, 2013)

Made in the USA
San Bernardino, CA
19 November 2019

60137885R00151